Love,

Lies &

Laurie

Jill Millar

For the girls of the '*wine-o'clock club*'.

Chapter 1

Laurie Kerr never intended to have five kids and it wasn't that she didn't know how to stop it happening; it was just that every time she had one she knew without a shadow of a doubt that she wanted another. It was the best sort of addiction, and the worst, and she was totally obsessed. Personally, she blamed it on the hormones that raged through her body for nine months. Not for her the morning sickness, lethargy and tiredness that plagued other woman, oh no, she buzzed like an adrenalin junkie on speed and that was before she even had the gas and air! Was it any wonder she wanted more when for nine months she was invincible. She was never stressed, never tired, no task was too big, no job too small. She was on a permanent high, the best friend, wife and lover any man could wish for, or so she thought.

Of course, if you're going to end up with five children it doesn't do any harm to have a husband like Will who's as horny as a prize stallion at a stud farm. The thought of all that 'practising' was simply too much for him to resist.

It turned out however that Laurie was one of the most fertile women in Ireland and conceived almost immediately. When she told Will the good news she wasn't sure whether the shadow of disappointment that crossed his face was because he wasn't quite ready for a baby or the fact that his high hopes of passionate sex for at least eighteen months had been completely dashed. Other than his joyous belief that he possessed 'super sperm' poor Will hadn't really been sure whether to be delighted or distraught.

Nonetheless looking back Laurie felt sure that Will was one of the lucky ones. Both Laurie and Will had heard rumours that women went completely off sex once they had conceived but whoever made that one up clearly forgot to fill Laurie in. It soon became apparent that the hormones raging through her body had simply bypassed those other woman and made a beeline for her. Laurie was amazed to find herself in the role of rampant sex vamp just waiting for her husband to walk through the door so she could get a much needed fix.

Will who had previously been the one to instigate the majority of bedroom activity in their house suddenly found he was struggling to keep up with the sexual prowess of a wife who must have had a double dose of Viagra. His boss, thinking he was overworked, suggested he take some time off. Will, thinking that a fortnight at home with Laurie might actually finish him off completely, declined the kind offer. By the end of nine months you really would have wondered who had given birth, Laurie was glowing, her husband was a broken man.

Within a year her yearning for another baby had once again overpowered her mind and convinced her that it was time to try for number two. Her husband's half-hearted pleas to wait a while simply fell on deaf ears.

Kids two and three appeared in pretty quick succession and just as Laurie was getting her head around the fact that three kids was going to be her lot in life, by some quirky twist of fate the twins appeared. For Laurie this was the ultimate high, for her husband it was the proverbial straw that broke the camel's back. Will finally realised that the only chance of stopping the fruit of his loins continuing to appear with a frequency akin to snowflakes in a snowstorm was to book himself into the first available vasectomy clinic.

Laurie thought of how her friends looked at her with unmasked admiration when they learned that

Will had the snip and wondered why they in turn were not blessed with a male partner confident enough in his own manliness to put themselves under the knife. 'How' they often ask 'did you get him to agree to that?' and their open admiration turns to full blown hero worship when they learn that it was actually his idea. Of course, Laurie omits Will's little speech that he would rather 'cut through his own nether regions with a blunt knife than have any more kids', some things really were best left unsaid even among friends.

Laurie sleepily wondered what would have happened if Will hadn't resorted to that kind of drastic action. Would she ever have come to the point where she really didn't want any more kids? Ok, Ok so she knew that at some point Mother Nature had to get off her case and she had to get off the hormonal high, it's just she didn't realise that when she did her life would resemble that of a junkie in rehab.

'Mu-umm, Mu-ummm!' Laurie resignedly registered her son's voice piercing her semi-consciousness.

'Mu-umm,' her ten year old shrieked more insistently, 'Mum! You've gotta come now!'

Oh please no! Laurie screamed internally. Please don't let it actually be morning. There no way she could face another day just yet. Where had all the sleep hours gone to! Since she'd had kids there seemed to be a disproportionate amount of daylight hours and far too few sleep filled ones. Was this a phenomenon known only by parents?

A mother's life really had some uncanny parallels with that film 'Groundhog Day' she thought groggily. When Bill Murray woke in the morning to find himself trapped in the exact same day to the one he'd just had Laurie knew exactly how he felt. Personally though Laurie reckoned he was lucky. He certainly didn't have the day from hell which had become her groundhog day; meeting the demands of five over active kids; simultaneously acting as taxi driver, general dogs body and go between; referee, cook and housekeeper, not to mention (un)domestic goddess to husband and father of said five children. At the end of the day Bill Murray still looked like a man in charge of his own destiny not a harassed thirty six year old, recently trampled by a herd of baby elephants.

'Mum I really mean it you gotta get up. There's poo everywhere!'

Gingerly Laurie prised open one eye and squinted at the alarm clock whose reading, if it was to be believed, was 6.10am. She let out a long slow groan, but she was already stepping from the bed, un-gluing her sleep filled eyes and making her way downstairs.

Shane wasn't joking. The poo trailed from the cot where the twins slept all the way along the corridor, over her beige carpet (not one of her husband's better ideas) and into the kitchen. There stood the culprit happily smearing poo all over the kitchen cupboards like some modern day Michelangelo, the discarded nappy lying in a sodden stinking mess beside her.

'Cassie what do you think you are doing?' Laurie yelled

Clearly this was enough to set an already precariously balanced toddler over the edge and as she turned to look at her accuser she toppled backwards landing in a heap on the floor. Totally unperturbed she rolled onto her front, crawled through the nappy and hauled herself onto both feet using the hem of Laurie's pyjamas. Only then did Laurie see the traces of poo around her daughter's mouth and realised that at least one of her twenty-month old twins was as happy eating poo for breakfast as Cheerios.

By 6.45 the situation was under control and Laurie had one cherubic angel, scrubbed to within an inch of her life, sitting up eating porridge. She was just about to hop in the shower herself when the blood curdling scream emanating from Charlotte's bedroom had her hopping back into her poo stained jammies and tearing down the hall way.

'He took my Barbie!' screamed Charlotte.

'Well that's not the end of the world, Tom, give

it back.'

Tom appeared from under the bed with a smirk on his face which could only be described as gleeful carrying in one hand a pair of scissors and in the other a newly shorn Barbie sporting what was at best a short back and sides and at worst a crew cut.

'Noooooooo, noooooooooo, noooooooooooo!', screamed a now hysterical Charlotte. 'That's my favourite Barbie. I hate you, I hate you, I hate you'. Before Laurie could stop her Charlotte leapt on her brother like a lioness going in for the kill and Laurie knew her daughter had passed the point of no return. As six year old Tom writhed and struggled under the weight of his eight year old sister, Laurie hesitatingly wondered whether to leave them to it. It was a tempting thought and in fairness to Charlotte it was her favourite doll so strictly speaking she had every right to tear strips off her brother.

In general Laurie was all for the 'let's sit down and talk through our problems' type of attitude but when it came down to it was there really anything more satisfying than eking out your own revenge? And let's face it a girl does need to learn how to stick up for herself. Just as Laurie was about to step in, her fears for Tom's safety having now reached a critical level, she watched as Tom wriggled free from his sister's grasp, struggling for breath, while a sobbing Charlotte held Barbie's hair in one hand and a clutch of Tom's hair in the other.

'It wasn't my fault' squealed Tom, 'it's what Indians do to their prisoners, I had to scalp her.' At this point Laurie was glad that it was only Barbie he'd decided to scalp and not his sister.

'Tom you know you are not allowed scissors and you are certainly not allowed to cut off hair.'

Tom glared at his Mum in a way that could only be interpreted as you stupid woman what would you know.

'But Mum', he cried 'I can't be a real Indian unless I scalp my victims.'

Please let the cowboy and Indian phase die out quickly she thought to herself. 'Apologise to your sister now, Tom'.

'It was only a stupid doll' he yelled.

'Well then why don't we take one of your toys and give it to Charlotte to make up for it?' Tom nervously flicked a look over to his much loved cowboy 'Woody.'

Charlotte quick as lightening ran and grabbed the toy holding it high above her head. Tom knew when he was beat.

'Sorry' he mumbled.

'I didn't quite catch that, did you Charlotte?'

'Sorry' he said a little louder.

'Sorry for what?' Laurie asked.

'For taking her stupid Barbie and cutting her hair off.'

'Tom' Laurie said warningly.

'Ok, Ok I'm sorry alright.'

'You are never to do anything like that again, do you hear me? And you will pay Charlotte back every penny it takes to get her a new doll. Do you understand?'

'Yes' he squeaked.

'Ok now go and get ready for school.'

Laurie stole a quick glance at the clock. How had it got to 7.45. They needed to leave the house in under thirty minutes and Ellie, Cassie's easy going twin, wasn't even up and dressed yet.

As Laurie walked into her daughter's bedroom she suddenly appreciated that these were the moments which made it all worthwhile. Her beautiful daughter lay curled on her stomach, her tiny fingers entwined in her favourite blanket, her blond hair curling gently around the nape of her neck, the perfect picture of innocence. She allowed herself one brief moment to treasure her still sleeping form and promised herself that no matter what else happened today she would carry this moment with her.

Almost as if she could sense Laurie's presence

her baby stirred, opened her eyes and smiled directly at her. At twenty months she could switch on a megawatt smile of pure delight that made Laurie's heart flip over. In an instant her baby's arms were stretched towards her and Laurie enfolded her tightly to her chest allowing herself to breathe in every inch of her before giving herself up to the chaos. She kissed her gently on the forehead and carried her to the kitchen while her baby babbled away incoherently in her ear.

The kitchen was worse than she feared. Someone had upturned a half-finished bowl of cornflakes and the contents dripped over the table and onto the floor; porridge seemed to be sticking to every surface; the cereal boxes lay in disarray; Shane had the TV turned up full volume in an attempt to drown out Cassie's shrieking and Charlotte and Tom were still fighting with each other and demanding to be fed before they 'die of hunger.' She glanced at the clock and realised she now had twenty minutes to get three of her five children fed, dressed and ready for school. She still had three packed lunches to make and with a lurch realised that Shane had a spellings test today and she had forgotten to test him.

Multitasking began as you have never seen it before. The TV was harshly turned off much to Shane's dismay, spellings were shouted in between pouring cereals, filling juice bottles and making packed lunches. Laurie had little or no idea what she put into said lunch boxes working more on the theory that something was better than nothing. Uniforms were dragged from the tumble drier - every mother's faithful friend - children cajoled and coaxed into getting dressed; shoes found; consent forms signed; PE kits stuffed hastily into bags; swimming kits; football kits and library books located.

Laurie chanced another look at the clock and realised she should have left ten minutes ago. She dreaded yet another note from her children's teacher politely but condescendingly reminding her that her children had not once made it into school in time for assembly this term. There was nothing else for it they had to leave now. Kids were hastily bundled into coats and strapped into car seats and somehow in the process Laurie's car keys mysteriously disappeared. She felt her heart palpating in her chest and the sweat trickling down her body; she wanted to scream at the top of her lungs but realised she had to keep it together if there was to be any chance of getting the kids to school 'almost' on time. She dashed up the stairs located the spare keys and leapt into the car (now only twenty minutes behind schedule). She set off down the road well in excess of any acceptable speed limit and hoped against hope that there were no police officers waiting to nab her.

About one mile from school Laurie heard the unmistakable thump, thump, thump of a flat wheel. She resolutely hoped she was mistaken; after all it could conceivably be the pounding of her stressed out heart beating against her ribcage.

'Mummy, what's that noise?' shouted Charlotte.

Laurie successfully ignored her question four times before Shane, her very knowledgeable ten year old tutted and revealed with an air of disdain that the car had a flat wheel. He then scathingly informed his mother that she shouldn't be driving on a flat wheel as everyone knew it would break the rims and cost far more to get fixed in the long run.

Laurie silently cursed his father for imparting such knowledge to his son but knew without a shadow of a doubt if they didn't stop the whole sorry tale of how Mummy wrecked the car would be recounted to her darling husband. Had Shane not landed her in it Laurie would happily have driven the car to school and home again regardless of noise, smoke, damage to rims or dismayed pedestrians.

With a sigh Laurie pulled over and hopped out to inspect the damage. Sure enough the back wheel was completely flat and she hadn't the first baldy notion how to change it.

Laurie was just about to sink to her knees and bawl her eyes out when she spied the Nixon's gleaming 4x4 pull in behind her.

She breathed a sigh of relief and sent a short but very heartfelt prayer skyward. Whoever said there was no such thing as a knight in shining armour had clearly never met Doc Nixon.

Brian Nixon was the local GP and unsurprisingly Laurie had struck up quite a rapport with him over the past few years. Of course Laurie realised that this was probably something to do with the fact that she was an almost weekly visitor at his practice. Given the number of babies she'd produced not to mention the various emergencies, check-ups and jabs which regularly propelled her to his surgery it was hardly surprising that she was on first name terms with the man.

What never ceased to amaze Laurie was the fact that the very affluent Doc Nixon had enrolled his two kids in the local primary school instead of the very posh nearby Prep. This in itself was testament to his down to earth, easy going personality and the decision was very clearly his as his uber- posh, uber- stylish totally up her own arse wife, Cynthia Nixon, would have her precious darlings enrolled in the private Prep school in the blink of an eye.

Laurie never ceased to wonder how someone as kind and soft natured as Brian could end up with his polar opposite as a wife. Mrs Cynthia Nixon aka the dragon lady was every normal mum's worst nightmare. Not only was she always perfectly and immaculately groomed with all the latest designer labels befitting her 5ft10 skinny bitch frame, but she had a stare that could cut through glass and a personality to match. Laurie had long since learned the benefits of ducking for cover when Mrs Nixon was in the vicinity and as such she had only ever had the misfortune to witness her unbridled contempt being dished out to others. Laurie's particular sympathies lay with those wholly unsuspecting victims who attempted to curry favour with 'the wife of the local GP' and who more often than not came away a shaking, quivering mess. Even those unfortunate enough to witness her verbal assault on others verified that the experience did not leave you unscathed.

Laurie jumped to her feet and went to meet Dr Nixon who was now exiting his jeep. As she caught a glimpse of his brown booted leg she had only an instant to wonder whether he had recently had a fashion makeover before his wife's perfectly styled head appeared.

Laurie choked back the panic she felt taking over her body and forced herself to plaster a smile on her face, close her mouth, square her shoulders and prepare for the onslaught.

Chapter 2

'Well, well, well,' intoned Mrs Nixon 'this is quite a mess.'

'Yeah I know I've got a flat!' Laurie croaked, amazed to have found her voice at all.

'Nooo dear I wasn't talking about the car.' She fixed Laurie with her steely gaze and then slowly drew her eyes from the soles of Laurie's feet to the top of her head. Laurie felt the heat blushing up her neck and knew that by then her face was inevitably as red as her pyjama top.

Pyjamas! Pyjamas! Oh please no, please don't let me be standing here in the middle of the road at nine in the morning in my shit covered pyjamas Laurie silently begged. She chanced a look down and her worst fears were realised. Laurie was beyond

15

humiliated. She had Will's oldest trainers hanging loosely on her feet. She had one pyjama leg partially stuffed into a green sock and glimpsed the blue one peeping below her pyjama leg on the other foot. Her red satin pyjamas, aside from being old, bedraggled, and covered in poo, also had a fair splattering of hardened porridge, looking remarkably like snot, and numerous other unidentifiable stains covering the surface. Her pyjama top had a button missing and her pale, sun deprived flesh glowed translucent through the gaping hole. Without the aid of a bra her boobs were swinging like giant pendulums and she sensed rather than knew that Cruella de Ville was very much aware of the fact that she was totally knickerless.

'This is definitely a repair job.' Intoned the dragon lady looking directly at Laurie's horrified face.

'Yes, yes I couldn't agree more,' Laurie stammered in panic, 'it's just I didn't have time to change this morning or put on my make-up and obviously I wasn't expecting something like this to happen'.

'Nooo dear' she whined,' I was referring to the car, it at least appears to be repairable.'

If Laurie was a woman on the edge before Cynthia Nixon arrived on the scene she was now very definitely off the edge and hurtling towards oblivion. Until now she hadn't realised that a verbal assault could quite literally take your breath away. She felt as though she was physically suffocating and she realised that her only hope of survival was to keep her mouth firmly shut and practise breathing through her nose.

As Mrs Nixon ordered, cajoled and bossed Laurie's three kids into her car Laurie simply stood back and nodded like an escaped mental patient, obviously the pyjamas went a long way in assisting with that look.

Laurie silently admitted to herself that if Mrs Nixon told her that she was driving her children to Outer Mongolia she would have readily agreed. She could not think beyond getting the miserable woman out of her sight and out of her life so she could set about restoring what was left of her dignity.

Just as Mrs Nixon slammed the door of her luxury jeep and Laurie thought she was finally free of her, tragedy struck.

'I'll just drop the children off at school. You should wait in the car until I return.' Mrs Nixon ordered.

'Returned' Laurie thought as the woman blazed away. Please don't let her return. One encounter was bad enough; two in one day would surely be a fate too painful to contemplate.

Laurie's shocked and befuddled brain seemed to be incapable of forming a single coherent thought never mind an escape plan. But escape she must. She had no intention of hanging around waiting for the demon from hell to return and abuse her all over again.

Think Laurie! Think! she urged her brain. Typically Will was out of the country with work and not due back until later. But Kerry would rescue her. She could always count on Kerry in an emergency. Laurie and Kerry had been friends since Primary school where they had bonded over bottled milk and spellings tests. With a bit of luck Kerry could nip out of the office and whisk her away before Mrs Nixon returned.

Laurie reached for her bag and realised with a lurch that she'd left it at home, along with her mobile and her purse.

There was no possibility of escape!

Laurie groaned inwardly at the thought of what awaited her. In all honesty death row would have been preferable.

Oh well she thought miserably, at least she could try and improve her current 'homeless woman meets bag lady' look.

Laurie knew that right now she looked a fright. But given the right beauty products and a bit of time she had been known to look quite attractive. Ok so her hair tended to be a bit frizzy at times and her skin did go a little blotchy when she was under stress, but in general she had pretty attractive features: green eyes; blond hair - well at least it was when she didn't need her roots done; her nose while not exactly 'buttonish' kind of suited her face, and her friends were always telling her it added 'character'. And while she realised there was no possibility of her ever becoming Ireland's next top model, or topless for that matter given the state of her boobs after breast feeding five children, she toyed with the thought that she wasn't wholly unattractive. Yes, a bit of confidence was all she needed to bolster her self-esteem right now. She may be completely inappropriately attired but that didn't mean she was unattractive.

'I am an attractive woman' she incanted to herself.

'I do possess inner beauty' she chanted, as the twins giggled delightedly at Mummy losing her last vestiges of sanity.

But as Laurie peered self-consciously into the drivers mirror a hot flush of shame again engulfed her. She was definitely NOT an attractive woman and no self- help mumbo jumbo was going to change that!

'No' she hissed, 'please no!'

Was there no end to the humiliation? Who in the great beyond could she possibly have pissed off enough to deserve degradation on this scale? This 'thing' she saw before her was obviously a mirage.

There was absolutely no possibility it could be Laurie Kerr. 'It' stared at her with two haunted eyes, highlighted in their awful intensity, not with perfectly applied eye make-up, but with dark shadows underneath deep enough to sink a submarine. A little green gunk had gathered at the corner of one eye. Yesterday's foundation had solidified in clumps on her cheeks and was perfectly complimented by the dry, flaky skin trailing both sides of her slightly upturned nose. Purple blotches were scattered unevenly over her face and the beginning of a cold sore adorned her top lip. On one side her hair was matted flat against her head; on the other it frizzed like static electricity and her hair was definitely past 'just needing its roots done'.

How was this possible? She asked herself in astonished disbelief. And then it dawned on her, Bloody Barbie that's how! If it hadn't been for her she would have jumped in that shower and been at least clean and fully dressed.

While she knew in her heart of hearts the damage was irreparable, she managed to locate a baby wipe in the glove compartment and began removing yesterday's makeup and other traces of sleep detritus from her eyes. She had no brush so she tried scrunching up her matted hair on one side while simultaneously smoothing out the frizz on the other. When she was done she still resembled a homeless woman dragged through a bush backwards but she could do no more.

The twins, having had quite enough of their car seats, were now starting to whine and Laurie realised with a twinge of guilt that Ellie had not yet had her breakfast. Laurie searched the car and triumphantly produced a chocolate bar she found in the side pocket and guiltily stuffed it into Ellie's hand.

By this time Mrs Nixon had returned and Laurie again sceptically wondered why this psycho-hose beast was even bothering with her. Oh well thought Laurie at least she could borrow the woman's mobile phone and call for help.

'Right' said Mrs Nixon immediately, 'get in my car and I'll drive you home.'

'Oh no' Laurie said perhaps a bit too quickly, 'I couldn't possibly put you to so much trouble, you've done quite enough already.'

Yeah thought Laurie the trouble you went to in damaging my self-esteem is definitely enough. 'If I could just borrow your mobile I'll telephone for help.'

Mrs Nixon however was clearly a woman on a mission. Without even bothering to acknowledge Laurie's pleas she started lifting the twins from Laurie's car into her jeep.

'I see healthy eating isn't practised in your house then' parroted Mrs Nixon as she spied Ellie's chocolate bar. The gall of the woman, thought Laurie who would have happily told her that she prioritised 'five a day' if only she could have found her voice.

Thankfully Ellie had no such misgivings about asserting herself in front of Mrs Nixon. As Mrs Nixon tried to prize the bar from Ellie's fingers she clearly didn't realise that Laurie's daughter had a penchant for chocolate matched only by that of her mother.

While she might be easy going, the one thing guaranteed to set Ellie off was to try and deprive her of something she loved. Ellie held on to her chocolate for grim death and screamed at the top of her lungs. The more her ladyship struggled to free the bar from Ellie's grasp the louder Ellie screamed, the bar was now melted mush in Ellie's hands and Laurie glowed with satisfaction as she noted the chocolate marks were smeared all over Mrs Nixon's face, hair and very expensive looking cashmere coat.

'Go Ellie' Laurie silently yelled. At least one of the Kerr women was oblivious to the dragon ladies slaying powers.

'Can't you control your children' screamed Mrs Nixon in frustration as she slammed the car door. Laurie chanced a quick smile at her daughter now happily ensconced in the back seat smearing chocolate all over the luxury car interior, and thought that her day was suddenly looking up.

Mrs Nixon settled herself in the driver's seat and

condescendingly exclaimed, 'Gosh Laurie, don't you ever change those children's nappies, the stench of pooh in this car is unbelievable.'

Laurie knew for a fact that neither of the twins had a dirty nappy as she'd checked them about five minutes previously. She was just about to retaliate that her kids were the epitome of cleanliness when she realised that whilst they might be she was very definitely not! Besides Mrs Nixon was right, there was an awful stench of poo, and it was obviously better that the woman thought the stench was coming from the twins than from her. Laurie opted for the safest option, mumbled something incoherent and shuffled a little further to her side of the car trying to hide the dark stains running down the front of her pyjamas.

As Mrs Nixon neared Laurie's house Laurie knew that she must at all costs ensure she didn't come in. She did a quick inventory of how things had looked when she left that morning and realised with abject horror that it closely resembled the aftermath of a bomb site.

'Thank you so much for the lift Mrs Nixon', Laurie gushed, as they drew up to the front door.' I can manage from here.' Laurie leapt out of the car with the speed of an Olympic athlete and started unbuckling the twins.

Mrs Nixon however was not to be deterred and, with a quickness that surprised Laurie, she unbuckled

Cassie - Laurie noted she didn't make the mistake of tackling Choco-baby again - and insisted on helping Laurie inside.

In a moment of clarity Laurie knew with absolute certainty that this woman had not finished with her yet and was hell bent on gaining access to her house to humiliate her further. Little did the stuck up cow know that she hadn't a snowball's chance in hell of seeing the inside of Laurie's home.

Laurie took comfort in the fact that she had securely locked the door before she left and the only way Mrs Nixon would be gaining access was if she prised the keys from Laurie's cold dead fingers.

Mrs Nixon reached the door first and set her hand on the handle. To Laurie's horror it immediately swung open.

'Nooooo' Laurie screamed 'I locked it, I'm sure I did.'

'You don't think you've been burgled do you' asked Mrs Nixon nervously. 'We were burgled about a month ago and I can't tell you what a nightmare it was. Goods are replaceable but when they ransack the place you love..... well.... let me tell you I'm still recovering.'

Laurie suddenly felt nervous. She didn't fancy walking into her house with two toddlers to find burglars at work and she really was absolutely certain that she had locked the door.

'Do you think we should call the police?' asked Laurie anxiously.

'Well, perhaps we should chance a quick look first?' suggested Mrs Nixon. 'We don't want to call the police unnecessarily. Why don't I take a quick look inside, while you wait with the twins?' I'll leave my mobile with you and if I'm not out again in a minute call the police.'

Laurie thought about the state of her house, but before she could argue, Mrs Nixon was half way through the door.

Minutes later she reappeared.

'I'm sorry' she said 'but you've definitely been burgled. I can't see any sign of them though so I suggest you take a quick look around and see what's been taken and then we'll call the police.'

Chapter 3

This was turning into the day from hell thought Laurie as she cautiously entered the hall.

'Whatever you do, don't touch anything,' instructed Mrs Nixon. 'The police will need to check for fingerprints. Also, you should prepare yourself for a bit of a shock, it's even worse than my place when it was done over.'

Laurie wasn't quite sure what to expect as she walked through the kitchen. The place was pretty much as she'd left it, pyjamas were lying discarded on the floor, cereal boxes were strewn carelessly over the table, the cornflake bowl was still overturned and the milk spilt all over the floor, last night's dishes were piled in the kitchen sink, the only thing untoward was that a few of the drawers had been pulled out. Laurie couldn't even be sure that they weren't like that when she left as she remembered Shane had been hunting vigorously for his football cards. Of course there really wasn't much in the kitchen for them to take she thought silently as she made her way to the living room.

Laurie expected their 50 inch TV to be wrenched from the wall and her husband's state of the art stereo system to have been carried off, but surprisingly they were still intact; the kid's games consoles and Laurie's laptop also seem largely untouched.

'It's strange they haven't touched the electronic stuff' commented Mrs Nixon, echoing Laurie's own thoughts. 'I'd say that's a definite sign they were after smaller items they could carry off. By the state of your sofa I'd say they were searching for cash.'

'Yeah' Laurie mumbled, 'you're probably right'. Inwardly though Laurie was beginning to get more than a little nervous. She hadn't admitted as much to Mrs Nixon but the sofa cushions were on the floor because the kids had been making a tower out of them the night before and Laurie hadn't had the energy to tidy up before she went to bed. Nothing seemed to have been taken and if it wasn't for the door being inexplicably unlocked Laurie really would be thinking there hadn't been a burglary at all.

'Maybe you should check if any cash is missing' suggested Mrs Nixon.

The only cash Laurie kept was in her handbag and as she'd almost tripped over it when she walked into the house she felt pretty sure her purse hadn't been taken. Ironically, Laurie now found herself hoping that her purse had been stolen, at least then there would have been a real crime and she could pretend her house was in the state it was because of the burglars.

Unfortunately Laurie's purse and all her money were intact.

Laurie felt her panic rise. She had to rescue this situation. She didn't know how her door unlocked itself but she did know she hadn't been burgled.

'Shall I call the police now?' suggested Mrs Nixon.

'No, no ' Laurie found herself saying, 'Really nothing's been taken. I think something must have disturbed them and they've run off before they've had a chance to take much. The police will only spend half the morning getting in the way and you know as well as I do, they never get these people anyway. Even if they do, all the culprits seem to get is a slap on the wrist.'

'Oh tell me about it', she replied, 'My husband sees it all the time, these young addicts doing anything to get money for their next fix. Well......... I suppose if you're sure nothings been taken there really isn't much point in calling the police. I'll go and let you get started on clearing up this mess.'

She was just about to leave when they both heard the thump. There was definitely something or someone up Laurie's stairs.

Laurie's pulse skyrocketed and she instinctively grabbed Shane's baseball bat from behind the door. Unfortunately, as she did so she knocked her elbow on the door jam and emitted a yelp in pain. That was enough to set off a chain of events from which Laurie felt she might never fully recover.

They heard a muffled sound and moments later Laurie's husband shouted, 'Is that you baby? Boy am I glad to be home. I'm a poor sex-starved man who hasn't seen his gorgeous wife for over a week.' he joked.

Never mind sex starved, thought Laurie, he's going to be sexless by the time I've finished with him, she vowed, blushing furiously. She couldn't believe he'd just said that in Mrs Nixon's hearing. Well in any event that explained how the door had mysteriously unlocked itself.

Laurie cringed inwardly as she heard Will, who had evidently just stepped out of the shower, thumping down the stairs before appearing absolutely and totally butt naked in full view of Mrs Nixon.

Seeing Mrs Nixon, Will halted abruptly and hastily grabbed his nether regions in both hands before manfully shouting 'Who the hell are you?'

Mrs Nixon despite looking more than a little awe struck at the sight of Will's toned and naked body, quickly regained her composure gave Will a quick once over and feistily replied in a voice dripping with innuendo, 'Whoever the hell you want me to be.'

Will who was always a sucker for a good one liner immediately saw the funny side and hooted with laughter.

Laurie in the meantime stood in stunned silence. Whilst she'd never thought of herself as being particularly prudish there was just something about this particular exchange that made her blood boil.

Firstly, she had had the morning from hell which could largely be attributed to this woman who was now openly flirting with her husband. Just who the hell did she think she was? She had absolutely no right to stand in Laurie's house and come on to her husband.

Secondly Will was his usual composed self, seemingly oblivious to his nakedness. This irked Laurie more than Will would ever know. Laurie had given birth to five children and had the scars, stretch marks, saggy boobs and tummy roll to prove it. Will was the father of said five kids and looked as good now, perhaps better, than he had when she first met him. While Laurie realised that she could not blame Will for the pitfalls of being female and the unwelcome side effects of bearing five children in ten years she still harboured massive resentment against the male species in general, and Will in particular, that he had escaped the whole baby making process pain free and bodily unimpaired.

Thirdly, she knew that had she found herself in the situation where Will had unwittingly walked into the house with a male acquaintance only to find her stark rollicking naked that she would have shrivelled up and died with shame. Where was the justice? How could Will stand there absolutely naked and totally unselfconscious and openly flirt with the dragon lady who had in turn morphed into Jackie Collins. And worst of all neither of them even seemed to give a damn that Laurie was standing there witnessing the whole thing.

'So what brings you to this neck of the woods Cynthia?' breezed Will.

'Well,' she said, 'I was just helping Laurie home after her car took a flat, and then when we discovered the door unlocked and the house burgled I thought I'd better stay to make sure everything was alright.'

'Burgled' said Will, 'We haven't been burgled. I unlocked the door myself when I got in about ten minutes ago.'

'No, no you don't understand' said Mrs Nixon 'the whole place has been done over, didn't you see the state of the place when you came in?'

Laurie recognising the light dawning in Will's eyes looked at him pleadingly, hoping against hope that he would come up with some very convincing and believable lie as to why the house was in its current disaster status. But did he take heed? Like hell he did. Laurie knew when she saw the grin building on Will's face that he was about to drop her in the proverbial right up to her neck.

'Ahh I see you've become acquainted with my wife's housekeeping skills,' he said laughingly.

'Buutttt' stammered Mrs Nixon, 'it couldn't be……' ' I don't understand….?'

Laurie knew her husband's genitals had been under the knife once already but he didn't realise that she was about to subject them to the same kind of treatment all over again and this time without the anaesthetic.

For once it was obvious that Mrs Nixon was somewhat at a loss for words. She let her gaze drift around Laurie's house in absolute bewilderment before eventually fixing Laurie with a comprehending nod and a knowing smirk.

'I don't know why I'm surprised. Of course, I should have realised immediately,' she said smugly, 'but really I do think it was wrong of you to mislead me knowing how upset I was at having my own place burgled last month', and with this she turned and blinked tearfully at Will.

'Laurie how could you be so thoughtless?' said Will, 'and after Cynthia went out of her way to help you. I think you owe her an apology.'

Laurie couldn't believe what she was hearing. How the hell did this suddenly become her fault. I'm the victim here she screamed silently. Typical bloody man! Laurie was angry beyond the point of rationality. Why were men such imbeciles? An arrogant, overbearing bitch of a woman played to his ego for five minutes and consequently he fell hook line and sinker for the teary eyed, poor me routine.

'Don't you think you should put some clothes on' she growled at Will.

He glanced down, as if only just remembering he was naked, gave a casual little shrug at Mrs Nixon and strolled off up the stairs.

'Thank you for your help this morning.' Laurie said tight lipped to Mrs Nixon.

'Is that it?' she snarled, obviously thinking she was owed some kind of an apology, but Laurie was damned sure she was not going to grovel to this woman one minute longer.

Laurie walked pointedly to the door and opened it for her.

Mrs Nixon gave one final lingering look at the chaos that was Laurie's home and finally made to leave.

'I really can't understand how a man like your husband can tolerate this' she said witheringly.

'Likewise' snapped Laurie as she closed the door firmly on Cynthia's self-satisfied smirking face.

Wow! Who would have thought that she would get the parting shot Laurie thought miserably before collapsing in a sobbing heap behind the door.

Chapter 4

Cynthia Nixon liked to think she was not a woman to be trifled with. She couldn't believe she had allowed that cultchie bitch Laurie Kerr to lead her such a merry dance. Did she really think Cynthia had nothing better to do than run around after her all day rescuing her from her silly little dramas? The audacity of the woman was simply unbelievable. Really if the stupid woman took a bit more time over her own appearance and the state of her home and less time breeding like an over fertile rabbit maybe she would actually have a life. Quite frankly Cynthia could do with less of her amateur dramatics. The only reason she had stopped with the maudlin cow in the first place was because she'd been hoping to get an introduction to her gorgeous hubby whom she'd seen dropping the kids off at school on a couple of occasions. Thankfully at least that had paid dividends and fortunately she got more than she'd bargained for in that department.

The man was an Adonis. Absobloddylutely gorgeous with a body to die for. He obviously kept himself in pretty good shape. What the hell he was doing with tatty, batty Laurie she simply couldn't imagine. Quite clearly the man needed a proper woman to steer him onto bigger and better things. He had the looks, the charm and the charisma to sell snow to the eskimos. In fact, she had an inkling that he actually did do something in sales and if memory served her correctly it was quite possibly something in the pharmaceutical business. If that was the case she could almost certainly give his sales a bit of a boost. She and Brian had substantial influence in the medical field and she was confident she could put a bit of business his way. Yes it was definitely about time she took a bit more interest in her husband's business affairs and if that meant she could have a little affair of her own, so much the better.

It had been a bit of a dry spell in that department for Cynthia. She hadn't had a dalliance in quite some time and she had no doubt that Will Kerr would be more than up to the task. The fact he was married suited her perfectly. Married men she found were much more discreet and much less likely to bring her own world crashing about her ears. Last time things had got a little too close for comfort. She really thought Brian had begun to put two and two together. Admittedly it wasn't her best idea to have an affair with his business partner. Ian was definitely a risk she shouldn't have taken. She should have listened to her instincts which warned her he was too young, too single, too immature and worst of all too connected to her husband to risk having an affair with. Unfortunately, his good looks and sex appeal had overshadowed her better judgment and she'd decided to risk it. She had no way of knowing the inane boy would actually fall in love with her and when he did he had turned into a most unattractive leach. She hadn't been able to shake him off and she was pretty sure that Brian must have had some inkling of what was going on.

She hadn't liked setting Ian up for a malpractice claim but what other choice did she have? She had a very carefully constructed house of cards and she wasn't about to let Ian's needs bring it all crashing about her ears.

Fortunately, Brian had listened to her advice and agreed to dismiss Ian from the Practice before things got out of hand. She liked to think the fact that she had arranged for the patient to drop the malpractice claim benefitted both Ian and Brian in the long run.

No, she wouldn't be making that mistake again. She had definitely learned her lesson about taking, single men as lovers. Will Kerr on the other hand was an entirely different proposition. She was fairly sure that a hard-working father of five would be very amenable to a little extra marital fun. Goodness knows he couldn't be getting all his needs met by Laurie Kerr. It was quite obvious that the woman couldn't even get herself dressed in the morning never mind meet the needs of a very virile male. The poor man had sounded pretty desperate for a bit of action when she'd met him earlier.

It was unfortunate that she and Brian didn't have a sexual relationship anymore. She knew it really wasn't all down to him. It seemed that the attraction within their marriage had been stamped out about the same time as child birth. She didn't think there was a link between the two things but she could remember a definite shift in her feelings towards him after Rory was born. She had definitely stopped wanting him. Sex had become more of a ritual than a pleasure after that. He was the father of her children but it was a long time since he had made her heart beat faster and her body yearn for him. In fact, having sex with her husband had about as much appeal as sticking her arm in a pot of boiling water. And yet she knew she still had a need for physical touch, she was a woman in the prime of her life, burning with passion. And so, it was with significant trepidation that she had first taken the risk of engaging in her little dalliances. Fortunately, they had proved fairly successful in staving off her restlessness. Certainly she felt more satisfied when she took a lover. It brought her life into focus and ironically it made her appreciate her husband all the more. She loved the fact that he provided for her and the kids. He was an easy companion and friend. He wasn't too demanding as a husband, he allowed her total independence and there was more than enough money in their joint bank account for her to take pleasure in all the little luxuries that afforded her. As long as he continued to provide a good home for her and her boys she wasn't about to rock the boat.

No, she thought. She was very happy with her life and very keen that it should continue in the manner in which she had grown accustomed. She had no doubt that Brian must also feel a little dissatisfied with the state of their relationship but what could she do about it? The spark just wasn't there anymore. She couldn't provide a solution because she didn't have one. She supposed that at some point he would take a lover as well. She just hoped, that when he did, he had the common sense to pick up someone who would appreciate the sex and leave the rest well enough alone. She had no intention of allowing her life to be turned upside down. She loved her life. She loved her home. She loved her children and in her own way she loved Brian and she wasn't about to give him up for anything or anybody.

Her extra marital affairs were just what she needed to keep her libido satisfied and now that she had seen what a fine specimen Will Kerr was she had him locked firmly in her sights.

Much as it pained her to have to do it she could

see no other option than to invite Will and unfortunately his despicable wife to one of the Practice's corporate events along with a few of their well-oiled contacts. If Will was the sales man she thought he was she knew he wouldn't be able to pass up an opportunity to charm and impress. She needed to become as useful to him as she was to her own husband and then who knew what would happen…………..

Chapter 5

Kerry realised things were really bad when Laurie had been on the phone for over fifteen minutes and she was still urging her friend to take deep breaths into a paper bag. Even worse was the fact that Laurie was still talking in short outbursts of gobbledegook. The last time she and Laurie had spoken in that lingo they'd been about five years old.

'sheso….horribledrag…….ladyandWillasbad..not …….know………..wado' she sobbed.

'Ok Laurie breathe. I really can't make out what you're saying. Who is the bag lady?'

'Ohhhhhhhh' sobbed Laurie 'Yes I…. baglady and she really 'orrible ……. dragonlady.'

'Laurie, Laurie please you're not making any sense. You need to stop crying now and try and tell me what's happened. Is it something to do with the kids?'

'No s'not. Is her……… all her fault. She ………..sadist and now invite us to dinner and Will want to go…………… and I not fit any clothes……………. and he says I must goooooo coz bad if I not there. Oh Kerrieeee help meh..eee.'

'Yes I'm going to help Laurie just as soon as I find out what the hell you're talking about. A dinner invitation sounds like a good thing and we'll get you something to wear. Don't worry it'll all be ok. Right listen, is Will at home?'

'Yeessss'

'Right good. I'm coming to get you. We are going to get as much alcohol as possible into you in as short a time as possible and then you are going to tell me all about it. I will see you in thirty minutes – be ready.'

Sixty minutes and five vodkas later and Laurie was like a new woman. The whole episode with the dragon lady had come pouring out and Laurie was now laughing in drunken hysteria as she struggled to tell Kerry in small irrational drunken outbursts how she and Will had now received an invitation to a Charity Auction and Dinner Dance from Cynthia Nixon which Will was hell bent on attending.

'OK Laurie listen carefully. This is what you're going to do. You are going to go to that dinner looking sensational. You are going to show that no good interfering bitch exactly how gorgeous you really are. I know she caught you at a bad moment, let's face it pyjamas are never a good look on anyone, but that is no reason to be brow beaten and bullied into submission by that stuck up know it all.

You are a beautiful, sexy mother of five gorgeous kids and wife to scrummy Will. You have everything to be proud of and nothing to be ashamed of.'

'But my house Kerry! If you had seen the state of it, she thought it had been burgled. And the way she flirted with Will. She was just so intense. I can't compete with someone like that.'

'Laurie you don't need to compete with her. Her behaviour to you was despicable and totally unforgivable and that's all the more reason for you to go to her damned Dinner Dance looking sensational. Besides Will can look after you and there's bound to be someone else there you can talk to. What about her husband Dr Nixon. He sounds alright.'

'Yes, he's lovely.' she sighed drunkenly

'Well then girl what are you waiting for. There will be plenty of lovely people there for you to talk to without having to even speak to that woman. You and Will haven't had a decent night out in ages. Go and enjoy yourself and show her the glamorous, confident, beautiful Laurie Kerr.'

'Ok.'

'Ok?' 'Really?'

'Yes! Really! I am sick, sore and tired of being treated like a door matt. You are damned right! I am going to show her what I'm made of! I am no push over! I am going to go and show her the real Laurie Kerr! But I do need a drop dead gorgeous dress and I have no money and no time to buy one and I'll never lose two and a half stone in three weeks.'

'Laurie you don't need to lose two and a half stone,' Kerry laughed. 'Have you actually looked at yourself in the mirror recently? Admittedly though you really do need a haircut.'

'I know but there are just not enough hours in the day anymore.' Laurie sighed.

'Well first thing tomorrow you and I are going shopping and if we've time we are definitely getting your hair sorted.'

'I can't tomorrow,' Laurie groaned. 'Will is away in Frankfurt tomorrow for three days and I absolutely refuse to go shopping with five kids.'

'Well what about your Mum could she take them for a bit?'

'Well yes. I suppose I could ask her. It's just I don't like to impose. She has enough to do looking after Aidan's wee boy.'

At the mention of Aidan's name Kerry's heart gave a little flutter. She had had a crush on Laurie's little brother for as long as she could remember and try as she might she couldn't get him out of her system. Laurie used to tease her ragged about it when they were younger but she really had no idea that Kerry still felt as strongly about him. She could never admit to Laurie that when Aidan had announced he was marrying his childhood sweetheart she had locked herself in her room and cried solid for three whole days.

She actually never really believed that Aidan and Angela were all that well suited. Of course that could have something to do with the fact that she harboured a secret fantasy that one day Aidan would wake up and realise that he had got the wrong girl. Unfortunately things never work out like that in real life. Angela had fallen pregnant, Aidan had announced their engagement and six months later he found himself the very proud father of little Michael.

Two years later Angela decided she had settled down too soon. She needed to make something of her life and had taken herself off to New York leaving Michael at home with his Dad. Predictably Aidan was heartbroken and soon found himself struggling to juggle the demands of a challenging two year old and a full time job. If it hadn't been for Aidan and Laurie's mum Maggie being there to look after Michael, Aidan would never have been able to cope. Now nine years on things appeared to have settled into a routine. Angela visited Michael from time to time. Maggie took care of the daily demands of a wonderful eleven year old little boy and Aidan was a devoted and loving father. Somehow though Kerry never did get her chance to declare her undying love to Aidan and her hidden crush remained deeply buried.

Kerry forced her thoughts back to the present. 'I'm sure your Mum wouldn't mind, and anyway, Michael probably loves playing with his cousins.'

'Ok, ok I'll ask her. You have no idea how much I need a break. Don't get me wrong I love my kids to bits but I just feel so totally exhausted all of the time. There's always so much to do and no time to do it. I feel as if I'm letting them all down. If I spend some quality time with one of them I feel guilty for not devoting the same time to the other four. If I do something with all five of them everything else becomes unmanageable, we end up eating pot noodles and the house looks like an advertisement supporting the work of Environmental Health.'

'Does Will know how you feel?'

'Will is never there! He seems to dash from one flight to the next with barely a moment to see me or the kids. When would I even get a chance to talk to him? And anyway he reckons I brought it all on myself. If we didn't have five kids we might actually have a life!'

'Laurie he is the father of those five kids. How

dare he say that! They are his responsibility too you know.'

'Well, ok so maybe he hasn't actually said that in as many words but I know he's thinking it. And anyway how can he spend more time at home. It's his job. If he doesn't work we don't eat.'

'I know Laurie but I just think you need to take the time to talk to him about how you feel. Maybe you could get some childcare sorted or take on a part time job, or at the very least get a cleaner to help about the house.'

'A part-time job! Don't you think I have enough to do already?'

'Laurie I didn't mean it like that. I just meant that maybe you need to get out of the house a bit. Get some time to yourself.'

'I knew it. You think I'm a bad mother. You think I'm not coping either. I knew I shouldn't have told you. '

'Laurie, I think you're a wonderful mother. I don't know how you do it. I think you are amazing and I'm sure Will does too. You're just in a bit of an emotional rut at the moment. You need some 'me' time.'

'Do you really think so?' Asked Laurie blearily.

Kerry nodded.

'I knew there was a really good reason why you're my best friend', Laurie smiled woozily as her head dropped onto the table and her eyes slid shut..........

Chapter 6

Ohhh why do I call that woman my best friend Laurie groaned. She did this to me. I am never ever going to drink again.

'Ok honey I'm leaving now. The kids are up but not dressed and its 7.30. I thought you deserved a bit of a lie in. Have a great day with Kerry. What time is she picking you up?' Will asked breezily.

Laurie couldn't answer. She knew if she tried she would vomit all over his lovely shiny shoes. She couldn't talk and she couldn't move. She just had to lie still until the pounding in her head had receded to a mere thundering din. In fairness, she did try to grunt at her husband before he disappeared out the door for four full days but the effort was just a step too far. She felt the bile rise in her throat and made a supersonic dash to the bathroom just in the nick of time.

Two paracetamols, two pints of water and a hot shower later Laurie was beginning to feel almost human again. If only she could have another little sleep she felt sure she'd be almost back to normal. She would lie down on the bed for just a second and then she really would have to get the kids sorted………………..

'Laurie, Laurie are you ok?' asked Kerry anxiously shaking her gently on the shoulder.

'Oh shit, shit what's the time' yelled Laurie jumping up before remembering the delicate state of her head.

'Mummy said a bad word. Mummy said a bad word' shouted Charlotte joyously.

'No way' yelled Shane pounding up the stairs two at a time.

'Ok you two, Mummy needs to get dressed and you two need to help me get the twins ready for your trip to Grandma Mags.'

'Yessss' yelled Tom from the bottom of the stairs. 'I love Grandma Mag'

'Oh Kerry, I'm so sorry. I just lay down for a minute. I must have dozed off. What time is it?' mumbled Laurie.

'It's 9.30 but don't worry everything's fine. You

take your time and get ready and I'll drop the kids off to your Mum.'

'Did I ever tell you that you are my best friend in the whole world.' Laurie sighed contentedly as she let her head flop back onto the pillow.

'Yeah you may have mentioned it,' laughed Kerry. 'Just don't push your luck. Be awake and dressed by the time I get back. Ok?'

'You got it' said Laurie who found herself looking forward to a leisurely hour getting ready and then a full day shopping in Belfast. Oh the things I used to take for granted she mused as she gingerly eased herself out of bed for the second time.

How the hell did Laurie do this on a daily basis Kerry wondered frantically as she encouraged, cajoled and blackmailed all the kids into Laurie's monstrous people carrier.

Kerry felt she had probably burned up more calories in the past forty minutes getting five kids organised than she would have running the Belfast marathon. No wonder Laurie was in such great shape.

Kerry, distracted and all as she was with five chattering kids in the car knew that deep down her motives for offering to drive them to Laurie's Mums were not totally selfless. She was hoping that Aidan might be there. She hadn't seen him for about six months and she wanted to see if her attraction towards him had waned. As Kerry drove up the rough country lane towards Maggie's little cottage she was disappointed to see that Aidan's car wasn't there. The kids bolted from the car as soon as she drew to a stop and ran into the house shouting for Grandma Mags. As Kerry unbuckled the twins from their car seats Laurie's Mum came out to meet her.

'How are you pet?' she said giving Kerry a quick hug. 'I haven't seen you in ages. Have you time for a quick cup of tea before you head off again?'

'Just a quick one Maggie or the day will be over before I even get Laurie to Belfast.'

'You know I'm so glad you're taking her out for the day. To tell you the truth I've been a bit worried about Laurie.'

'Really, why's that?'

'Do you not think she's been a wee bit down on herself lately? It's as if she has lost all confidence in herself.'

Kerry, thinking back to how Laurie had been after her recent run in with the dragon lady, found herself reluctantly agreeing with Maggie.

'You know, lots of women lose their self-confidence after having children. It happened to me after I had Aidan. I think it was a mixture of post pregnancy hormones and finding myself the mother of two young children who seemed to need me every minute of the day. I think Laurie must be under a lot of pressure with Will being away so much and so many little mites depending on her for everything. She really doesn't have much in the way of adult company. I'm just worried she's not getting enough time to do the things she used to love doing. I'm really so glad you're taking her out for the day. It'll do her the world of good.'

Kerry felt guiltily of how little she'd been there for her friend recently. She had been so wrapped up in her own social life and her job that she had sort of forgotten that Laurie might need her. 'I really should be doing more to help her' Kerry said blushing. 'I think maybe I haven't been there enough for her lately. She does seem a bit down.'

'Now don't you go beating yourself up about that Kerry love. You know how stubborn Laurie can be. She thinks if she doesn't do it all by herself that she's failing. I'm amazed you even managed to get her agree to me having the kids today. I offer all the time but she hardly ever lets me help.'

'I think she just thinks it's a big ask for you to take five of her wee ones and Aidan's as well.

'Aye well it is a bit tricky but there's no reason I couldn't take the twins off her hands a couple of mornings a week while the others are at school to let her have a bit of time to herself. You will keep an eye on her for me, won't you Kerry? I'm more than a wee a bit worried about her truth be told.'

'I will Maggie. I've been trying to convince her to get a bit of help about the house or even to take a part time job.'

'Ummhhh bet that went down like a ton of bricks.'

'Yeah she did seem a bit put out that I'd suggested it. Anyway thanks for the tea Maggie, I need to get going or our shopping day will be over before it's even started.

Just as Kerry was walking through the door she crashed straight into a big hulking figure coming in the other way. As her nose bumped his chest she caught the scent of him and a rush of adrenalin coursed through her body. As she stepped back to adjust her footing her eyes roamed up over Aidan's body coming at last to rest on his twinkling green eyes creased with the hint of a smile. 'Woah slow down there Kerry. Are you trying to tackle me out the door before I'm even through it,' he said laughingly.

Kerry felt herself grin inanely up at him. Why was it that he had the effect of instantly setting all her senses on high alert? That smile, those eyes, even the very scent of him. He was six foot three of pure unadulterated gorgeousness. From the curling tips of his jet black hair to his rolling biceps and solid rugby playing frame. She felt her heart jumping about madly in her chest. 'Hi Aidan, how are you doing? I haven't seen you in ages.'

'I'm doing well thanks Kerry. What about you? What are you and that mad sister of mine up to this weather?'

'Just heading up to Belfast today to do a bit of shopping.'

'Good on you. Be sure to enjoy yourselves. What time will you be back? Sure I can drop Laurie's kids home later when I'm picking up Michael it'll save Laurie a drive over.'

'Probably about eight or so, that'll give us time to get something to eat. Would you mind? '

'Not at all. It'll give me a chance to catch up with you both. You will still be there won't you?' he asked smiling.

Was it Kerry's imagination or was there a little glint in his eye when he said that.

'Yeees' she stammered and she could have sworn he held her gaze just a moment more than necessary.

'That's great. I'll see you later then,' he said holding the door open and stepping aside to let her pass.

Kerry couldn't really remember the drive back to Laurie's. She was replaying the scene with Aidan over and over again in her mind. Was she just kidding herself, reading far more into his intentions than was really there? Perhaps it was all just wishful thinking on her part. At the end of the day he was only offering to drop Laurie's kids home. But there was that look! She was sure he had held her gaze longer than necessary.

Chapter 7

By the time Kerry and Laurie reached Belfast it was already heaving with shoppers which neither of them felt ready to tackle until they'd had a slap-up lunch and a good strong cup of coffee. Laurie was in great form, just getting out for the day without the kids had her spirits soaring. Kerry was still mulling over her encounter with Aidan and with her mind not totally on the conversation Laurie guessed something was up.

'Earth to Kerry' she said waving a hand in front of Kerry's face and only then did Kerry realise just how distracted she was.

'Gosh you've got it bad' Laurie laughed. 'Come on spill the beans, who is he?'

Kerry felt the blush rise up her neck, a sure give away that Laurie had hit the nail on the head.

'There's nothing to tell' mumbled Kerry looking

down at her lap hoping that somehow Laurie would miss her giveaway blushes.

'Kerry Ford. Don't you dare give me that line, I've known you far too long to be fobbed off. You're mind has been elsewhere since you got back from Mum's this morning. What's the matter? Did you meet a tall handsome stranger on the way over and fall instantly in love?' Laurie laughed.

Kerry felt her face burn the deepest shade of crimson imaginable and suddenly the penny dropped in Laurie's mind.

'It's Aidan isn't it?' Laurie gasped. 'You have a thing for Aidan?' she asked incredulously.

Kerry was mortified. She knew there was no way she could deny it now and suddenly she wanted Laurie to understand. She raised her head and locked eyes with Laurie. 'Yes' she croaked 'It's Aidan'.

Laurie leaned back in her seat, a look of total disbelief on her face. 'But why Aidan, why now?'

'It's always been Aidan' said Kerry mournfully, willing her friend to understand.

'What do you mean, 'always'? I know you two got on well when we were kids but that was years ago, before he even started dating Angela.'

'The thing is Laurie. I liked him back then but I wasn't brave enough to do anything about it. Then he met Angela and I never got my chance. I tried to push him out of my mind. He had a wife and child and I knew it was futile to go on harbouring feelings for him. I met plenty of other guys but never the right one. Part of me still keeps wondering how things would have turned out if I had plucked up the courage to ask him out when we were younger. If he hadn't been your little brother I would have asked him out without a second thought but I knew you wouldn't want him hanging around in case he blew the whistle on all you were up to. So I decided I would wait until you went away to college. I reckoned that once the summer was over he was fair game, he'd be turning seventeen and even you wouldn't see him as a kid anymore. I'd be nineteen and I reckoned that once you were at Uni you wouldn't have such a problem with it. But of course Angela got her claws into him before I could do anything and the rest as they say is history.'

Laurie was unusually silent as Kerry's hasty outburst ground to a halt.

'I need some time to take this in' she said at last. 'I really never suspected you genuinely liked him. I remember the pair of you were always together that summer and I used to tease the two of you rotten but I never really thought you could be serious about my nerdy little brother.'

'He wasn't a nerd' Kerry said defensively.

'Oh I know that really' Laurie smiled. 'Aidan was

great. I guess it's just that typical brother sister thing. When you watch your little brother go through puberty and you feel you've long since tackled the whole thing it's nearly impossible to see them as anything other than nerdy. Looking back now I know Aidan was cool. He never grassed me out to our parents and he pretty much left me to my own devices, but at the time, I couldn't think of anything worse than Aidan hanging around. But Kerry do you really think anything could happen between you and Aidan now?' Laurie asked.

'I don't know, but I'd like it to. Do you think you could get your head around that?' asked Kerry cautiously.

'The thing is Kerry, Aidan hasn't had much luck on the relationship front and he's running scared. If he feels himself getting close to someone he backs off faster than you can say the word 'relationship'. It won't be easy for either of you trying to sort through his emotional baggage. And then there's Michael to consider. Aidan's priority is to make sure his life is disrupted as little as possible. It's not easy for a kid that age to come to terms with the fact that his mother abandoned him. Aidan isn't keen to let Michael get close to any of his female friends in case the relationship ends and he feels he's being rejected all over again. You're my best friend Kerry. I would love for you to meet Mr Right and settle down. But Aidan and Michael have been through so much. I don't want to see any of you with your hearts broken.'

'But what if it all worked out Laurie? What if Aidan is my Mr Right? How great would that be, for Aidan, Michael and me? I've tried so hard to put him out of my mind. I meet a new guy and we start dating but no matter how much I like him I find myself constantly thinking about Aidan and comparing the two of them. I think that's why I've never been able to settle down. I know that the chances of us having a successful relationship are pretty slim but it's got to the point where if I don't know for sure one way or the other I think I'll never be able to settle down with anyone else. I need to find out whether we would actually be any good together. I can't go on with the uncertainty of not knowing, I just can't do it any longer.'

Laurie was beginning to wonder how she had never guessed the depth of Kerry's feelings for her brother. She didn't think she'd ever seen her friend so animated. She had also caught the steely glint in Kerry's eye, a look Laurie was all too familiar with. Kerry had already made up her mind about dating Aidan and Laurie realised it was futile to try and dissuade her.

'Well I guess if you feel that strongly about things then maybe you owe it to yourself to give it a go.' Laurie said cautiously.

Kerry breathed a sigh of relief; at least with

Laurie grudgingly on board she had one less thing to worry about.

As Laurie made a quick dash to the ladies before they tackled the shops Kerry found herself thinking back to that gloriously fun filled summer. She had just finished her A levels and felt totally free for the first time in her life. Laurie and Kerry decided that they would hightail it to Laurie's family caravan pitched just outside Portrush for the entire summer and after that life became one endless party. There were numerous nightclubs and bars dotted all around the area and nights were spent crawling from one bar to the next before landing at whatever nightclub eventually took their fancy. When they woke in the morning the caravan would be littered with beer cans and bodies. They always seemed to end up with at least five or six overnight guests. Some were friends from school. Some were simply people they'd picked up along the way who couldn't be bothered getting a taxi home and so had crashed at the caravan.

If the weather was good Laurie and Kerry would head down to the beach and meet up with the guys who ran the local surf school. Laurie had started dating one of them and when he wasn't working he spent his time giving them free surfing lessons. Aidan was also on the scene quite a bit because, despite Laurie's protests, her parents insisted that Aidan was just as entitled to use the caravan as she was. Their one concession to Laurie was that Aidan wouldn't be allowed friends to stay over as it would be too crowded and Laurie thanked her lucky stars that her parents had no idea just how many people were unofficially 'staying' at the caravan.

Even though Kerry already liked Aidan, that summer cemented her feelings for him. His long hours spent on the rugby pitch had paid dividends. Whereas he previously had the rangy teenage look, his shoulders were now broad and his forearms had taken on a muscular quality that made him very easy on the eye. His thighs were solid muscle and Kerry who always had a thing for a nice bum could hardly tear her eyes away from Aidan's very pleasing derriere encased in his ripped denim jeans. He was well on his way to being drop dead gorgeous.

But it was more than his looks that had Kerry intrigued. Aidan was the sort of person Kerry could talk to for hours. She felt herself open up to him more and more that summer as they discussed their plans for the future. He was, she realised a very mature, almost seventeen year old. He liked a good time but certainly was never going to be the party animal that Laurie was. He had a gentle nature which appealed to Kerry but also a really sharp mind that often had Kerry challenging her own previously formed opinions. As Kerry found herself spending more and more time with Aidan she felt the physical attraction between the two of them grow. Somehow Kerry knew that she would have to make the first move if anything were to happen between them, there was no way he would embarrass himself by taking a knock back from his big sisters friend.

The sexual chemistry between them by the end of that summer was at fever pitch. It was definitely true that forbidden fruit was the most desirable. If they accidently brushed against each other the electricity fizzed between them. Their eyes seemed to seek each other out and hold just that little bit too long. Kerry found her body physically aching for him because she wanted him so badly but she was reluctant to risk spoiling things between them and she was afraid of Laurie's reaction. She had no doubt Laurie would be less than pleased and that it would end up driving a wedge between her and Aidan. She wanted it to be perfect and because of that she determined to wait it out until Laurie went off to University in Edinburgh. Kerry for her part was going to study law at Queens in Belfast and she decided that once she had settled in she would invite Aidan up to visit her.

Sadly, she never got her chance. The summer ended all too quickly and by the time Kerry had settled into halls she had received a letter from Laurie indicating that Angela Devine had taken a shine to her little brother and that she thought they were dating.

Kerry thought it would all blow over quickly and Aidan would soon be available again but that didn't happen. As Kerry got on with student life and the fun but casual relationships that accompanied it her familiarity with Aidan lessened and she put her feelings for him down to a teenage crush. But when she met up with Aidan again at Laurie's wedding she realised her feelings for him were as sharp as ever. Unfortunately, Aidan was by then nursing a broken heart and already struggling to bring up a child on his own. It was definitely not the time to consider a relationship.

During the intervening years Kerry would see Aidan intermittently at Laurie's kids various christenings and birthday parties and each time she felt a sharp pang of regret at what might have been. Recently though she thought the spark had come back into Aidan's eyes and she vowed that if anything was ever going to happen between them it would be now, and if it didn't, she would put any thoughts of a relationship with him out of her mind for good.

Chapter 8

Buzzing with coffee fuelled adrenalin the two women hit the shops. Laurie was willingly dragged from one boutique to the next trying on anything and everything that Kerry thrust upon her until at last they found the perfect dress. Had Laurie been shopping on her own she would never have given it a second glance but Kerry had a great eye for beautiful clothes and could instantly see what Laurie could not.

The dress was a rich emerald green which seemed to compliment Laurie's mesmerising green eyes perfectly. The material was light gossamer which gathered firmly round the bust before floating gently and ethereally to just below Laurie's knees. It was the perfect mix of classy and chic and Laurie loved it from the very second she slipped it over her hips. She instantly looked and felt ten years younger. Kerry knew with the right shoes and accessories Laurie would outshine any other woman in the room.

Luckily, they were able to lay their hands on the perfect pair in the stores own shoe department. The gorgeous silver Sergio Rossi shoes set off the dress beautifully and really did highlight Laurie's long slender legs to perfection. It had been a while since Laurie had worn six inch heels but years of practice in her teenage years enabled her to carry it off with ease.

Fortunately, Kerry had the good foresight to book Laurie a hair appointment at Belfast's top salon. There was no way she was going to risk Laurie turning up at her Charity Dinner without her hair being totally restyled and coloured and Kerry knew that with Laurie's tendency to leave things to the last minute there was a very real possibility she may not get it done at all.

Frank Malloy - or Franco as he liked to call himself nowadays - was a genius with hair and had a reputation of being the finest in the business. It was rumoured that he had been offered a once in a lifetime opportunity to set up business with one of the celebrity stylists in London but his partner George had point blank refused to leave Ireland and as a result Franco turned down the offer. London's loss was definitely Belfast's gain. Franco had a knack of knowing instantly what style would suit a client and his magic scissors seemed to take on a life of their own as they carried out his bidding. Kerry had met Franco years before when he was struggling to climb the ladder to success and she was literally a down and out student with nowhere to live. When Franco had offered her his small bed sit above his hairdressing salon Kerry gratefully took it and the two had become firm friends.

Franco loved to play on the fact that his mother was half Italian and insisted that his accent was merely a result of his mixed heritage but Kerry was one of the few people who knew it was entirely fake. Nevertheless Franco insisted that his strong Italian accent had played its part in helping him establish such a successful business and had no intention of dropping it.

'What is this specimen you have brought to me?' barked Franco as an awestruck Laurie was scrutinised intensely in the chair in front of him.

'Pah, there is no excuse for a woman siz beautiful to have siz terrible hair. It is a shame, no? How as dis happened?' he growled at Laurie.

'Go easy on her will you Franco? The woman has five kids and not a minute to herself'.

Seeing the look of fear and uncertainty on Laurie's face Franco winked at Laurie conspiratorially. 'Ahhh now I understand. But my darling you must promise me that if I use my magic scissors you will never again allow siz terrible hair. Yes? You understand I cannot have my name and siz….. siz frizz' he said holding Laurie's hair loosely in his fingers as if he feared contamination by mere touch, 'linked to ze name of the great and wonderful Franco.'

Laurie nodded in shock, more than a little dumbfounded as to know what to say next.

'No matter my dear we will have you looking beautiful again. Now vat hairdressing miracle would you like me to perform?'

'Ummmhh maybe just a trim and a bit of colour?' Laurie said uncertainly.

'Nonsense child! Siz hair cannot be remedied by a 'trim and a bit of colour" he mimicked. 'It needs 'ze Franco' do you permit me to give you 'ze Franco' my dear?'

Laurie stole a glance at Kerry who was struggling in vain not to laugh while she nodded her head at Laurie.

Laurie squeaked her consent and Franco taking that as a yes began his magical transformation.

Three hours later Laurie could hardly believe that the sleek, blonde, elfin beauty looking back at her from the mirror was actually her. She turned her head left and right trying to ascertain where the real Laurie Kerr had gone to. The transformation was beyond anything she could have hoped for and she felt her eyes brim with tears of gratitude.

'Franco you are a genius' Kerry gasped.

'Si, Si, I know he said proudly. But truly it is my pleasure to find such a stunning beauty hidden beneath the dross. It is like magic, yes?'

Never in all her years had Kerry seen Laurie look so good. Laurie had always been pretty but with this haircut she was stunning. The lank heavy locks of hair that had seemed to weigh Laurie down had been replaced with silky, mellifluousness and the gorgeous honeyed tones and edgy cut had totally transformed not just her hair but the very shape of Laurie's face. Her cheekbones were startlingly pronounced and her eyes, no longer hiding behind a curtain of hair, were strikingly soulful.

'Franco I love you' cried Laurie 'and other than my husband you are the only man I've ever said that to.'

'Well then bella I am truly honoured. Your eyes may be ze window to your soul but your hair ezz your crowning glory. Now you must come back to me soon' he said smiling. 'It is always a pleasure to see a true beauty emerge from the ashes.'

Chapter 9

High on success after their incredible day they decided to grab a Chinese take-away and a few bottles of wine rather than eat out at an expensive restaurant. Laurie whose credit cards were maxed out was extremely relieved and Kerry was hoping to get back early to freshen up before Aidan's arrival.

By the time Aidan dropped the kids back the two women were already on their third glass of wine. Kerry felt she needed all the Dutch courage she could muster and Laurie was so overwhelmed by the day's events that she had thrown caution to the wind. Aidan, star that he was, summed the situation up in sixty seconds flat and quickly put the younger kids in bed and a DVD on for Michael and Shane to watch.

When Aidan finally re-emerged in the kitchen he was ready for a drink himself and Kerry was quick to offer him a glass.

'Hey sis what happened your hair?'

'Don't you like it?' asked Laurie fearfully touching her new cut self-consciously.

'It looks great', said Aidan 'takes years off you. Why'd you not get that done ages ago?'

'Oh I don't know probably something to do with the fact that I never have the time what with having five kids and Houdini as a husband' she said laughingly.

'Well he'll Houdini himself right back here in an instant once he knows how great you look. In fact he may never let you out of his sight again in case some young buck mistakes you for a twenty something and sweeps you off your feet.'

Laurie laughed merrily at the very suggestion but she was secretly thrilled to bits that Aidan had paid her such a great compliment. 'Well it's all thanks to Kerry really. She's the one that arranged everything.'

'Is that so Kerry? I might have guessed that you'd have a hand in it,' he said playfully meeting her gaze.

Laurie hastily mumbled her excuses and left.

'I think she needed a bit of a lift' said Kerry truthfully, making sure Laurie was definitely out of ear shot. 'I'm just glad the new hair style seems to have done the trick.'

'Aye Mum was saying something the same to me the other day. She thought maybe Laurie was a bit down in the dumps,' he said a small frown creasing his brow. 'Do you think she's alright?' he asked concerned. 'I mean you know her better than anyone.'

'I'm not sure' said Kerry. 'I hope so, but she certainly hasn't been herself lately. I'm a bit worried she's not coping as well as everyone assumes she does.'

'I think I'll have to pop in and see if I can help out a bit more' said Aidan. 'I've been listening to her rhyme off a list of jobs that Will was supposed to have done and hasn't for so long now it's just become a kind of background noise.' he smiled.

'What like the replacing the bulb in the hall?' asked Kerry grinning.

'Aye, or maybe putting up those photo frames of the children?' suggested Aidan.

'Or maybe fixing the lock on the bathroom door so she doesn't have to keep singing every time she takes a wee.' Kerry bounced back.

'Yeah or maybe building the trampoline the kids got for Christmas last year and ....'

'....have never had so much as a bounce on yet' interrupted Kerry finishing off his sentence.

'Oh yes I think I know that list of jobs she has for Will better than he knows them himself.' grinned

Aidan.

'Sometimes I think she doesn't need a husband so much as an entire entourage' laughed Kerry lovingly.

'Aye that's my big sis for you, always did have a list as long as her arm for other people to do' he grinned.

'Yeah but I wouldn't change her for the world' said Kerry matter of factly.

'I know you wouldn't Kerry. You've been a great friend to her. She's lucky to have you' he said meeting her gaze.

As Kerry's eyes locked on his she felt that old familiar feeling well up inside her. What was it about him that made her insides melt and her brain turn to mush.

'I've missed this' said Aidan.

'What?' asked Kerry hoarsely.

'You and me, having a bit of banter, putting the world to rights. It seems like forever since we've had a proper conversation and yet,' he said wistfully,' it feels like yesterday.'

Kerry nodded mutely, reluctant to break the connection between them.

'You must know I had a massive crush on you when we were younger' he said colouring slightly.

Kerry knew if she really wanted to find out how Aidan felt about her she would never get a better chance. Screwing up every ounce of courage she could muster she held his gaze 'had?' she said playfully. 'I was rather hoping you still did.'

'Really?' he asked disbelievingly. 'You'd never consider going out with the likes of me Kerry?' He asked doubtfully.

He watched her as a slow blush crept up her neck. 'I'm sorry Kerry I didn't mean to embarrass you. Are you......? ... I mean are you interested in me as more than a friend?' he stumbled.

Kerry nodded.

'Even though I have Michael and everything?' he asked disbelievingly. 'Really?' he grinned as he began to register from the look in her eyes that her interest in him was genuine.

Aidan stepped closer to her and gently tucking a stray tendril of hair behind her ear he whispered 'Kerry could I take you out to dinner sometime?'

As Kerry looked at Aidan she wondered how he could ever doubt her interest in him. He was a unique combination of gentleness and manliness; his sparkling green eyes radiated tenderness quite at odds with the overpowering physical strength that emanated from him. His hesitant smile hinted at a man completely unaware of his own attractiveness, yet his muscular body and chiselled features betrayed him as the red hot male he really was. As far as Kerry was concerned he'd be desirable to pretty much any woman with a pulse.

She reached up and touched him gently on the cheek allowing herself the pleasure of feeling his beautiful face beneath her fingertips. 'Aidan' she said slowly and deliberately 'I'd love to go out on a date with you, in fact I couldn't think of anything I'd rather do.' she said happily.

'Dad?' said Michael excitedly bursting into the room and unwittingly breaking the spell. 'Dad you've got to see this. Batman is totally kicking superman's butt….. I mean…… Batman is totally winning. This DVD is awesome! Quick Dad! You've got to see this! It's the best fight scene ever!' As Aidan reluctantly allowed himself to be dragged away he turned and smiled at Kerry mouthing 'I'll call you.'

Kerry couldn't believe it. She was actually going on a date with Aidan! All those years of wondering 'what if' and now it was finally going to happen.

Although now she had a whole new list of 'what ifs.' What if she had only imagined the chemistry between them. 'What if' they were better suited as friends. 'What if' she'd wanted him to be 'the one' so much that she'd ignored any possibility that they weren't right for each other?

Chapter 10

Kerry was buzzing with adrenalin. She'd been running an internal battle with herself for the past week and was still yo-yoing between the risks that she was jeopardising her friendship with Aidan to allowing herself the luxury of dreaming of her happy ever after. She had always believed in destiny but when those long held dreams suddenly become a possibility, the fear that she might have pinned all her hopes on the wrong man threatened to engulf her and steal away her joy. That old saying her Dad was so fond of, 'don't back the wrong horse,' had inserted itself in her brain and was on constant replay. How would she survive the crushing disappointment that would come if Aidan wasn't her destiny after all?

She was more relieved than excited when Aidan had texted her to say he had finally managed to get a babysitter and was taking her out to dinner. The suspense of waiting, not knowing whether she had made a terrible error of judgment was threatening to engulf all her common sense. She had finally reconciled herself to the thought that surely it was better to have tried and failed than never to have tried at all. Yes their date might be a complete disaster but it might also be the best thing that ever happened to her. Kerry had never ran away from a challenge in her life and she wasn't about to start now. She would worry about the possibility of dealing with crushing disappointment if it arose. She wasn't going to let some erroneous fear spoil everything.

Kerry had invested in a gorgeous rust and black colour-block dress for the occasion which she had paired with her black block heel ankle boots and her favourite black duster jacket. She was hoping the look was understated but sexy. The last thing she wanted was to look like she was appearing in court for a client. Why she was taking such care with her hair and makeup when Aidan had seen her a thousand times before with little more than a pony tail and touch of mascara she wasn't quite sure. She supposed she was hoping to mark the change from friendship to relationship. Suddenly the thought of what she and Aidan could become gave her heart a little flutter.

When she opened the door to Aidan he gave a long slow whistle and insisted she give him a little twirl.

'Kerry' he said looking at her with wide eyed appreciation 'you are looking absolutely gorgeous. If I wasn't such a gentleman I might try and persuade you to skip dinner altogether and jump straight to dessert.' he said grinning.

Kerry loved his gentle teasing; she found it impossible not to flirt back. He opened up a side to her that others rarely got to see. She relaxed in his company, her slightly on edge 'lawyer persona' slipped away leaving her character softer and more feminine.

'You're looking pretty hot yourself Aidan' she said appreciatively taking in his crisp white linen shirt and his textured grey slim fit jacket, mid washed jeans and brown leather shoes. 'If I wasn't such a lady I might take you up on that offer' she said lightly, linking her arm through his and steering him down the driveway towards his car.

Aidan had booked a table for them in a beautiful little restaurant in the picturesque village of Portballintrae. In the summer month's tables booked up weeks in advance but fortunately in late winter it was handed back to the locals for a few months. They were fortunate enough to be seated by the window overlooking the pretty little harbour, which thanks to the huge full moon hanging lazily over it, meant it was not yet lost to the inky blackness of the night. Little candles glimmered at the table and a warm fire roared in the restaurant's open hearth.

Kerry couldn't believe how seamlessly she and

Aidan slipped back into their old way of chatting. It was almost as if the intervening years had never been and yet they had so many years to catch up on they hardly paused for breath. Kerry had forgotten what a natural story teller he was, how he liked to draw out the details others would have glanced over, spinning out a story in such a way you were held captivated until he let you go. He had a fantastic memory too retelling stories from their youth that Kerry had long since forgotten. Kerry knew she was falling head over heels for him and no matter how much she urged herself to be cautious she just couldn't help the way she felt about him. He wasn't just handsome as hell and fit to boot he was actually decent company too. Kerry couldn't remember the last time she had enjoyed a date so much.

The evening flew by and before they knew it they were the last remaining guests and the long suffering waiter was giving them begging looks to hurry up and leave. Finally taking the hint Aidan settled the bill and the two of them walked out into the chilly night air.

'It's such a shame it's too late and too cold to go for a walk along the beach.' sighed Kerry longingly.

'You always did love the sea' said Aidan smiling. 'I remember you being totally stressed out in the middle of your A-levels and the only thing that ever truly relaxed you was going for a walk along the beach.'

'How do you remember these things?' asked Kerry amazed yet again by the things he'd recall from their youth.

'Kerry' he said seriously 'what you don't realise is that I was a little bit in awe of you. I pretty much noted everything you said or did back then. Sorry,' he laughed 'that makes me sound like a stalker.'

'I think I'm safe enough' said Kerry. 'You're not really the stalker type. I'm actually quite flattered. And you're right by the way. There's just something about the sea that relaxes me. I guess it must be the island mentality. I don't think I could ever live anywhere that was completely landlocked. I'd go stir crazy if I had to live somewhere without seeing the sea from one end of the year to the next.'

'I get that' said Aidan as he kindly opened the car door for her and then settled himself into the driver's seat. 'In fact, if the weather picks up a bit we should come back and have a good long walk along Runkerry Beach. It's been a while since I've taken the time to do that' he said longingly.

'Sounds great' said Kerry smiling.

It only took forty minutes to reach Kerry's house and she couldn't help wishing it was longer. She really didn't want the night to end. 'Do you have to get back for Michael?' she asked 'or do you have time for a coffee?'

'No luckily he's at a sleepover at his friend's so I'm free all night' he said grinning.

Kerry's heart skipped a beat. Did he want to stay over with her? Was she ready for that? Luckily she caught Aidan's eye before she opened her mouth and said something stupid, she knew that mischievous glint of his and the hint of a smile that played around his mouth reassured her that he was just teasing.

She hit him playfully on the arm. 'I'll make you de-caff' she said. 'I wouldn't want you to be up all night with no one to keep you company.'

Aidan laughed and followed her into the house.

As Kerry put a pot of coffee on Aidan made himself at home. 'This is a lovely place you have here Kerry', he said taking in the squashy sofas and thick pile rugs and warm earthy colours which definitely gave the place a homely feel.

'Thanks' said Kerry. 'I love interior design and after living in poky rented flats for so long I just couldn't wait to buy my own place and finally get the opportunity to put my stamp on it. I was fortunate enough to buy just before the house prices went through the roof, which is just as well; because I could barely afford the mortgage repayments even then.'

By the time Kerry had finished making the coffee Aidan had got a fire going and it struck Kerry yet again how natural it felt to be with him. It was so easy spending time with him. She had the vague sense that he had already slotted seamlessly back into her life only this time definitely as something more than a friend she thought as she watched his taut thighs and firm bum lean forward to throw another log on the fire. Aidan turned and caught her staring. Kerry felt her face flush but she couldn't turn away. For once the power of speech eluded her and much as she wanted not to be standing there like a gormless teenager she found herself incapable of stringing together a single coherent sentence.

The air was electric, it sparked and danced and fizzed between them. As Aidan silently crossed the room, his eyes never once leaving her face, Kerry felt the hairs on the back of her neck rise on end, her body shivered in anticipation of his touch and when it finally came, his lips tenderly searching out her own, his hands powerfully holding her to him; her heart raced within her. She lost herself entirely in his kiss, she could not hold back the fierce fire that ignited her from the inside out. Just as Kerry thought her body might actually combust with longing Aidan gently released her. He drew back looking every bit as stunned as Kerry felt. He tenderly cupped her face in his hands and smiled at her.

'Wow' he said. 'I know wow doesn't cover a kiss of that magnitude but I have no other words.

'Ummhhh' said Kerry shakily, 'amazing might

cover it, or possibly incredible, delicious or wonderful but actually I think 'wow' pretty much sums it up' she said smiling.

'I'm sorry Kerry' said Aidan 'I should probably have asked permission before I took advantage of you like that but honestly I don't think I was capable of getting the words out, I don't know what came over me.'

'Oh you had permission alright' said Kerry laughing. 'What I'd like to know is when can we do it again?'

'How about right now?' suggested Aidan as his lips once again found hers and Kerry succumbed to the overpowering desire that engulfed her.

'You are very, very addictive' grinned Aidan when he eventually surfaced for air. 'If you keep that up I might forget that my intentions are entirely honourable' he teased.

'Ummhh' said Kerry still dazed from the rollercoaster of emotions his gorgeous mouth had taken her on.

'Now while I would very much like to just keep on kissing you I don't think I can be responsible for my actions if we keep doing that.'

'Right now I'm not sure if I want the honourable Aidan or the irresponsible one' whispered Kerry pulling him towards her lips once more.

'Kerry' he moaned. 'Please don't do this to me. I don't want to rush this. You're sweet and funny and gorgeous and I don't want you to wake up in the morning thinking you've made a massive mistake.'

Kerry shook her head uncertainly. 'I won't' she breathed.

'You might' sighed Aidan. 'I don't want to mess this up. You're too important to me.' He said gently.

Was there ever more of a turn-on Kerry wondered than having a man who you knew wanted to sleep with you but was doing his best to resist? The more he tried to do the honourable thing the more irresistible she found him.

Aidan kissed her again and Kerry felt she was floating on air. It had been a long time since anyone had kissed her like Aidan did. Actually, strike that. She didn't think anyone had ever kissed her like Aidan did.

'Ok' he said gently releasing her. 'That was your goodnight kiss. Not because I don't want to stay here all night long but because I do' he said softly. 'I'm at the point of no return Kerry, my body wants all of you and my mind is telling me that's not a good idea just yet.'

Kerry was no longer capable of rational thought. He'd turned her brain to mush just as quickly as he'd turned her legs to jelly. Deep down she knew she didn't want to rush this but somehow every fibre of her being was telling her that she did. Right now, she trusted his judgement more than her own so reluctantly she nodded her agreement.

He touched her softly on the cheek before casting one longing look behind him as he closed the door and left. Kerry stared after him a joyous quivering mess of a woman, a slow smile playing on her swollen lips.

Chapter 11

The Charity Dinner Dance of which Cynthia was chief fundraiser and organiser was being held in the luxurious surroundings of Riverview Resort and Spa just outside Ballymena. Cynthia had decided that since she had gone to so much trouble organising the event it was only fitting that the patrons of the hotel should offer her free accommodation for the evening and fortunately for Cynthia the owners had generously agreed.

Brian had made it clear that he had no intention of leaving the children with a babysitter overnight, being of the view that they were being minded by babysitters far too often in the first place and Cynthia was equally adamant that she fully intended to stay in the hotel with or without him.

Cynthia had been sure to check in early and take advantage of the wonderful Spa and was currently basking in the glorious Hot tub before her appointment for a Coral Serail and Hot Lava Shell Massage.

She found herself idly wondering whether Will and batty Laurie would actually show up tonight. She had phoned Will earlier in the week and he had assured her they were going to attend but it was such a shame he was bringing his wife. It would have been the perfect opportunity for Cynthia to get to know him. On the plus side, she would at least get a chance to talk to him and to let him know how much she could offer him in terms of business as well as pleasure. She had selected Will's table with great care ensuring that he was placed with herself and Brian as well as the owners of a very lucrative private medical hospital and a major Drug Manufacturer. Cynthia had done her homework. She knew exactly what type of products Will's firm were trying to sell and she knew for a fact that once the owners of these companies knew what he had to offer them they would jump at the chance of trying to out-do each other. If Will played his cards right this could prove to be a very lucrative evening for both him and his employer.

While Cynthia Nixon was basking in the luxurious Spa, being pampered to within an inch of her life, Laurie Kerr was battling to remove the detritus of spaghetti bolognese from her five children. Why she had decided to cook her special 'spag bol' tonight of all nights she'd never know. Of course the children had never before decided to start throwing their food all over each other and what seemed to have started as an accidental spillage when Cassie tipped her bowl over Tom's head had suddenly escalated into a food fight of World War Three proportions. Not a surface was left unmarked; not a child left unscathed and not an adult left with one iota of sanity. Even Will who normally breezed in and out of the children's lives without fully appreciating the trail of destruction these children could leave in their wake appeared more than a little shell shocked when he saw the spaghetti dripping from the light fitting and the TV covered in red sauce. He was amazed when he couldn't even identify which twin was which below the mask of spaghetti and mince streaked hair.

Surprisingly, Will had actually managed to make himself useful by sticking the kids in the bath leaving Laurie to try and salvage the kitchen. How she was going to restore some semblance of normality and get herself ready for her ladyship's dinner dance was beyond her comprehension. Just as Laurie pulled on her rubber gloves in anticipation of tackling the mammoth task before her, the doorbell rang and the cavalry arrived in the form of Kerry and Aidan.

Kerry instantly took in the state of the kitchen and the fact that Laurie was treading that very thin line between sanity and insanity and ushered her out of the kitchen with firm instructions not to reappear until she was styled to within an inch of her life.

Luckily Kerry had anticipated that Laurie wouldn't allow herself enough time to get ready for her night out and so had the foresight to arrange that she and Aidan turn up an hour earlier than planned to take over baby-sitting duties.

Within sixty minutes the kitchen again resembled an inhabitable space and Kerry was impressed at how quickly Aidan had got stuck in to the task at hand. Kerry's normal experience with the opposite sex had led her to believe that they fled from anything of a domestic nature, but then Aidan wasn't like any other man she had ever dated.

Kerry still felt as though she were living on cloud nine. She knew it was still early days with Aidan, she hadn't even seen him since the night at the restaurant, they'd both been so busy with work and it wasn't always easy for him to find a babysitter in the evenings, but somehow it just felt right. He texted her every morning with a little 'Morning gorgeous' message and just having someone who thought about you as soon as they woke in the morning made her feel special. She'd lost track of the number of men she'd dated who promised to call her and then hadn't bothered so having someone spontaneously text or call because they actually wanted to was a treat in itself.

Luckily for her Aidan loved a bit of flirty banter just as much as she did and she was discovering that it was an easy way to transition from being just friends to something more intimate. Besides it was a welcome relief to finally date someone who didn't expect you to jump straight into bed with them before you even knew how you really felt about them. She knew exactly how she felt about Aidan. Her problem was trying to rein herself back so she didn't either scare him off completely or end up wanting to spend every minute of her time with him.

Tonight was only their second date and the reality of having six children to look after wasn't so much a date as a baptism of fire. Somehow they had both agreed it would be easier for Laurie to head out and enjoy herself knowing the kids were looked after rather than worrying about them all night. Kerry had agreed to stay the night at Laurie's and Aidan had suggested that he and Michael stay for a while and then call back in the morning and take all the kids for a walk along the beach. It would be a nice surprise for Laurie to wake in the morning and realise she and Aidan had taken the kids out for the day. It certainly wouldn't do any harm to give Will and Laurie a much needed lie in and some quality time together.

When Laurie reappeared in the kitchen Laurie looked better than Kerry had ever seen. Will who had dashed down the stairs moments before let out a long wolf whistle and watched as Laurie's face broke into a beatific smile. Little Charlotte gazed wonderingly up at her Mum and shouted gleefully, 'Mummy is a Princess!'

'Yes, she is my dear' said Will affectionately. 'Do you think I should be her Prince Charming and take her off to the ball?'

'It isn't a Ball Daddy' said Charlotte knowingly 'It's a dinner dance. But I think you should definitely take her there Daddy because she looks so lovely. '

'Very well my dear' said Will 'your chariot awaits' and as he held out his arm for Laurie to take, Laurie just had time to deliver quick kisses to all the little ones before Will swept her out the door.

Laurie was overjoyed with everyone's reaction. It had been a long time since Will had paid her a genuine compliment.

As if reading her mind, he turned to her.

'You really do look beautiful you know Laurie. I could quite happily skip this function and spend the night at Riverview Manor with you instead.'

Laurie laughed wickedly, 'Ah now, but what about 'all these important contacts' you 'just have to meet' that you've been wittering on about all week? What about 'the importance of making a good first impression' and 'not doing anything embarrassing?' Laurie teased.

Will had the good grace to look humbled. He really had misjudged Laurie. He sometimes forgot that underneath the everyday chaos that his wife found herself in, she still possessed the characteristics that had attracted him to her in the first place. She was utterly gorgeous, especially when she made the effort for nights like tonight and she was intelligent, humorous and fun. The fact that he so often found himself surrounded by high flying business woman meant that he had somehow forgotten that his own wife could compete with the best of them.

'I'm sorry Laurie' he said humbly. 'I've been unfair to you recently. I'm really glad you agreed to come with me tonight.'

'Do you really mean that Will?' asked Laurie. 'It's just that sometimes I feel as though you'd rather do anything else other than spend time with me.'

Will felt a pang of shame. 'It's not that Laurie' he sighed. 'It's just I never seem to have the time to do all the things I want to do. Of course I want to spend more time with you but I'm always so tied up with work I never seem to get the chance.'

'I'm busy too Will. It's not easy managing all on my own. Sometimes I feel like you only notice me as the woman who looks after your children.' Laurie sighed.

'How could you even think that?' asked Will disbelievingly.

Laurie shrugged half-heartedly. 'You need to work out how you can make more time for me and the kids Will,' she said, 'because I'm not sure how much longer I can cope raising our family on my own.'

Will gritted his teeth. He knew if he said anything else he and Laurie would end up having a massive row and that was not how he wanted to spend his evening. Did Laurie really think he enjoyed all the travel his work entailed? How could she not see that he was just trying to provide for her and the kids?

Thankfully just then they arrived at Riverview Resort and Spa. Maybe if Laurie had a few glasses of wine she'd ease up a bit and get off his case.

Chapter 12

The newly refurbished interior of Riverview Resort and Spa was so stunning it almost took Laurie's breath away. She stepped onto white carpet so lush she literally had to dig her heals back out of it. The chairs were covered in sumptuous white leather and the gilt-edged tables added to the feeling of luxury. The ceiling was adorned by some of the most gorgeous chandeliers that Laurie had ever seen and the glass wall offered a stunning view of the waterfalls lit up by coloured lights strategically placed along the line of the river Braid which passed through the grounds of the Manor itself. Everything about the place spoke indulgence and decadence and it suddenly struck Laurie how great it was to be out of the house with her gorgeous husband on her arm.

As the waiter offered her a glass of pink champagne Laurie hesitated. She was tonight's designated driver and as she had an alcohol tolerance equivalent to a newt she wasn't sure she could even have the one tempting glass of bubbly. Will sensing her hesitation grinned and breathed those wonderful words 'Let's just get a taxi home.' Laurie joyfully downed the champagne in two healthy gulps and sought about retrieving another glass from a passing waiter while Will excused himself to mingle. Laurie spotted Dr Brian Nixon and gave him a friendly wave. Gentleman that he was and seeing her standing on her own he immediately headed over to her and kissed her on the cheek.

'Hi Laurie, it's lovely to see you and might I say you are looking absolutely stunning tonight.'

'You may indeed Brian' said Laurie smiling, instantly loving his unusual mix of old fashioned gentlemanliness and modern-day friendliness. Brian Nixon had an uncanny knack of always making people feel at ease. He was a man genuinely comfortable in his own skin and his relaxed and easy warmth had the immediate effect of putting a smile on Laurie's face.

'I take it that Will is here too?' asked Brian.

'Oh yes he's about here somewhere trying to mingle.'

'Well I hope he doesn't leave you on your own for too long because I can see that there are at least a dozen men in this room just dying to sweep you off your feet.'

Laurie laughed disbelievingly and catching the wicked twinkle in Brian's eye he whispered into Laurie's ear 'Oh look here comes one now'.

Laurie watched as a very rotund bearded man approached them both. It struck her that if Santa ever retired this man would make a perfect substitute. It wasn't just his round, rosy face and grey-white beard that made him the perfect candidate but the way his eyes danced as he took in every detail around him. While he was far from attractive there was something uniquely charming about him that seemed to compel Laurie to look at him.

'Hello Brian. Well aren't you going to introduce me to this handsome lass you're with?' he asked.

'Of course,' said Brian, 'this is the beautiful Laurie Kerr, wife of Will Kerr who works with Worldwide Pharmaceuticals. Laurie this is Chris Jingle owner of Canton Global Medical. Laurie spluttered and her mouthful of champagne went down the wrong way causing her to choke. She looked at Brian incredulously, was he serious? Was the man really called Chris Jingle as in rhyming with Kringle? Brian's eyes just twinkled mischievously in response.

'Now lass don't you mind him, that's just his wee joke cause everyone says I look like Santa Claus. I can't see it myself' he said merrily 'but Brian here likes to wind me up about it, don't you lad? My real name is Chris Canton and I have to say if I was ten years younger I'd sweep you off your feet' he said roguishly. 'You're the prettiest woman in the room by miles' he said kindly.

'Did I hear someone mention the prettiest woman in the room?' said a shrill voice from behind Laurie.

Laurie felt the hairs on the back of her neck prickle warningly. How typical of the dragon lady to make her presence felt just as Laurie was starting to unwind. Laurie couldn't help but feel she wasn't the only one adversely affected by Cynthia's presence. Brian's face had paled, his jaw had tensed, almost as if he was gritting his teeth and his soft, laughing eyes had hardened instantly. Laurie who herself had been dreading hearing that voice all week sobered up immediately. She knew only too well that with Cynthia Nixon on the prowl she needed to keep her wits about her.

Fortunately, Chris came to the rescue, seeming to have suddenly picked up on the frosty atmosphere.

'Of course,' he said lightly 'there is always a beautiful Queen to every Princess' he said charmingly.

'I do hope you're not comparing me to the wicked stepmother.' said Mrs Nixon laughingly.

Laurie sensing that that was exactly what he was doing tensed immediately.

'Of course not my dear' said Chris secretly giving

Laurie's arm a meaningful squeeze. 'I only mean that I am privileged to be surrounded by beautiful women.'

'Beautiful women!' said Cynthia disbelievingly as she looked at Laurie properly for the first time. 'Oh my goodness is that really you Laurie? I hardly recognised you, if I remember correctly the last time I saw you, you were standing in the middle of the road in your rather unseemly pyjamas at 9.15 in the morning. It's so lovely to see you in some proper clothes, although I'm sure you don't wear them half as well as those tatty old pyjamas.' she laughed casually.

Laurie felt herself shrivel with shame. Please don't let them ask for details thought Laurie pleadingly.

Fortunately, Chris sensing her discomfiture said easily 'Well I think Laurie would look good in whatever she was wearing' he grinned 'but with legs like hers I'd rather see her in a pretty negligée than pyjamas any day.'

'I hope you're not lusting after my wife's legs' said a voice to Laurie's left as Will approached 'that's definitely my job' he said smiling and reaching out his hand for Chris to shake. 'Nice to meet you by the way. I'm Will Kerr' he said pleasantly.

'Pleased to meet you. Chris Canton' he said by way of reply.

'From Canton Global?' asked Will

'The very same' said Chris.

'Ah then you're just the man I was looking for. I was just chatting to a colleague of yours, Dan Bridges, and he said I'd better speak to you, apparently you're the man who makes things happen?'

'Well I have been known to' said Chris amiably.

Laurie, grateful that the talk had moved onto business and more than a little relieved that the tension had been broken, quickly excused herself and went to the ladies' room.

Thankfully her hair and makeup were still intact all she needed to do was top up her lippy. How did Brian live with that woman on a daily basis she shuddered? She was more than just unpleasant, she was venomous. She seemed to go out of her way to impress those she liked and destroy those she didn't. She was cunning and devious and Laurie knew better than to underestimate her. She had witnessed both the Cynthia who could tear people to pieces and the one who oozed fake charm, compliments and goodwill; fooling even the most sceptical of her peers about her sincerity. She also flirted with abandonment and men seemed incapable of seeing beyond the charming side of her character that she presented to them. She supposed that was how poor Brian had been fooled.

Brian was the most genuine person Laurie had ever met. In some ways she understood how a man like Brian so totally without guile or pretence himself would ever suspect that others could be so deceptive. Laurie had no doubt that Cynthia had reinvented her character to become exactly what she knew Brian would be looking for in a wife. She could quite easily believe that Cynthia's cunning and deviousness had been so complete that Brian had no idea as to her true character until it was too late to do anything about it. The fact that she was a beautiful woman with a great body and a fantastically fashionable dress sense would also no doubt have played its part. Brian certainly wouldn't be the first naïve man to be beguiled by a beautiful woman pretending to be everything he ever wanted. Laurie felt nothing but sympathy for Brian whom she sensed was a very unhappily married man and was far too lovely to have landed himself someone as vindictive and malicious as Cynthia Nixon.

After tonight Laurie planned to stay out of her way as much as possible. Clearly her only chance of survival tonight was to drink copious amounts of alcohol and avoid her at all costs.

By the time Laurie made her way back into the great hall the guests were already seated. Hastily Laurie found her table and was relieved to find that she was seated between Brian and Chris. Will was sitting beside Cynthia and Dan Bridges the man whom Will had been speaking with earlier.

The meal was absolutely delicious, made all the better by the pleasant company Laurie had on either side. She quickly realised that Chris and Brian were firm friends who sparked off each other in a way that was both fascinating and entertaining. The pair were evenly matched in terms of wit and intelligence and playfully engaged Laurie in their banter. Just as Laurie found herself nodding in agreement with the argument one of them presented the other would put forward an equally compelling argument to the contrary and Laurie found herself agreeing instantly with the other. The two men seemed to thrive on their ability to make her change her mind and she found herself compelled to do so frequently and unrepentantly. The more alcohol Laurie consumed the more she felt like a ping pong ball being batted back and forth between the two men as part of a fun, fast paced game. Their table was attracting more than its fair share of attention given the two men's easy and engaging repartee.

Unfortunately, in her somewhat drunken state Laurie had failed to consider the effect her fun was having on a very jealous hostess whose own temper was becoming more and more frayed by the minute. Cynthia had felt sure that placing Laurie between boring Brian and cumbersome Chris would have had a stupefying effect on Laurie whom she had been quite sure would have nothing to contribute to the conversation. She hadn't bargained on the three of them being the life and soul of the party.

Her mood was dampened still further because she couldn't believe how well Laurie was looking. While Cynthia wouldn't go so far as to say that Laurie was beautiful, she was looking better than Cynthia had given her credit for. Worse still, she seemed to be attracting an awful lot of admiring glances from the few men she had glimpsed glancing over at their table.

Of course it was clear to Cynthia that Laurie knew exactly what she was doing, flirting and laughing in that completely false and unrealistic way. She obviously wanted to be the centre of attention and Cynthia was just beginning to wonder if Laurie Kerr was deliberating trying to irritate her.

To top it all off, things with Will were not going as well as Cynthia had hoped. He was certainly playing the salesman bit to the hilt but she couldn't understand why he kept sliding away from her hand subtly placed on his arm or lingering momentarily on his firm thigh. Maybe she was rushing things with him a little, but it seemed to her that he was distracted by the seemingly humorous chitchat at the opposite side of the table and she thought he had looked slightly longingly in that direction from time to time. Surely he couldn't realistically think that he was better off with batty Laurie and the dismal duo than he was with her. Ridiculous as that was, nevertheless Cynthia thought that it would be better all-round if Laurie toddled off home where she belonged. Just as Cynthia was wondering how she could arrange that she was called upon to introduce the charity auction.

Chapter 13

'Ladies and gentlemen thank you all for coming tonight. I'm sure you'll all agree that the evening has so far been a wonderful success and I'd like to thank the owners and staff of the hotel for their generosity and support in providing us with such a beautiful venue and delicious meal.' Cynthia paused to allow the shouts and applaud to die down before continuing. 'And now that you're all well fed and hopefully too drunk to know how much money you're spending ......' shouts of 'here, here' and laughter floated up to Cynthia just as she had hoped. 'I would like to encourage you all to find it in your heart and your wallet to lend your support to what is a very worthwhile cause. As many of you here tonight are from a medical or pharmaceutical background I know you are all very much aware of how important fundraising is to the parents and children, staff and patients of the special care baby unit at the Royal

Victoria Hospital. These much-needed funds can be a lifeline to families whose children would otherwise not survive being born prematurely or who are born with life threatening conditions. And so, it is my pleasure to hand you over to Mr Williams our auctioneer for the evening and I would ask you all to dig deep to support this most worthwhile cause.'

Enthusiastic applause greeted Cynthia's little speech and she was glowing in her own success as she took her place beside the auctioneer ready to perform one of her final duties of the evening, recording the names of the various bidders. Thankfully local industries and local celebrities had contributed some very appealing items to the charity auction and there was a plethora of restaurant vouchers, helicopter rides, hotel stays, and a luxury Mediterranean cruise to tempt even the most hesitant of bidders.

As bidding got underway for the fifty or so items generously donated the atmosphere in the great hall became almost electric. Rival firms battled to outdo each other in a well-intentioned camaraderie of spirit. Items worth perhaps £30 or £40 were going for almost three times that amount. Larger donations worth hundreds of pounds were selling for two or three thousand.

The atmosphere at Laurie's table where Brian and Chris were engaged in an outrageous battle of bidding wars, not to actually win the items but simply to run up the bidding as high as possible before bailing out just before final bids were taken, was electric. They had easily doubled or even tripled the value most items were fetching and seemed to thrive on the adrenalin rush of knowing just when to exit. Neither of the two men had yet been stuck with the item but Laurie was convinced it was only a matter of time. Will, who had drawn his chair up beside Laurie, clutched Laurie's hand feverishly, a sure sign that he was as excited as the rest of them. He placed a number of bids himself though not having the funds to actually risk being stuck with an item he couldn't afford he was careful only to join the bidding in its very early stages and well before the item reached its ultimate value. Laurie more than a little drunk on champagne was enjoying watching the drama unfold immensely. It was years since she had enjoyed herself so much. She really should thank Cynthia Nixon after all, because without her Laurie would have been stuck at home with a bottle of wine and a DVD.

The all-expenses paid cruise in the Mediterranean was the ultimate prize in the charity bidding. The holiday alone was easily worth £5000 and that was where the bidding started. Not even Chris or Brian dared to take the bidding beyond the £9000 mark, both of them assuring Laurie that neither of them really needed a holiday that badly. Bidding seemed to focus on two middle-aged gentlemen towards the front of the hall whom Brian knew to be age old rivals. Will who had been dying to go to the toilet for the past half hour suddenly decided that he couldn't wait a moment longer and excused himself from the table just as the bidding reached the £10,000 mark. Surely it wouldn't go much higher thought Laurie earnestly.

Laurie was so caught up in the bidding that she didn't notice that the leg of Will's chair had caught on her dress. Unfortunately, as Will pushed his chair back, Laurie's dress made a large ripping sound. Laurie sprung out of her seat in an effort to save her dress ripping further, toppled over the chair Will had carelessly left behind her and found herself on a heap on the floor. Both Chris and Brian jumped up to assist her and Laurie found herself gesticulating wildly and somewhat drunkenly that she was fine.

Unfortunately for Laurie, Cynthia seized her opportunity pointed the auctioneer in the direction of the new bidder and at Cynthia's insistence wrapped up the bidding in three seconds flat. As Laurie righted herself on her chair she heard the Auctioneer call out the words 'Sold to the lady in the green dress for the amazing sum of £10,500. Ladies and gentlemen please put your hands together for the generous lady Mrs… ummh Mrs … '

'Laurie Kerr' hissed Cynthia.

'Mrs Laurie Kerr' said the Auctioneer. Please all give Mrs Kerr a round of applause for her unstinting generosity to such a worthwhile cause.'

As the whole room stood to its feet to applaud her, Laurie's face drained of colour. 'Oh shit' she thought, how in the world was she ever going to get out of this and how was she ever going to tell Will. With the thunderous applause still ringing in her ears Laurie slipped into a dead faint and slid off her chair for the second time in under three minutes.

Chapter 14

When Will returned from the toilets he was somewhat surprised to see a rather subdued table. When he had left them the atmosphere had been positively adrenalin fuelled.

'Well' he demanded earnestly 'Who won the cruise?'

No one spoke. Five heads bowed to the floor. Laurie looked a deathly shade of white and for a moment Will wondered what on earth he'd missed. 'Laurie are you alright?' he asked.

Laurie didn't answer.

'Laurie what's going on? Who won the holiday?' Will asked again totally perplexed.

Laurie raised her eyes to look at Will 'We did' she said meekly.

'Ha,ha' Will guffawed. 'Good one Laurie. I

wondered why you guys were being so quiet. You really had me going for a second there.'

Laurie looked at Will pleadingly.

'Ok Laurie you can drop the act now you've had your little joke' said Will laughingly as he plonked himself down on his chair. 'Anybody fancy some more champagne?' offered Will generously.

'Did I hear the word champagne?' intoned a whiny, nasally voice. 'Are you celebrating winning your wonderful holiday darling?' Cynthia asked shrilly.

'You're a bit slow on that one Cynthia' grinned Will. 'This lot have already had their little joke.'

'Joke, what are you talking about Will?' asked Cynthia. 'I don't think any of us regard saving the lives of those little babies as some sort of joke. I think what Laurie did was truly wonderful.' she said giving Laurie the most vicious, supercilious smile Laurie had ever seen.

Laurie could see Will's face pale as he started to reassess the situation, she knew just how he felt.

'Laurie' he croaked. 'I think we need to talk.'

Chapter 15

Laurie had never seen Will so angry. His face was deathly pale. His lips were drawn in a thin hard line. She could see him struggling to keep his voice down given the fact that they were standing in the front foyer of the Hotel but his anger was bubbling over causing him to raise his voice and gesticulate furiously drawing more than one concerned glance from the other hotel guests. This was a domestic on a scale Laurie had never encountered before and she didn't know whether to be more concerned that for the first time in her life Will actually looked as though he wanted to hit her or the fact that she had just spent £10,500 of money that they just didn't have on a holiday that they would never go on, with no possibility of a refund.

Will was currently shouting furiously at her because apparently there was no way in hell he could run grovelling to the Charity Board to explain the whole thing had been a terrible mistake, especially not in light of the fact that Laurie had been given a bloody standing ovation for her unstinting generosity. Even if by some unlikely stretch of the imagination they were willing to believe that the whole thing had been a terrible mistake the Charity would be left with a gaping ten grand hole in its finances.

'Just what the hell did you think you were doing Laurie?' Will shouted furiously. 'I turn my back for less than three minutes and you somehow manage to bankrupt us. I knew I couldn't trust you. Why did I ever credit you with having the intelligence to come with me tonight. I might have known what a mess you'd make of everything – you always do! Poor blundering Laurie always 'accidentally' messing things up. Always leaving me to deal with the shit you leave behind! Always Laurie, bloody always, well I'm sick of it. I'm sick of the whole fecking thing. You're an embarrassment to yourself and to me and I've had enough.

'Please Will!' Laurie pleaded 'if you'd just let me explain.'

'Explain Laurie! How the hell can you possibly explain your way out of this one. Is this some sort of joke to you?'

'But Will I didn't mean to bid on that holiday. I really didn't I still don't understand how the auctioneer thought I was placing a bid. It really wasn't my fault.'

'No Laurie it never bloody well is! But you know as well as I do that this is a professional auctioneer, not some bloody amateur so obviously any dimwit would realise he's not about to take 'accidental' bids from people.'

'But Will please you've got to believe me it really was an accident. I fell off my seat and the next thing I knew the auctioneer had pointed that little stick of his and was banging it on the table.'

'And just what the hell were you doing lying on the floor in the first place Laurie. I suppose you were so pissed you couldn't even keep your backside on the seat,' Will glowered. 'I knew I should never have agreed to you having a drink Laurie, you're silly enough when you're sober never mind when you've had a few glasses too many. There was me thinking that for once you were making an effort to impress and what do you do, you not only ruin the whole bloody evening but our finances for the foreseeable future as well. I should have known I couldn't trust you enough to bring you somewhere like this Laurie, it's clearly more than you're able for', shouted Will.

'What's that supposed to mean?' asked Laurie as the first tears began streaming down her cheeks.

'You know exactly what I mean Laurie. You're a disgrace, an unmitigated disaster an ....'

Laurie never did get to hear what else she was, she had convulsed into floods of tears and Brian Nixon, sensing Will was out of control had quietly but assuredly stepped between Laurie and Will.

'I think you've said enough' stated Brian calmly. 'Laurie has endured enough ridicule for one night don't you think?'

It was as though Will suddenly tuned back in to his surroundings, as if a switch flipped back to off in his head. His eyes lost the vicious edginess of moments before as he suddenly seemed to realise where he was and what he was saying. Will turned to look at Laurie as if only realising what a state she was in. 'Oh Laurie, he said 'I'm sorry, I'm so sorry, I don't know what came over me.'

To be fair Will looked every bit as shell shocked as Laurie was feeling. But for the moment Laurie was unable to see anything beyond her own fear and humiliation.

'I think you need to give Laurie a little space here' said Brian, as he gently placed a hand on Will's shoulder and steered him towards the bar.

'Laurie' called Brian over his shoulder. 'Just wait there. I'll be right back.'

Laurie stood stock still in complete shock until she realised that there were at least a dozen pairs of eyes staring straight at her. It was enough to force

Laurie's mind to kick into action and somehow convey to her feet that they needed to get out of there as quickly as possible. Laurie dashed out the doors into the now pouring rain, which suited Laurie perfectly well because at least no one was likely to come looking for her, and furthermore, it would disguise the snot and tears streaming down her face. Laurie found herself running blindly to the car park where she sank down at the side of her car realising she had no keys, no money and no means of escape.

Chapter 16

Laurie wasn't sure how long she sat hunched by the side of their car but it felt like forever. Eventually she realised Brian was crouched down beside her, rain running down his face in unceasing rivulets. He was speaking to her but it was as if his voice was coming from a long way off. Her body was shaking so hard that she absently wondered if she was having some sort of fit. Brian tried to coax her towards his car but she couldn't seem to get her legs to move. She was vaguely aware of him half carrying, half dragging her to the passenger seat but she was shivering so uncontrollably she was totally incapable of speech. Thankfully Brian seemed to realise this and drove in silence.

At some point, she recognised they'd stopped moving and that Brian was helping her inside; but it wasn't until the fiery hot liquid Brian was feeding her hit the back of her throat and burnt its way to the pit of her stomach that Laurie began to really felt anything at all. And then the impact of feeling again hit her like a body blow; scenes from her disastrous night floating past her eyelids in slow motion, at first the laughter; the feeling of being high on adrenaline and alcohol and then her fall from her chair, the awful realisation her bid had been mistakenly taken, the standing ovation, her fainting, the look on Will's face when he realised what she'd done and worst of all the way he belittled her, shouted her down and scarily lost control.

It was some time before Laurie's mind caught up with the present and the shaking in her body subsided as she gradually felt some warmth return to her. Brian stood silently by allowing her time to adjust, supplying her with a warm jumper to slip on, thankfully one of his and not his wife's, lighting a fire to keep her warm and lift her spirits. She was glad he was there; a solid reassuring presence; grounding her back in reality. Eventually Laurie found her voice. 'Thank you Brian she said humbly. I'm sorry to be such a bother.'

'It's no bother Laurie but I'd be happier if you'd stay here a while longer until I'm certain you're not going into shock again. It's not a good combination suffering an incident like you did and then getting soaked to the skin in the pouring rain. I was minutes away from taking you to the hospital.' He admitted.

'Really?' Asked Laurie hesitatingly. 'I had no idea' she shuddered.

As the two of them sat in a companionable silence before the fire Laurie noted that Brian seemed as lost in thought as she was.

'Laurie' said Brian eventually. 'How well do you know my wife?'

'I don't really know her at all Brian' she said shakily 'I only met her in person last week when she rescued me after my car took a flat.' She said cautiously.

'Do you have any reason to think that she may dislike you?' he asked gently.

Laurie wasn't quite sure how to answer that. She thought it was part of Cynthia's genetic make-up to dislike most people on sight but she could hardly tell Brian that. 'I'm not sure' Laurie replied, thinking guiltily of Cynthia's reaction to her deliberately misleading her about the burglary.

'It's just …. Laurie I have a suspicion that the auctioneer would never have thought you were bidding unless someone was directing him to take a bid from you', he said cautiously.

'What do you mean Brian?' Laurie asked.

'I mean that I think my wife deliberately instructed him to accept your bid.'

'No' said Laurie. 'Why would she do that?' she asked incredulously.

'That's the one thing I haven't quite figured out yet, but I have my suspicions', he said hesitatingly. Forgive me if I'm speaking out of turn but I… I think she may want to….well….to get to … I mean…to become more intimately involved with your husband' he said shakily.

Laurie could see the raw pain in his eyes.

Brian looked away and dipped his head. 'I've known for a while now that my wife has …..problems. I'm not sure how much of it stems from her personality and how much has set in since she had the children. When I first met Cynthia she was confident and self-assured, but she also seemed to be thoughtful and considerate or at least I believed she was' he said doubtfully. 'I'm not sure when I began to think that maybe she wasn't the person I believed her to be. She suffered from post-natal depression after the children were born and I prefer to think her personality somehow underwent an irreversible change rather than I had misjudged her all along. All I really know for sure is that she is not the woman I thought she was when I married her. She is I'm ashamed to say, ruthless, vindictive and selfish. She doesn't want me anymore, at least not the way a wife should want her husband, and so what I'm trying to say Laurie is that…………well………….. she takes her pleasure elsewhere.'

Laurie saw the pain and shame etched in Brian's face. She realised how much this was costing him to share with her. She felt a well of sympathy rise up in her for this lovely man who wanted to help her in spite of the pain and humiliation it was costing him personally. She didn't know what to say. She reached out and hugged him to her. She felt his body relax against hers and in that moment a shared comfort seemed to pass between them. She rested her head against his chest enjoying the soothing rhythm of his heartbeat, the heat of his body against hers. They stood like that for a long time, neither of them speaking, each deriving comfort from the others presence.

At length Laurie began to feel the anger bubbling up inside her, against Will against Cynthia. Brian was right this was all Cynthia's doing, she had deliberately instructed the auctioneer to take her bid knowing full well that Laurie hadn't been bidding at all. She wanted to cause trouble between Will and her so she could get her claws into her husband. 'How could she?' raged Laurie. 'How could she do this to us?' she cried as she pushed herself up into a sitting position.

'I'm sorry Laurie' said Brian.

'You aren't the one who needs to apologise' said Laurie. 'That woman, your wife, has absolutely no idea what she has put me through tonight. How dare she do that to me? Will works all the hours God sends, we hardly ever see him because he's always away on some business trip or other and in a single moment your wife has managed to bring our carefully balanced finances crashing around our ears. We can't afford to pay for that damned holiday Brian. We'll have to re-mortgage our house to pay for it' Laurie sobbed.

'Hush Laurie, please don't upset yourself again. It'll sort itself out. I'm sure I can have a word with the Charity and explain that you didn't actually mean to bid on the holiday and that it was all a big mistake. I'm sure they'll end up cancelling the bid and saving the holiday for auction at another time,' he soothed.

'Do you really think so Brian? It's just that Will said...'

'Will said a lot of things tonight Laurie that he most definitely shouldn't have said and if you ask me he was bang out of order!' Brian said angrily.

'He.. he's not normally like that' stumbled Laurie. 'I've never ever seen him that angry before.'

'I should bloody well hope not' Brian replied indignantly. 'Laurie you had done nothing wrong. None of this was your fault. Don't you see Laurie?' he said holding her squarely by the shoulders and forcing her to look him in the eyes. 'This was all one big set up.' Cynthia had already picked her target, all she had to do was get rid of the competition', he said gently.

'Wha….. What do you mean?' Laurie stuttered.

Brian sighed heavily and released Laurie's shoulders. He rubbed his hand across his face and suddenly he looked utterly defeated.

'Laurie' he stumbled. 'I know this has been a hell of a difficult night for you already and I'm not sure whether you really don't see what I'm trying to tell you or whether you don't want to see, but I think deep down you know what I mean.'

'No. Laurie breathed. Will would never cheat on me. He would never do that to us, to his family. I trust him completely.'

'Good' said Brian. 'That is really good, because I do not trust my wife at all and I can tell you now Laurie that when she puts her mind to something she is a very difficult woman to refuse.'

Chapter 17

It was after two in the morning before Brian dropped Laurie home. The house was in darkness. She wondered if Will was home yet and dreaded the thought of seeing him. She just couldn't face another row, at least not tonight.

Laurie felt as if she had been hit by a ten-tonne truck. Her face was swollen with tears, her head was throbbing, her body still felt chilled to the bone and her mind was in so much turmoil she knew that she would never sleep. As she crept quietly up the stairs she decided she needed a good long soak in a hot bath before she did anything else. As she let her body glide into the wonderfully warm water she forced her mind to think of anything but tonight's events; but try as she might she really could not help replaying some of the horrible things Will had said to her. Was she really such a disaster that Will felt ashamed of her?

Deep down Laurie knew that Will was right, without him around, her life descended into chaos. He was her rock; he was the strong, sensible one while she was impulsive, spontaneous and scatty. That was how it had always been with her and Will. She flitted unwittingly from one disaster to the next, Will would steam roller along behind, smoothing things over. In fact Will's ability to rescue Laurie had been evident from the first moment they met.

Laurie let her mind drift back to those earlier happier times when she and Will had first met. It turned out that they both attended Edinburgh University, although they didn't actually meet until their third year. Laurie had, as usual, been out on the tiles with the girls and was heading home from some night club or other at about three in the morning. Of course she and the girls were all totally hammered, singing along at the tops of their voices, when somehow Laurie fell a little behind the rest of the group - probably something to do with not being able to handle alcohol and six inch stilettos at the same time.

On this occasion however Laurie's stiletto's proved quite fortuitous. She had somehow managed to get her heel stuck in a crack in the pavement and was struggling in vain to free herself when Will stumbled out of a bar and walked straight into Laurie's jiggling perpendicular bottom. Will made some wise crack about normally having to work a lot harder to get women to bend over like that for him. Laurie, realising that this guy was drop dead gorgeous instantly decided she would bend in any position he wanted her to.

However, given the number of guys she'd taken back to her flat after a night out only to wake in the morning and realise she had very definitely had her beer goggles on Laurie urged herself to be cautious. So bad was her track record at picking up nerds, losers, pompous gits and even on one occasion a homeless man, whom thankfully she managed to ditch before reaching her flat, that her friends now insisted in vetting every guy she met on a night out. She was then only allowed to take things further if at least three out of four of them agreed he was dateable. This in itself was a fairly lengthy process, each friend having to rate him on looks; likeability; number of zits; height; hair style and overall dress sense or lack thereof. Needless to say she had yet to meet a man who passed muster by one friend never mind three and her dating record was therefore dwindling at the rate of a gay man in a straight bar. This time though she didn't have a friend in sight, she could have been raped and murdered for all those drunken good for nothings would know, but she was fairly sure this guy was good to go.

He looked to be about six feet tall, piercing blue eyes, longish blond slightly curly hair, a strong jaw and a smile that was pure unadulterated Brad Pitt.

Laurie was already head over heels in lust. The only problem was she knew he was way out of her league. There was no way a guy this good looking would look twice at a girl like Laurie. She was plain Miss Bingley to his Mr Darcy.

Not only that but he was also clearly gentlemanly enough to help a damsel in distress. He struggled for a good ten minutes to free her heel from that grating. Little did he realise that was probably eight minutes more than necessary as Laurie was enjoying the feel of his hands on her leg so much she deliberately pushed down as hard as she could to ensure it stayed exactly where it was. Laurie reckoned he had twigged what she was doing eventually but by that time he was enjoying the feeling of his hand on Laurie's leg as much as she was and didn't give a damn.

Obviously, gentleman that he was, he apologised profusely when he accidently snapped Laurie's stiletto in half. Laurie explained that unfortunately his negligent behaviour meant that he was honour bound to walk her home. They walked, or rather he walked and Laurie hobbled, back to her flat. To this day Laurie still can't recall what they talked about, so awestruck was she to have this gorgeous specimen of a man attached to her arm. She did remember that he laughed a lot and whether she really was the funniest woman in the world or he just brought out the humorous side in her she still didn't know. What she did know was that by the time they made it back to her flat she was loathe to let him slip through her fingers. So when she chanced her luck and asked him in for a coffee she was at once delighted and astonished that he actually said yes.

Needless to say there was no coffee (quite literally as her flatmates had finished the jar) so when he insisted that Laurie make it up to him she did exactly what any self-respecting woman in her position would do and made him a cup of tea instead. Laurie's tea making skills must have been better than she had given them credit for because he liked it so much he decided to stay for dessert and luckily Laurie was on the menu.

The sex was mind blowing. Laurie could still remember the raw hunger of that first night. She wanted him with an all-consuming passion she never even knew she possessed before. If she could have bottled that feeling she would have made her fortune in sales.

Amazingly though it really wasn't just about the sex, it was so much more than that. It was as if their souls had already connected on some supernatural plain way before they ever met. And right then, she knew she had found her soul mate. This was it. This was what all the fuss was about. When you found someone that just totally fitted it was like past, present and future suddenly made total and perfect sense. And the really great thing was it wasn't just her thinking this. Will had felt it too.

'What just happened?' he said breathlessly.

'I'm not sure' Laurie gasped 'did the earth just move?'

'No I'm pretty sure that was just the leg falling off your bed.'

'Shit! Did it really. My landlords going to go nuts again.'

'Seriously though that was pretty amazing Laurie, I've never really had that whole out of body experience before.'

'Yeah, I know but I think I really need to check whether it was just all the blood rushing to your head with the bed at that angle' she giggled. 'Better let me check to see if the experience is repeatable' she said kissing his gorgeous full mouth and once again sliding her hand over the taut muscles of his gorgeous body.

'Hey, give a guy a minute will you', he said but he was already kissing her back deep enough to make her body ache.

And so it was that Laurie and Will became a couple.

Their friends were delighted of course. But Laurie often wondered if they really thought it would last. Will had been very much a ladies man and it was a big adjustment for the lads heading out without their lethal pulling partner.

Laurie was vaguely aware that somehow other woman saw Will with her and viewed her as competition not to be taken seriously. She knew they were trying to assess how someone as stunning as Will could really be serious about someone like her. She was attractive and good natured but definitely not in the drop dead gorgeous category. They discarded her as irrelevant and went straight in for the kill.

Will went on oblivious to all of this as only a man can. He was happy, and amazingly despite feeling a bit insecure so was Laurie. She didn't know where this experience was going to take her but she knew that a life without Will was unthinkable. Laurie was quite aware, at her friends insistence, that she was more than likely going to end up with a broken heart but this was one rollercoaster she couldn't get off and so she resolved to take her chances.

She couldn't eat. She couldn't sleep unless she was in Will's bed, wrapped up in his arms and then she slept like a baby. She practically moved into his place much to the undisguised disgust of his 'lad about town' flatmates.

Three months became six and then they were suddenly celebrating their one year anniversary and still they were happy. More than that, they were in love. Laurie wanted to take Will back to the North of Ireland and show him off to her parents. He was keen to go and so it was they set off on a plane to the Emerald Isle.

Will fell in love with Northern Ireland just as quickly as he fell in love with Laurie. They spent weeks on the North Antrim coast in their little two-man tent. They travelled through the luscious Glens of Antrim and did a whistle-stop tour of Cushendun, Cushendall and Ballycastle. Will joked that the people of Cushendall would never give him directions. Laurie challenged him on that one, but he was right, they wouldn't, they insisted on walking him to wherever he wanted to go and stopping off at the pub on route to show him a bit of Irish hospitality.

The weather, for once, was brilliantly warm and sunny and they spent days on Portstewart beach the Whiterocks and Portballintrae. He drank it all in as eagerly he would a pint of Guinness; the golden beaches, the awesome views and stunning scenery. He surfed, learned to speak Ulster Scott's - not too much of a problem for a Scotsman - and drank like a native.

One summers evening Will took Laurie to Mussenden Temple right out on the cliff, high above the golden sands of Downhill beach. He pulled her to the edge and when Laurie dared to open her eyes she saw the sands lit up with candles in jars spelling out the words 'Marry Me'. For once in her life Laurie was speechless. She nodded her consent and then burst into tears. Of course Will knew the best way to calm her down and right then Laurie decided she liked making love to him even better as a betrothed woman than she did as his girlfriend.

Ten months later they graduated and returned to Northern Ireland to get married in the exact same Mussenden Temple at which he had proposed. Their Scottish friends more used to seeing Northern Ireland in the headlines for the bomb and the bullet couldn't believe the beauty of the place and most extended their planned two-day visit to give them time to take in the Giant's Causeway, Carrickfergus, the Mourne Mountains and the beautiful Fermanagh Lakes. Laurie felt as though she should have been receiving commission from Northern Ireland tourist board but she was just too happy to give more than a passing thought to anything but the dream she was living.

They honeymooned in Vegas. Spending their days lazing by the pool, their afternoons luxuriating in each other's bodies and their nights in the Casinos gambling money they didn't have.

They came home stony broke but glowing in that way only the truly happy can. Within two weeks their tans had faded along with their glow.

Reality had struck big time.

They had no money, no jobs and nowhere to live. Their wedding gift money had long since disappeared and they literally couldn't even afford to buy food. Their dole money hadn't yet come through because of a delay in being assessed. They were staying in a little borrowed campervan in Laurie's Mum and Dad's front garden, and while as students they could have lived pretty much anywhere the dynamics had somehow changed. For the first time they felt the pressure of living in the real world with the need to support themselves. As singletons they could have relied on the good nature of their respective parents to pave the way financially until they found their feet, but as a married couple they were loath to ask for hand-outs. They both felt that their parents had done their bit. Now it was time to see what they were made of and their pride would not allow them to fail.

Only then did they question the wisdom of doing a Business and Management degree (Will) and an English degree (Laurie). Why had no one ever advised them to do something that would actually make them employable? They just wanted to make money but they couldn't figure out how to get their hands on it.

Unfortunately, it appeared that they had dossed for four years doing degrees that neither of them now gave a toss about while their peers who had left school at sixteen seemed to be raking it in as interior designers, builders, and even amateur property developers. Ireland was just at the beginning of the economic boom and those with a bit of a head start in the property business were making more money than they knew what to do with while Laurie and Will were in a rut and they both new it. They realised with a pang that perhaps it wasn't the most sensible idea to get married straight out of Uni with no jobs and no prospects. The arguments which had never previously featured in their relationship had begun to appear with increasing regularity. They were always short with each other, quick to see the faults which had previously remained hidden. The glow had most definitely begun to fade from their relationship and all they really wanted was to reclaim the perfection that had once been flowing in abundance. In reality they were both grieving for the relationship that once was and that was the saddest and most difficult thing of all.

Will was the one who eventually pulled them out of the quagmire they had found themselves in. Typically it wasn't his amazing CV or his cushy first class honours that landed him his first job. No, it was the fact that Laurie's brother knew a man who knew a man who had just set up his own business selling IT equipment and needed someone who could take on some of the sales work while he dealt with the admin and suppliers.

And so it was that Will ended up working twelve hour days for less than he could have got on the dole. Of course Will had that certain charisma which made him just the right fit for sales. The female buyers were wooed by his charm and good looks, the male buyers latched on to his confidence and good humour and soon he had them eating out of his hand.

He was, it has to be said, a totally gifted

salesman. Hardworking, warm-hearted and genuine. Of course his boss was a smarmy git and miserable as sin but after three years sorting out all the dross his boss left behind he finally had enough experience and confidence to land himself a job as sales rep with a major pharmaceutical company.

In his first year he outsold any other sales rep by fifteen per cent, in his second that figure increased to thirty per cent and his bosses, keen to hang on to him, promoted him time and again. He was doing good.

Married life was looking up too. They moved into their own little rented flat in Belfast not too far from the city centre and their jobs. Yes jobs because by then Laurie had also secured herself a job as a para-legal working in a Belfast law firm. Thankfully you didn't need a law degree to work there you just needed to be a pretty faced female in a too short skirt with a self-depreciating sense of humour. In an economy that was booming Laurie knew that if she could work up a bit of experience everything else would fall into place. And so it did.

After working for a few years Laurie got the baby bug and soon after she and Will began making babies at a rate which left both of them reeling. Even now Laurie couldn't quite believe that she was the mother of five kids and not for the first time did she wonder whether their arrival in such quick succession had been too much too soon? Of course she knew that it was almost entirely her own doing but if truth be told she had been wondering for some time now whether Will was really happy. Sometimes it seemed like he couldn't wait to get away on his next business trip just to escape the chaos that was their home life. And while she knew that deep down Will loved his kids fervently she often wondered what had happened to the glorious relationship they once had as a couple. When you had once been in love so completely and so all-consuming was it even possible to be satisfied by something so much more humble and mundane?

As Laurie shook herself from her reverie she realised that tears were once again spilling from her eyes. She really would have to get a grip, being an emotional wreck was not something she was used to. The problem was, she realised she no longer knew her husband and she was no longer completely sure of his heartfelt loyalty.

Chapter 18

Will rolled over and reached for Laurie. He was so hung over even the struggle in doing so almost made him wretch. He wasn't yet at the stage where he could risk opening his eyes as his head was spinning so badly that the effort was sure to be a step too far. He felt Laurie snuggle up to him and realised that she had for the time being at least decided to forgive him. As he felt her hand travel down his torso he couldn't help a small groan of satisfaction escape his lips. He reached for her drawing her naked body next to his and gingerly opened his eyes.

'Holy shit' he cried 'what the hell do you think you're doing?' he yelled as he threw his arms out and roughly pushed the woman who was lying on top of him off his body with such force she landed on the floor.

'Bollocks' he shouted 'what the hell is happening

here?'

'I would have thought that was pretty obvious' Cynthia replied sharply, rubbing her hurt elbow gingerly.

'What…? How…?' Will stammered, looking around in bewilderment as he attempted to take in his surroundings. 'Did we just…?' 'No, no, no' he panicked, 'this isn't right, this can't be' he muttered, stunned to find himself in bed in a hotel room stark naked with a woman who clearly knew her way about his body.

'What's the problem Will?' Cynthia smiled. 'You weren't complaining last night now where you?' she simpered.

Will who couldn't even take in what had just happened in the last five minutes never mind what had happened last night felt the bile rise in the back of his throat and ran for the bathroom throwing up just as he reached the toilet. What had he done he wondered miserably? Had he just spent the night in bed having sex with this woman? He bolted the door and turned on the shower trying to give himself some thinking space.

He remembered rowing with Laurie and for the first time in his life he felt truly mortified at how he had treated her. After Brian Nixon had steered him to the bar, he remembered downing his drink and ordering another pretty quickly. The truth was he was ashamed of the things he had said to Laurie. Of course he was damned angry with her too but he felt guilty at the way he had dressed her down in front of all those people and he was also more than a little concerned that he had let his temper get the better of him like that. He was disappointed in Laurie but strangely he felt even more disappointed in himself.

He remembered drinking at the bar for some time before Cynthia joined him.

'There you are Will I've been looking all over for you' she said. He remembered wishing she would just clear off but good manners prevented him from ignoring her and besides it struck him that she might know where Laurie was.

'Have you seen Laurie?' he asked.

'Oh you poor dear, I heard about your little disagreement, but don't worry Will I saw Brian rush out after her and I'm sure she's in very good hands. I'm more concerned about you to be honest, you look absolutely miserable' she crooned.

'I feel pretty shitty actually' Will admitted. 'I had a real go at Laurie for bidding on that holiday.'

'Oh darling is that all you're worried about?' she asked. 'You know, I am co-ordinator of the charity dinner, I'm sure we can sort something out about that.'

'Really?' Will asked hopefully. 'You've no idea

what that would mean to me.'

'Well let's have a little drink and a chat and then I'll try pulling in a few favours to see if we can't get this little misunderstanding cleared up.'

Will wasn't sure how much more he had to drink after that. In fact he was struggling to remember almost anything after that. He recalled Cynthia persuading him to follow her to her hotel room because she had some telephone numbers there that she needed before she could let him know whether anything could be resolved about the auction. Will wanted so much to be able to tell Laurie that everything was sorted out that he didn't hesitate to agree. He remembered having a few more drinks in her hotel room but after that he was drawing a complete blank.

How could he have been so stupid? It was bad enough that he had torn strips off Laurie last night but to sleep with someone else was something he knew she would never forgive. Of course the fact that he had never done anything like it before wouldn't cut any ice at all. He may not remember much about last night but what had gone on this morning was all too vivid.

For the first time in his life Will didn't know what to do. Unfortunately turning back time wasn't possible, although that, more than anything was exactly what he wanted to do.

Chapter 19

'Darling, are you leaving so soon?' Cynthia purred as Will exited the bathroom and hurriedly began getting dressed. He had spent so long in there that Cynthia had long since reached the end of her tether. Of course, if he had left the door unlocked she would have joined him for a little bit of fun. His body was even better than she remembered. He was perfectly toned, just the right mix of bulging bicep and sexy six pack. His waist unlike her husbands had not yet given way to middle aged spread and his thighs were long and strong. The only problem was that she really wanted to enjoy him a lot longer. This morning hadn't worked out at all as she had planned. She really didn't know what had gotten into him and she certainly didn't appreciate being dumped unceremoniously on the floor especially when she was just starting to really enjoy that tasty body of his.

'This was a mistake Cynthia. I shouldn't have come to your room last night and I'd appreciate it if you didn't mention it to anyone.'

'Oh darling there's no need to be so churlish. I have no intention of mentioning it to anyone. I'm married as well you know. It wouldn't exactly do either of our reputations, not to mention our marriages, any good if I went around telling all and sundry now would it' she purred as she found his tie and began wrapping it sexily around his neck. 'You seem exceptionally tense this morning Will. I think I liked it better when you were relaxing into my body last night,' she purred rubbing her leg sexily up and down his thigh.

To her shock Will hastily pushed her away and began searching for the rest of his clothes. 'I don't think you understand' he said gruffly. 'This shouldn't have happened. I love my wife. I'm not about to throw it all away on some pathetic one night stand.'

'Now just hold on a minute Will. Don't start taking it out on me just because you can't keep it in your pants. You were only too happy to come back to the room with me last night and let's face it you really couldn't get enough of me, so there is absolutely no point making out that you hadn't intended for any of this to happen. And as for being a one night stand, well I'm not into those either. I wouldn't have allowed you to stay the night except you were so persuasive and I must admit I was rather flattered when you told me how much you wanted me and how much it would mean to you if we could spend the night together. And now in the cold light of day you just want to pretend like it never happened; that it didn't mean as much to you as it did to me' she said tearfully.

'Oh hell Cynthia, I'm sorry, I didn't mean to make you cry' Will sighed as he sat down heavily on the bed and gingerly placed his arms around her as she sobbed on his shoulder. 'Hush now, really I am sorry to have upset you. It's just….. well…… to be honest I can't really remember an awful lot of what I said last night, or did, for that matter, so it's going to take me a while to get my head around it.'

'But Will' she sobbed, 'it just meant so much to me. And everything you told me about how lonely you get and how poor Laurie is always so exhausted, well I suppose I just felt I had found a kindred spirit. I thought we were both lonely hearts who could take a little comfort in each other from time to time. I mean, where's the harm in that? Neither of our partners really seem to notice us anymore and you agreed that as long as no one got hurt it wouldn't do us any harm to well….. you know…. get together occasionally.'

Had he? Oh hell, he had no idea what he had said last night but being shitty to Cynthia wouldn't change what had happened. 'Listen Cynthia, I'm really sorry about how I've treated you. I really never meant for any of this to happen, but right now I've got to go. I need some space to sort myself out' he said.

'Of course Will, I understand' stammered Cynthia. 'I'll call you in a couple of days and let you know how I get on about withdrawing Laurie's auction bid.'

Will hesitated. He really didn't want Cynthia to call him, but he was anxious about the inevitable financial ruin which would result if the bid couldn't be retracted, so he nodded his agreement, gathered the rest of his things and left.

No sooner had Will closed the door than he heard the lift ping. Hot footing it as fast as possible Will made a bee-line for the stairs. The last thing he needed was to be caught leaving Cynthia's room by someone he knew.

Chapter 20

Brian sighed. Things were worse than he feared. He was glad that at least it was him and not Laurie who discovered Will high tailing it down the corridor just as he arrived. It didn't take a genius to work out where he had spent the night.

'Oh darling, you've changed your mind' Cynthia crooned as she opened the door to his knock.

'I take it you were expecting lover boy then?' Brian said angrily.

'I don't know what you're talking about Brian.'

'I'm talking about the fact that I just witnessed Will Kerr leave your bedroom.' Brian hissed furiously.

'Oh don't be silly darling. Honestly Brian you have such a suspicious mind! Will just popped in this morning to see if I could lend a hand in having Laurie's auction bid retracted that's all.'

'I wasn't born yesterday Cynthia and I've had enough of your little games. You don't get to play God with other people's lives you know.'

'What's that supposed to mean?' snapped Cynthia.

'I think you know perfectly well what I mean. You instructed the auctioneer to take that bid, didn't you?'

'Really Brian, I have no idea what you're talking about'

'Don't play the innocent with me Cynthia. I know what you're like remember. Have you any idea how distraught Laurie is?' he asked angrily.

'Oh poor Laurie' spat Cynthia. 'The way you were cosying up to her last night was embarrassing. I really don't know what people will think.'

'People can think whatever the hell they like' Brian said furiously. 'The girl was in bits Cynthia and all because of your little scheme to steal her husband. What sort of a woman are you? Were you ever anything other than a vicious, malevolent, selfish bitch?' he spat.

'How dare you speak to me like that' Cynthia raged. Don't forget that I made you the man you are today. I gave you two children and I have taken the Practice from strength to strength. If it wasn't for me you'd be a failure Brian, a loser, a nobody.'

'Yeah, well I've had enough of your games Cynthia. I'd prefer to be a loser and a nobody than to have to put up with you for the rest of my life. The sooner you pack your things and leave the better.'

'Oh I'm going nowhere Brian, and if I do I'm taking everything you own with me.'

'Do you know what Cynthia? I've decided that it'd be worth it just to see the back of you' he raged angrily before storming from the room, slamming the door so hard it rattled on its hinges.

Chapter 21

Amazingly Laurie had fallen asleep as soon as her head hit the pillow, a combination of shock, alcohol and exhaustion had obviously taken their toll and knocked her out completely for a full eight hours.

When she at last awakened the house was deathly silent and the space beside her where Will should have been lay tellingly empty. Laurie determined that she would not let herself dissolve once again into floods of tears, forced herself from the bed and tentatively made her way downstairs to ascertain where her family was.

She picked up the note that Kerry had left and silently blessed her for taking the kids out for the day. She had obviously been so comatose that even their normal morning exploits had failed to waken her.

As Laurie made herself a much needed cup of coffee, she heard Will's car draw up outside. She braced herself for his onslaught, but surprisingly when Will made his appearance he looked as miserable as she felt.

'Laurie, I'm sorry about last night' he said coming forward and wrapping her in his arms.

As Laurie relaxed against him the smell of perfume emanating from his clothes instantly overwhelmed her. The scent, like the woman who wore it, was pure Poison. Laurie drew back as if she'd suffered an electric shock. Brian's words of warning were still ringing in her ears and although up until this moment she had never doubted her husband's fidelity, she did now.

'Where were you last night?' Laurie asked sharply. 'Why didn't you come home?'

'I thought I'd give you some space' Will replied easily 'so I stayed the night at the hotel.' Laurie noted that although the words slipped easily from his mouth he couldn't make eye contact with her and his features were awash with guilt. In that moment, she knew he hadn't spent the night alone.

Laurie felt her knees buckle beneath her and gripped the worktop for support. She felt the bile rise in the back of her throat; she couldn't breathe, Will couldn't look her in the eye and what's more she couldn't bear to tackle him about what he'd really got up to the night before.

Will's own conscience was bearing down on him. He felt as if he were suffocating, he couldn't deal with this, he couldn't bear to think what he'd done to Laurie.

'I need to pack' he said, more sharply than he intended, 'I have to be in Germany for a meeting first thing tomorrow and I have a one o'clock flight' he said quickly leaving the room and heading for the stairs.

Within thirty minutes Will had packed his bag and gone. Laurie sat at the kitchen table too shell shocked to do anything. Her brain had gone numb; she only wished her heart would follow so that she could no longer feel the pain of it breaking in two.

Chapter 22

Kerry had always believed the beaches in Northern Ireland were some of the best in the world and as she and Aidan drifted along the golden sands of Runkerry she lamented the fact that she rarely had the time to enjoy them. Of course, this was no romantic stroll, not by any stretch of the imagination, as six overexcited children scrambled over rocks and into rock pools with alarming speed. Kerry was used to Laurie's bunch by now but normally they were contained in a building of some description, here there seemed to be no boundaries and the children appeared to make the most of every opportunity to get up to mischief.

'Relax' Aidan teased, seeing Kerry once again scrunch her face against the sun to do her twentieth head count in as many minutes.

'I can't' she mumbled apologetically, 'It's as if

they're deliberately disappearing just to wind me up.'

Aidan threw back his head and laughed. 'Oh Kerry' he grinned 'you have a lot to learn about kids. They'll be fine, well maybe it would be a good idea if the twins didn't pick up those cigarette butts and eat them.'

'No' Kerry screamed as she ran towards the twins at full pelt to rescue them.

'Just joking, just joking' Aidan shouted after her just as she reached them.

'I am going to kill him' muttered Kerry mutinously as she saw the twins' toothless grins and realised they weren't eating anything more harmful than a bit of sand. I will get him back for that Kerry vowed.

Aidan who was now standing by her side and looking contrite wrapped his arms around her 'awh forgive me sweetheart, I couldn't resist teasing you, just a little.' Kerry walloped him on the arm but luckily for Aidan she was too overjoyed by his use of the word 'sweetheart' to do him any real damage.

'Aidan, Aidan' shouted the boys eagerly 'You've gotta come see this, it's awesome.' They waved their hands in the air frantically and beckoned him over to the rock pool they were gathered around looking intently at something caught in their fishing net.

'Ok I'm coming' grinned Aidan as he gave Kerry

a quick peck on the cheek and bounded over to the boys like an over excited puppy.

'Right girls, time for some ice cream' Kerry decided as she and the twins dandered off in search of the nearest ice cream van.

Ten minutes later Kerry realised it was not a good idea to try and carry eight ice creams and two toddlers! Eventually she gave up and decided to let the twins eat their cones on the way back down to the beach. The only problem was they were so absorbed in eating they couldn't seem to walk at the same time so a trip that should have taken about two minutes ended up taking twenty and by the time they arrived back at the beach Kerry had as much ice cream on her as was left in the cones. How do normal people do this? Kerry wondered for about the hundredth time as the kids spying the ice cream left what they were doing and hurtled towards her at a hundred miles an hour. Poor Aidan was left to release their captured sea creatures back into the wild and just as she thought he was about to join them she heard him give an almighty howl.

'What's wrong?' Kerry shouted anxiously.

'Damn jelly fish just stung me that's what wrong' he shouted in reply.

'Ooh must be bad' exclaimed Michael 'Dad never swears, well at least not in front of kids at any rate.'

Bet if you went a little closer you'd get an education in swear words thought Kerry knowingly.

'Let's see, let's see' shouted the kids excitedly, as Aidan made his way towards them clutching his right hand.

'I was trying to get it out of the net, I thought it was dead' he said miserably, 'and the next thing I knew it stung me.'

'Wow said the kids' gathering round.

'Impressive hand Dad', said Michael admiringly looking at the misshapen stub at the end of his arm were Aidan's hand used to be.

'Does it hurt?' asked Shane captivated.

'You could say that' replied Aidan grimacing.

'Oh Aidan, I leave you for ten minutes and look what happens' teased Kerry. 'Good job I know a great cure for jellyfish stings.'

'Really?' questioned Aidan, 'you aren't just going to kiss it better or something, are you?'

'Oooohhhhh kissy kissy' sniggered Charlotte.

'No' said Kerry indignantly, 'a real cure.'

'Great' said Aidan, 'what is it?'

'Pee' said Kerry.

'Sorry, what did you say?' asked Aidan, 'I thought it sounded like pee.'

'I did' said Kerry.

'Yeah right' scowled Aidan. 'I know I wound you up earlier about the cigarette butts Kerry but I'm not falling for that one.'

'Seriously Aidan the ammonia in the urine neutralises the sting. The stronger the urine the better' said Kerry.

'Wow', said Michael, Shane and Tom in unison, 'that's cool!'

'Yuck' said Charlotte, 'that's disgusting'

'I'm agreeing with Charlotte on that one' stated Aidan firmly.

'Awh Dad, go on it might help, be a sport,' whined Michael.

'Sorry to disappoint you Michael but you are not peeing on my hand' said Aidan forcefully.

'Suit yourself' said Kerry 'but if you want to get rid of the pain, the sooner they pee on it the better.'

'Awh go on Dad, it's worth a try' wheedled Michael.

'Are you sure about this?' asked Aidan.

'Yes, it's a well-known scientific fact.'

'Have you ever known anyone to try it and has it actually worked?' asked Aidan sceptically.

'Only one way to find out,' said Kerry impishly

'and the sooner you do it the better it works apparently.'

Aidan thought for a moment, whispered something to the boys and pointed back to the rock pools from where he had just come.

'Yesssss' said Shane excitedly as the four of them trotted off to the nearest rock already getting their weapons and anti-venom pistols at the ready.

'Does it really work?' whispered Charlotte to Kerry.

'Nothing to say it doesn't Charlotte dear' said Kerry with a wink.

'I feel sullied' cried Aidan in dismay as he and three very pleased with themselves boys returned.

'That was great' enthused Tom as he and Shane began arguing who had the best stream and who was the better shot.

'I can't believe you let us pee on your hand Dad' laughed Michael 'wait till I tell my mates about this one, you'll be a right laughing stock' he teased.

'Well did it help?' asked Kerry bemusedly.

'Can't say I notice any difference', said Aidan dejectedly. 'The only real difference is I now have a sore hand and stink of urine.'

'You are looking a bit pale' said Kerry, 'I tell you what we'll get some vinegar from the fish and chip van up in the car park, now it really does help with jellyfish stings,' and with that Kerry turned on her heel and marched off in the direction of the car park leaving Aidan gaping open mouthed in disbelief. As the penny dropped that he had been well and truly played he threw back his head and gave a great guffaw of laughter.

Chapter 23

'Nothing quite like a chip buttie to finish off a lovely day at the beach is there?' Kerry asked contentedly.

'Well it helps if you have a gorgeous woman on your arm' said Aidan 'even if she has the most wicked sense of revenge ever' he said teasingly.

'Awh come on Aidan, even you have to admit it was hilarious, I don't think I've ever seen Laurie's boys so excited' said Kerry.

'Yeah' agreed Aidan 'it'll certainly give them something to tell their mates about at school on Monday. I'll be a right laughing stock' he said miserably.

'Yep they should get good mileage out of that one alright' grinned Kerry entirely unrepentant. 'Anyway I'm bone tired; much as I love Laurie's kids I am seriously relieved to have dropped them off again.

I don't think I could have survived another 24 hours with them' said Kerry tiredly.

'You really are great with them' said Aidan sincerely 'and they think you are totally awesome you know.'

Kerry smiled up at Aidan 'You're pretty good with them yourself' she said admiringly.

'Ah but you see I've had a lot of practice with Michael to get me to this stage, but you', he smiled affectionately, 'are a natural'.

As Aidan leaned over Kerry on the sofa, gently pulling her in for yet another languorous kiss Kerry was acutely aware that even if she wanted to she was powerless to stop herself falling in love with this gorgeous man.

'Eeuucchhh, don't you two ever come up for air?' asked Michael as he wandered into the living room.

Aidan immediately sat bolt upright, 'Uhhh…. Sorry Michael I didn't see you there' he said flustered.

'Duhhh, that much is obvious' stated Michael bluntly.

'Ummhh look Michael there is something I wanted to talk to you about actually' said Aidan, who had now turned a deep shade of red. 'I mean it's about Kerry' said Aidan apologetically 'It's just .. ummhh….urrr…… well you see son it's just that we ummmh, urrrr, well you see son ..'

'Dad if you're trying to tell me that you and Kerry are seeing each other, well duhhh I'm not a thicko, I had already guessed that' said Michael 'so while I could enjoy watching you waffle on for the next ten minutes I am in the middle of a game and want to get back to my X-Box, like today!! So let me put you out of your misery, yes I know you're seeing Kerry and yes I am fine with it. In fact' he said looking directly at Kerry 'I think she's pretty great, so don't worry I won't give you a hard time about it' and with that he turned on his heel and hurried back to his game.

'Well that went better than I thought it would' said Aidan incredulously. 'Looks like you've been given the seal of approval then' he said thoughtfully to Kerry. 'I really never thought he'd take it so well. I've been so worried about telling him.'

'He's a great kid' said Kerry meaningfully. 'I guess we weren't as subtle about keeping it from him as we thought we were' she said.

'Well I suppose finding your Dad snogging on the sofa is a bit of a giveaway' he said flustered.

'Yeah but I think he had already guessed' said Kerry, 'he's an astute kid.'

'I feel a bit bad that he had to find out like this though' said Aidan, 'I probably should have talked to him before now' he said worriedly.

'Well, you know Aidan maybe it's for the best it happened this way, it saved a big ominous build up, this way he kind of just adjusted to it naturally and let's face it he seems pretty chilled out about it.'

'Yeah, I guess so' said Aidan thoughtfully. 'I think I might have a chat with him about it manno a manno in a day or two though. Make sure he really is as chilled out about the whole thing as he appears.'

'Does this mean we are officially an item then?' asked Kerry gently pulling Aidan towards her to continue where they had left off.

'I guess it does' groaned Aidan softly as Kerry's lips once again met his.

'Eucchhh not again' said Michael disgustedly as he once again breezed into the living room 'do you two never stop! No child should be exposed to this amount of snogging inside ten minutes' he said gleefully as he looked at the two embarrassed faces peering shamefaced over the back of the sofa.

'Just kidding' he laughed, 'I must have left my remote down here' and finding his remote he gave them one last elated look and swanned back upstairs.

'I think I'm scarred for life' groaned Aidan.

'Yeah you and me both' said Kerry, 'I feel worse than the time my Mum caught me snogging the boy next door when I was thirteen' she said and suddenly the pair of them dissolved into fits of giggles like a pair of naughty teenagers.

'Dad' shouted Michael. 'DAAADDDDDD'

'Sorry' said Aidan 'I just need to see what he wants. He's probably forgotten to charge the batteries in the controller's again.' he said reluctantly disentangling himself from Kerry.

Two minutes later Aidan reappeared with a massive grin on his face. 'I hope you don't mind Kerry but I need to pop out for a bit.'

Kerry couldn't help the shadow of disappointment showing on her face. She'd been so looking forward to snuggling up on the sofa with Aidan especially now they didn't have to worry too much about what Michael would think.

'You see that was Josh's Mum on the phone' said Aidan gleefully. 'Michael has just been asked to a sleepover at Josh's house and I said he could go.'

Kerry couldn't help mirroring Aidan's enormous grin. Much as she loved Michael she couldn't wait to spend some time alone with Aidan.

'No problem' smiled Kerry as Michael bounced into the room with his overnight bag hanging loosely over one shoulder.

'I'll only be ten minutes or so' said Aidan 'make yourself at home. I'll be back..' he mimicked in his best Arnold Schwarzenegger voice. 'Sorry, sorry' he mumbled, 'I've obviously been spending too much time hanging around kids.'

Kerry allowed herself a small smile before the door banged and Michael and Aidan disappeared.

Oh no thought Kerry dismally realising she'd been in the same sweaty clothes all day, never mind her most basic M&S underwear. She flew out of the house and just managed to catch Aidan before he drove off.

'What's up Kerry?' asked Aidan screwing down the window.

'I need to pop home' she said. 'Do you think you could drive over to mine after you leave Michael off?' she asked. 'I just fancy a shower and a change of clothes' she mumbled blushing, feeling sure Aidan already knew she was planning on changing out of her manky underwear. 'All that sand you know?' she said embarrassed.

Aidan grinned. 'Sure no problem Kerry' he said. 'I'll see you shortly.'

As soon as Aidan pulled out of the drive Kerry jumped into her little mini and sped off home. She wondered how on earth she was going to manage to shave her legs, wax her bikini line, have a shower and find some decent underwear before Aidan called round. Of course, she knew it was a bit of an assumption that he would want to spend the night with her but she wanted to be prepared just in case.

Kerry raced through her preparations in record time but even so she was just stepping out of the shower when she heard the doorbell ring. Quickly she grabbed her dressing gown and rushed down the stairs to let Aidan in.

'Did I call too early?' grinned Aidan taking in her soaking wet hair and flushed face.

'I just need five more minutes' gushed Kerry. 'Come in though I promise I won't be long.'

'You look pretty damn gorgeous the way you are' said Aidan taking in her flimsy dressing gown, which in her haste was loosely tied, barely covering her body.

Aidan's eyes flashed with desire; and as he allowed them to stray slowly over her body, the memory of their first kiss assaulted Kerry's senses and sparked a longing within her.

Slowly Aidan reached for her and as his lips hungrily met hers she was once again lost in the pleasure of his mouth. A low moan escaped her as his kiss deepened; teasing her with his tongue; his passionate need for her insisting she release her mouth to his control; his desire not permitting her to hold anything back. Her legs trembled; she could hardly bear the weight of her own body while his lips assailed hers; his arms held her powerfully to him; his lips never once slowing in their relentless pursuit of her.

Aidan groaned with desire, his hand slowly slipping between the folds of her gown, searching out the sweet softness of her skin. 'Kerry' he groaned. 'Do you want me to stop?'

'If you're able to stop you've a lot more will power than I have' she moaned. 'I want you Aidan.'

Aidan drew back. 'Are you sure?' he asked, his eyes betraying his desire.

Kerry nodded. He had opened up a well of longing in her. She couldn't stop even if she wanted to.

Aidan secured her body tightly to him and lifted her off the ground as though she were lighter than air. He carried her to the bedroom and laid her out gently on the bed.

Hastily he removed his own shirt and jeans revealing a chest so taut and toned that Kerry couldn't take her eyes off him. She ached to touch him, to feel his body underneath her fingertips.

As he kissed his way down her body Kerry's hands roamed freely over his smooth taut back. She revelled in his strength, in the warmth of his body, in the very maleness of him.

As she gave herself up completely to this beautiful man, she allowed herself to revel in the wonder of him. She knew then, without a shadow of a doubt, that he was the only man who could ever make her feel complete.

Afterwards Kerry lay enfolded in Aidan's arms, exhausted but content.

Aidan gently kissed the top of her head. 'You are incredible' he breathed. 'I don't know what you do to me but I seem to lose the ability to control myself when you're around. I really didn't intend for that to happen.'

'Do you know what' said Kerry 'I'm really glad it did.'

'Really?' He asked. 'You're sure I didn't rush you into it? I don't want you to regret it.'

'I promise you I won't regret it.' she grinned. 'It's not as if we've only just met Aidan. We've known each other for a long, long time.'

'If I'm being honest with you Kerry you've been my Achilles heel for as long as I can remember' said Aidan.

'Why did you never do anything about it until last week then?' Kerry asked confused.

'The truth is I never thought you'd look twice at someone like me. You've always been so.... so unobtainable I guess. Do you remember that summer when we were both staying in the caravan in Portrush?'

'Yes' Kerry smiled

'It was all I could do to keep my hands off you. I was sure you'd be horrified if you knew the lustful thoughts running through my mind.' he laughed. 'I know that to you I was just your friends little brother, but you had this way of making me feel like I was a man already. I knew you'd baulk at the very idea of us getting it together. You were this gorgeous, vibrant woman and I was just this dumb-assed kid with a massive crush' he chortled.

'What makes you think I didn't feel the same way?' she asked carefully.

'Well if you did why didn't you do something about it?'

'I was waiting for Laurie to go to Uni.'

'Well why didn't you get in touch after that?' he asked.

'By that time you were otherwise enthralled with a girl by the name of Angela' she replied.

Aidan winced at the mention of her name. 'Angela and I were never going to work' he said bluntly.

'It's ok Aidan I don't mean to pry. You don't have to talk about it.' Kerry said. 'I mean, I do know the gist of it anyway.'

'To tell you the truth Kerry it's really only

recently that I've been able to think things through clearly myself. It's taken me a long time to come to terms with the way things turned out. When I look back I can see the whole thing was doomed from the beginning. I only started going out with her because she kept pestering me and I was at a bit of a loose end. My friends kept telling me how gorgeous she was and what a fool I was not to do something about it. I was still reeling from the fact that I had fallen in love with this gorgeous, sexy, nineteen year old over the summer but there wasn't a hope in hell she'd look twice at me.'

Kerry's heart gave a little flutter. Did he just say 'fallen in love with'?

'Oh Aidan' sighed Kerry. 'If only you'd waited a little bit longer. By the time I got around to contacting you I'd heard from Laurie that you were going steady and I never got my chance.'

'You really would have gone out with me then?' he asked incredulously.

'Yes Aidan. I would have.' she said simply.

'If only I'd known.' he said wistfully. 'Things could have turned out so differently,' he sighed.

'But when you and Angela got married everyone thought you were so in love' Kerry said.

'Yeah well everyone thought wrong' he said bitterly. 'I was a damned fool to have anything to do with her in the first place. When I slept with her it was my first time and I didn't have a clue what I was doing. She told me she was on the pill so I thought everything would be alright. How was I to know that she forgot to take it half the time? Things went from bad to worse so quickly. Within weeks we found out she was pregnant.'

'When we told her Mum and Dad they went ballistic. They are really religious. Her Dad is an Elder in the church and I guess he thought that he would gain some sympathy from the congregation if he showed he wasn't going to tolerate his wayward daughter's mistakes. He chucked her out faster than you could say 'unmarried pregnant girl.' She was in a right state. She had no job, no money, no place to live and a baby on the way. She was so frightened. What could I do Kerry? I couldn't just abandon her.'

Kerry knew there was no way in the world Aidan would have left Angela to fend for herself in those circumstances. He was far too decent a human being.

'When we told my parents they were so shocked. By this time Angela had her heart set on getting married. I think she was just feeling so vulnerable that she craved the security that she thought marriage would bring. When we told my parents we were getting married they tried to talk us out of it. They said we were too young. They told us they would support us, help us all they could, but not to rush into getting married. They were right of course. We'd only been dating just over a year and the truth is if Angela hadn't found out she was pregnant I would have finished with her. I knew I didn't love her. But in an effort to convince Angela that I wasn't about to abandon her I agreed to get married.'

'Ha' he snorted. 'Isn't that ironic? I couldn't abandon her. I stood by her, gave up my own aspirations and within two years she had abandoned both me and the baby.' he said angrily.

'How did you manage Aidan?' Kerry asked.

'I didn't, not at first. I was a mess, trying to hold down my job in the joinery place I was working and look after a baby. If it hadn't been for Mum stepping in and minding Michael every day I don't know what I would have done. I was a wreck. I was spending every minute of every day either at work or looking after a baby while all my mates were out having a great time and acting like twenty one year olds should. I resented every minute of it and most of all I resented Angela for leaving me in that mess.'

'It was all such a shock. I just hadn't seen it coming. She left Michael with Mum one afternoon, said she needed to do a bit of shopping. By the time I got home she'd packed up her bags and left. I found a note on the table saying she was finding it all too difficult and that she needed a life of her own. She said I wasn't to try and find her because she wouldn't be coming back.

'We had no idea where she'd gone to. It was over a year before I heard from her again. She phoned on Michael's third birthday to see how he was. I was so angry I spent fifteen minutes shouting down the phone at her before hanging up. Turns out her Gran had left her a life Insurance policy and when Angela realised how much it was worth she saw it as her bid for freedom. She booked herself on the first available flight to New York and set about reinventing herself.'

'Of course she didn't think what that money would have meant to us as a family. No, it was all about her and her needs. I think I could have forgiven her for walking out on me. But I can't ever forgive her for walking out on Michael.'

'But wouldn't it have been worse if she'd left and taken Michael with her?' asked Kerry.

She saw Aidan blanch.

'If she'd tried to do that I'd have spent the rest of my life hunting her down' he said angrily. 'Things may not have been easy Kerry but I love my son. I wouldn't change that part of it for the world. I guess that's the only thing that makes me believe the whole sorry mess was worthwhile.'

'Well for what it's worth I think you've done a great job with him' Kerry said smiling. 'He's a lovely kid.'

'Yeah he is.' said Aidan. 'I just wish his Mum had

stuck around long enough to realise that. It's not been easy for him growing up without a Mum. He knows she left him and that's a difficult thing for a kid his age to get his head around. It's not as if she died or something, if that had happened he wouldn't have had a choice in the matter. It's the fact that she chose to leave him. You've no idea how much he tortures himself about the whole thing. I've tried to tell him that his Mum loved him and that she was just too young to deal with everything. But he knows his Mum was the same age as I was and I didn't leave him. Deep down he feels his Mum just didn't love him enough to stick around. And let's face it Kerry she couldn't have or she wouldn't have done what she did.'

Kerry could see how difficult this was for Aidan to deal with. She heard the raw emotion in his voice and realised how right Laurie was that Aidan was only beginning to come to terms with things. She turned around to face him and drew him close. Aidan seemed to pull his thoughts back to the present and eventually the anger left his eyes. He smiled gently at Kerry, and as his mouth found hers, Kerry felt her insides melt once more. This was their moment and Kerry was damned if she was going to have Aidan plagued with thoughts of Angela. Kerry determined this would be a long and glorious night. As she felt Aidan's hand move slowly down her thigh every negative thought was quickly swept away in a tidal wave of passion.

Chapter 24

'So how did Saturday night go?' asked Kerry 'you didn't say much about it when we dropped the kids back on Sunday.'

'Don't ask' muttered Laurie.

Kerry who had sensed there was something wrong with her friend from the moment she had walked in the door was suddenly more than a little apprehensive. Laurie looked wrecked, like she hadn't slept properly in days and hadn't had a proper meal in weeks.

'What is it? What's wrong Laurie?' asked Kerry anxiously.

'You know Kerry I don't think I can talk about it yet. It's still too raw' said Laurie her eyes once again mutinously filling up with tears.

That was the point Kerry realised it was serious.

Laurie never bottled things up, it wasn't in her nature. Normally all her thoughts bad, good or incoherent would come bounding out of her at 100mph whether she had intended to say them or not. Laurie was a talker, so for her not to want to talk about it sent alarm bells sounding in Kerry's head. Not only that, but Kerry was suddenly at a loss as to how to tackle her. Should she press her on it or let it go she wondered.

'Tell you what' she said at last, 'while the kids are at school why don't we bundle the twins up in their buggies and head out for a walk.'

Laurie didn't even answer. She stood unresponsive and dazed as Kerry took control, bundling up the twins, sorting their changing bag and even forcing Laurie's feet into a pair of trainers.

As they set off Kerry wondered just what the hell had happened on Saturday night to leave her friend a walking shadow of her former self. Finally they reached the park where the twins tottered over to the sand pit and although it had been a good ten minute walk Laurie still hadn't managed to utter a single word. Sure she smiled absently as Kerry retold the story of the jellyfish and her joy at Michael finally discovering the truth about her and Aidan but it was as if she was in a trance, just going through the motions.

'Laurie' said Kerry at last 'What is it? What's

wrong?'

Laurie turned to her friend dazedly 'I think …..I …ummh.. I think that Will has slept with someone else' she quivered at last, her eyes bubbling over with unshed tears.

'No' said Kerry emphatically. 'No, not Will, he just wouldn't. You are worrying about nothing' Kerry insisted. 'That man worships the ground you walk on, how could you ever think that.'

'Kerry he stayed overnight in the hotel on Saturday. He didn't come home until late Sunday morning and when he did he was reeking of perfume and couldn't look me in the eye. In all our years together I have never, ever suspected him of being unfaithful. Oh sure I get the fact that his business trips provide him with ample opportunity but somehow I just knew he would never act on it. Will isn't like some men who could cheat and it wouldn't affect him. Somehow I always understood that if he ever cheated on me I would know. He would be eaten up with guilt; his conscience wouldn't let him live with himself, and the fact that I never picked up on his guilty conscience always reassured me that he had been faithful. In all the years I have known Will I have never doubted his fidelity, I have never suspected him of cheating on me, until Saturday night. Suddenly all the things I suspected I would feel if he ever cheated on me overwhelmed me when he arrived home on Sunday. He couldn't look me in the eye. It was like a massive barrier had suddenly dropped between us and the guilt was oozing from him.'

'But how? Why?' demanded Kerry 'why would he choose Saturday night of all nights to be unfaithful? It doesn't make sense Laurie. The two of you headed off to that dinner on Saturday night like loves young dream. If he was going to cheat on you he wouldn't have done it then? Why would he sleep with someone else at a function that you attended with him when, as you say, he could cheat on any number of occasions when he's away on business and let's face it never risk being seen by someone, and never risk being caught either? What else happened on Saturday night Laurie? What went on that would cause Will to stay on at the hotel after you left? What haven't you told me?'

'Oh Kerry, it was my worst nightmare', said Laurie as she haltingly and tearfully poured out the rest of the events of Saturday that she hadn't even allowed herself to dwell on or think about. As she tearfully hiccupped and sobbed through the entire sequence of events Kerry felt a bolt of red hot anger surge through her on her friend's behalf. By the end of Laurie's tale Kerry didn't know who she felt madder at, Will for being such a rotten, selfish, inconsiderate plonker or the bitch from hell who Kerry would happily beat to a pulp.

Just then Laurie's phone rang. Laurie didn't

know whether she was hoping it would be Will on the other end or that it wouldn't be. Right now Laurie didn't have the energy to keep up a pretence about how everything was fine at home and how it would be lovely to see him when he got back. She sighed as she pulled out her mobile and looked at the caller display. But it wasn't Will, it was the school. Laurie felt her heartbeat quicken, had something gone wrong, had one of the kids had an accident? 'Hello' she answered anxiously.

'Hello is that Mrs Kerr.'

'Yes' said Laurie

'It's the school secretary Elaine here. I'm sorry Mrs Kerr but you're going to have to come and collect your children. All three of them are complaining of feeling sick and Shane has already vomited several times.'

'Oh no, said Laurie. I'll be right there.'

As Laurie quickly gathered up the twins and told Kerry what had happened. Kerry made an on the spot decision to stay and give Laurie a hand. It couldn't be easy under normal circumstances to manage three sick children and two toddlers, never mind trying to do that in the state that Laurie was in.

By the time they reached the school all three children had started vomiting and it was all Laurie and Kerry could do to get them home.

Laurie who had only brought one basin was simultaneously encouraging one child to vomit into it while coaxing Shane to stick his head out the window.

'Do you want me to pull over again?' Kerry asked for the third time.

'No just keep driving it's not far now' said Laurie 'we can't stop again or we'll never get home.

'Mum I am really going to be sick' gasped Shane.

'Well Charlotte is using the basin' said Laurie trying to stay calm.

Just as Charlotte heaved again into the sick basin Shane too felt the contents of his stomach rise to the surface and vomited forcefully out the window. Unfortunately for the car behind the wind carried the vomit all over its bonnet and windscreen. The driver sounded his horn angrily, set his wipers to fast speed and hit the wash-wipe but succeeded only in spreading the vomit further over the windscreen.

'Mum' said Shane querulously 'I just puked all over that car'

'Don't worry about it son I'm sure they'll understand'

Kerry who could see in her mirror that the driver had pulled over and was angrily shaking his fists at them wasn't so sure that he was the understanding type.

Kerry who had originally intended just to head into work a bit late soon realised she had no choice but to stay and give Laurie a hand. There was no way Laurie could deal with this by herself. As Laurie half carried the children into the house and started peeling off their vomit covered uniforms, Kerry set about finding pyjamas and towels and additional basins. Shane was a very strange colour of green and Charlotte and Tom who were pale at the best of times had turned deathly white. Meanwhile the twins started crying because they were hungry and Kerry who couldn't abide the smell of vomit never mind the sight of it quickly volunteered to look after the twins while Laurie set about tending to the sick. Thirty minutes later Laurie had finally worked out that she simply couldn't manage charging from one bedroom to the next and had to concede defeat and bring all the children downstairs into the one room so she could keep an eye on them all at once. Kerry meanwhile had realised that her chances of staying outside the vomit zone were absolutely pointless.

By 2am Kerry was as adept at emptying the sick buckets and mopping up after the kids as Laurie. The only plus was that as far as she could tell the kids were vomiting a little less frequently and she was hopeful that they might finally be able to get a couple of hours sleep. Laurie looked completely shattered and Kerry who had never experienced anything like the day she'd had knew exactly how she felt.

'That' said Kerry 'was the ultimate day from hell!'

'Welcome to my world!' mumbled Laurie exhaustedly. 'I couldn't have done it without you Kerry. I owe you big time.'

'We never even got a chance to talk about you and Will.' said Kerry wearily.

'It doesn't matter. In fact that was the only good thing to come out of today. I've been so busy I haven't even had a chance to think about it.'

'You need to talk to him Laurie. It might not be as bad as you think. Surely the not knowing is worse than confronting him?'

'I'm not sure it is Kerry. At least when I don't know for certain I can stay in the 'unpleasant but suspicious' stage. Once I know for sure then I have to move to the 'unpleasant but certain' stage.'

'Yes but at least then you would know Laurie! After all, you could be putting yourself through all this torture for nothing.'

'The thing is I already do know. He hasn't admitted it in so many words but I know I'm right and I don't want to have to deal with the reality of what that means. If I confront him about it I will end up having to choose whether or not to forgive him. If I choose not to forgive what will that mean for us, for our kids, our home, our whole way of life? If I do forgive him how weak does that make me? Poor

Laurie so needy and desperate she has to turn a blind eye to her husband's affair. Plus it might not even be a one off. For all I know he could be using this business trip as an excuse, maybe he's holed up in some hotel with that tart and just told me he was going away. Even if I do forgive him, how will I ever be able to trust him again? Perhaps now he's seen what's on offer he'll simply decide to make the most of it especially if his wife is unlikely to find out. Don't you see Kerry? It's a lose/lose situation. There is no happy ending to this one.'

'Will wouldn't do that Laurie. Come on, in your heart of hearts, you know he isn't that type of bloke. If - and it's a big if – something has happened it'll have been a one-time drunken mistake. He wouldn't repeat it. You know he wouldn't!'

'Oh so that makes it alright does it? Get drunk, find someone who's up for it and fall into bed with them, but hey it doesn't really matter because he was drunk and it didn't mean anything! Sure, even if the little wife finds out about it, she'll realise it was just a drunken mistake and she'll get over it! I can't believe you'd think that Kerry.'

'Laurie that's not what I mean at all! I'm just saying that there is a big difference between a one off drunken shag and a long- term affair.'

'Is there really Kerry? You really think that one type of cheating is easier to forgive than another?

Think about it Kerry. It's still deception, it's still shattering a loving marriage, it's still extinguishing a relationship built on trust and it's still destroying the respect that he had for me. If he really loved me and respected me he would never have done this Kerry!'

'You're right' said Will standing silhouetted in the doorway, his face pale and anguished.

Both Kerry and Laurie looked up in shock. Neither of them had heard him come in and there was no way of knowing how long he had been standing there.

Will fixed his eyes on Laurie's shocked face as Kerry gathered herself off the chair and silently made her way towards the door. 'I'm heading home now' she mumbled but neither Will nor Laurie even noticed.

'I'm sorry' Laurie. 'I'm really, really sorry' and the guilt and devastation on his face told Laurie all she needed to know.

Laurie crumbled. It was all too much, the exhaustion, the fear, the humiliation and the anguish had finally caught up with her. She could take no more. A sound rose up from the deepest part of her, a guttural roar of pure anguish, and as her body convulsed in despair she felt Will's arms around her, holding her to his chest as if he would never let her go. The love she felt for him overwhelmed her, she wanted to be with him so much she thought she would die - and yet she couldn't cope with his closeness, his familiarity; the smell of his aftershave; the heat of his body; the feel of his muscles under his thin cotton shirt. She loved him and yet she hated him. He had destroyed her, he had destroyed their love, he had destroyed their life, their family, and she couldn't endure the feel of him, his strength, his solidity, his presence, knowing what he had done.

She pushed against him, struggling to free herself but he refused to move an inch. It was as if he knew if he let her go he would lose her for good. And so he held her tight as she freed her arms only to punch him, slap him, and scream at him. And still he held her whispering words of love into her ear the whole time, words she didn't want to hear, words that sliced through the very core of her being because, although he had caused it, she still felt his pain and anguish and knew it matched her own. At last the fight left her body and she became still in his arms, exhausted, unable to bear anymore, she felt the strength leave her body as she crumbled against him completely spent.

As Will held Laurie's exhausted body in his arms he finally understood what it meant to feel your heart break. What had he done? How could he have done this to the woman he loved more than anyone in the world? He knew Laurie hated him for what he had done but she couldn't hate him any more than he hated himself. As he carried Laurie's exhausted body up to bed not for the first time he wished he had the ability to put things back to the way they were only a week ago.

Will heard a shout from downstairs and helped Charlotte find the sick basin just in the nick of time. As he finished wiping the vomit from her mouth she whispered sleepily, 'I love you Daddy, I'm so glad you're home, I missed you' and as she fell instantly back to sleep Will allowed himself to cry, for all that he had lost and for the love he didn't deserve.

Chapter 25

Aidan was still on a high from his weekend with Kerry. Well if the truth be known he had been on a high since Kerry had agreed to go out with him. He knew it was early days yet and let's face it quick one night stands and casual flings were more his style. He had point blank refused to let himself become emotionally involved with anyone since Angela. But this 'thing' he had with Kerry felt different. He didn't want it to be just a casual fling and yet as soon as he started to even think along the lines of this being something more, alarm bells sounded. His one and only long-term relationship had been with Angela and that had almost destroyed him. He couldn't allow himself to become too involved with Kerry not least because it scared the living daylights out of him. And yet he couldn't just give Kerry up. He'd been a little bit in love with her from the age of sixteen.

Huh? What did he know about love? It was

more likely these feelings he had for Kerry stemmed from a boyhood crush he'd never really gotten over. Anyway, he had Michael to think about. He was glad Michael seemed happy enough that he and Kerry were dating but he couldn't afford to get too involved with her. Michael had already been abandoned by his mother and the last thing he needed was to start viewing Kerry as some sort of mother figure only to have her walk out on him as well. He had to get a grip, he liked Kerry but Michael is his priority.

Aidan jumped into his car. He'd collect Michael from his mum's early today and spend some quality time with him this evening. He'd been so wrapped up with Kerry this weekend he'd hardly seen Michael and he wasn't prepared to push his son aside for any woman – even if that woman was Kerry.

'Well Mum have you got a couple of extra wee ones today?' Aidan asked seeing the twins tottering to the door.

'Aye Laurie's having a bit of a time of it with the older ones. They've got that vomiting bug that's going around so I said I would take the wee ones off her hands for an hour or two. Michael's been a great help entertaining them, haven't you Michael?' asked Maggie.

'Well I don't know if you can call it entertaining them exactly' Michael said laughingly. 'I made them some popcorn with the popcorn maker that Granny got me for my birthday. Isn't that right Ellie, didn't you like the popcorn?' asked Michael.

'Cockporn' said Ellie 'Cockporn, cockporn'

'That's right said Michael excitedly 'Did you hear that Dad, I taught Ellie how to say popcorn. I can't wait to tell Auntie Laurie. Ellie, say it again Ellie! Can you say popcorn?'

'Cockporn, cockporn' said Ellie excitedly.

'Oh dear,' whispered Aidan to Maggie 'Laurie's not going to like that one!'

'Grandma why has your face gone all red?' asked Michael. 'Are you not feeling well?'

'No, no, I'm fine' said Maggie 'it's just a bit warm in here that's all.'

'Cockporn, cockporn' said Ellie hopefully.

Not to be outdone, Carris suddenly also decided to join in 'Cockporn cockporn' she said holding out her hand to Michael.

'Wait till I tell Laurie' squealed Michael excitedly. 'Do you think that this is their first proper word?' he asked an increasingly red faced Maggie. 'Laurie will be so pleased with me', he said grinning proudly.

Aidan, who was reluctant to get into a detailed discussion with Michael on the meaning of those particular words, was trying in vain not to let Michael catch him sniggering.

'Are you sure you're alright Grandma?' asked Michael anxiously 'I don't think I've ever seen you so red. Do you need me to get you a glass of water?'

Maggie who was keen to change the subject at any cost hinted that a glass of water would be just the thing she needed and Michael purposefully strode off to the kitchen to get her one.

Aidan finally released the guffaw of laughter he'd been holding in and Maggie promptly clouted him around the ear.

'Oh come on Mum' grinned Aidan 'you've got to see the funny side'

'Indeed I do not!' said Maggie whose face was gradually returning to its normal colour. 'All I can think about is what poor Laurie's going to say when those two wee ones land home and their first ever word is cockporn. She'll wonder what on earth I've been letting them watch on TV. She'll never let them come the road o' me again.'

'Cockporn, cockporn' squealed the twins.

'Lord bless us all!' said Maggie pleading 'pray they'll forget that word by the time they get home.'

'Hardly likely' grinned Aidan. 'Not with Michael encouraging them. Do you want me to have a word with him?' he asked.

'And say what exactly?' choked Maggie. 'Isn't it bad enough that the two year olds are talking about

189

cock and porn without an eleven year old demanding all sorts of explanations? No you leave it be Aidan. They'll forget all about it soon enough. And as if I haven't had a bad enough day already' groaned Maggie.

'Why what happened?' asked Aidan anxiously 'I hope you haven't been taking too much out of yourself'

'Augh no it's not that. Well I wasn't going to tell you but I had a visit from the Priest earlier today.'

'Well sure Ma that'd make your day', said Aidan 'aren't you always saying that the new Priest Father O'Shaunessy never calls around as much as Father O'Brien did. Sure isn't it your number one gripe and has been for the last six months.'

'Aye well I could have done without him calling round when he did' complained Maggie. 'Sure wasn't I in the middle of giving Michael a right rollicking because he had just ran into the house slamming the door as usual and then he said the 'damn pony's head' is stuck in the gate again and typical wouldn't you know as I was telling him to leave the door on its hinges next time and to mind his language Father O'Shaunessy turned up and he says to Michael, 'son how do you expect to get into heaven if you use bad language and disrespect your elders?' Michael looks at him for a good long minute and he says 'Well Father I guess I'll run in and out slamming the door until Saint Peter says for heaven's sake come in or stay out' and sure with that he turned on his heel and ran back to the pony and I was standing there with my face as red as a beetroot. And Father O'Shaunessy he says to me 'You have your hands full there Maggie' and it was all I could do but to ask the good Lord to let the earth open up and swallow me there and then so's I would nay have to see the look on young Father O'Shaunessy's face. I was mortified so I was.'

Aidan cracked up completely and by the time Michael showed up with Grandma Magg's glass of water he wondered what on earth had happened to have his Dad clutching his sides and the tears rolling down his face and Grandma Mags looking as if she was just about ready to burst with laughter herself. Grown-ups! Who could understand them – one minute they were shouting at you for acting like a two year old and the next they weren't acting any better themselves!

Chapter 26

Kerry rested her head against the side of the toilet bowl unable to drag herself back to bed after her latest round of vomiting. Now she knew what Laurie's kids went through she felt even sorrier for them. She had started to feel a bit queasy yesterday afternoon but fortunately made it home from work before her vomiting began in earnest. She'd been dragging herself back and forwards to the toilet bowl ever since and it was now 8.30am. She knew she would have to call into work sick but the thought of even speaking to anyone seemed like a mammoth task.

Aidan had phoned last night and she had managed to speak to him briefly. He had offered to come round and look after her but she really didn't want him and Michael coming down with the bug too. Although the thought of someone calling round to take care of her was pretty tempting! She reckoned that Laurie's kids had vomited for about 14 hours so she thought perhaps she should turn the corner soon. Not soon enough she thought despairingly as her head disappeared over the toilet bowl for what felt like the hundredth time.

Eventually Kerry managed to drag herself back to bed and she must have fallen asleep because the next thing she knew it was 12.30pm and to her relief it had been a full four hours since she'd last been ill. Ugghh, she still felt like death warmed up though. After she had dragged herself from her warm bed and practically fell into the shower she began to feel a little bit more human and was just wondering if she could face having something to eat when the doorbell rang. She hauled herself downstairs to find an anxious Laurie standing at the door.

'Oh Kerry, I am so sorry!' she said. 'Aidan's just after telling me you weren't feeling too well so I thought I'd pop round to see how you are. I've brought you some soup, although I don't know if you're feeling up to it or not?' she asked questioningly. 'If not I'll just leave it here for you to have later and let you get back to bed.'

'I think I'm over the worst of it now Laurie and a bit of soup could be just what I need.' She answered gratefully. 'I haven't been that sick in years', she said miserably.

As Kerry sipped her soup slowly, testing the

delicate state of her stomach, Laurie filled her in on what had happened with Will.

'I still can't believe it' said Kerry. 'I am so disappointed in Will. Oh Laurie,' she said taking hold of her hand, 'what will you do?'

'I haven't got a clue' said Laurie, the tears once again pooling in the corners of her eyes. 'He says he can't even remember much about what happened because he'd had a lot to drink.'

Kerry gave Laurie an understanding grimace, feeling more than a little ashamed of the fact that she'd earlier suggested that somehow made a difference.

'Was he really with that bitch Cynthia Nixon?' asked Kerry.

'Apparently so' mumbled Laurie tearfully. 'It looks like Brian was right.'

'Brian?' asked Kerry. 'Have you already spoken to Brian about this?'

'No not since I found out. But on the night of the dinner dance he was very kind to me and…..' Laurie hesitated, not wanting to betray Brian's confidence, not even to Kerry '…. well he hinted that Cynthia has had her eye on Will for a while now and implied Cynthia would find some way of getting what she wanted.'

'Weeelll said Kerry slowly. That may be true but

she still couldn't force him to have sex with her. Will had to have played his part Laurie.'

'I know' said Laurie tearfully. 'I just don't know what to do about it Kerry.' The fact that I absolutely loathe the woman he slept with definitely doesn't make it any easier.'

'She sounds like an evil bitch' said Kerry loyally.

'It's like she's laughing at me and my pathetic life' groaned Laurie. 'Like she can click her fingers and take what's mine without giving it a second thought. It doesn't matter to her who gets hurt in the process; she doesn't care about her own husband and she certainly doesn't care about me and mine' cried Laurie miserably.

'What can I do to help?' Asked Kerry beseechingly. 'Do you want me to confront her Laurie because you know I'm more than happy to give the bitch a piece of my mind.'

Laurie shook her head dejectedly. 'You'd only make things worse for me', said Laurie despairingly. 'You know Kerry I've never hated anyone in my life but I really hate that woman with a passion. She's destroyed my marriage, she's humiliated me and she's ruined the life of my children all in one fell swoop and there doesn't seem to be anything I can do about it.'

'Oh Laurie' said Kerry consolingly as she

watched her friend dissolve into the tears that she could no longer keep in check.

Chapter 27

Cynthia had just finished her session at the gym and was trying her best to ignore the drivelling woman who always made a beeline for her at the end of every class. You would think that she would have learned by now that Cynthia was not the sort of person who wanted to associate with a woman who was three stone overweight, needed a facelift and whose clothes were quite obviously from Primark. Honestly the nerve of some people, thought Cynthia angrily as she saw the woman desperately looking around for her. It didn't seem to matter how many times Cynthia blanked her; the stupid woman kept coming back for more. Did the idiotic woman really think that she had nothing better to do with her time than to stand around making small talk with the likes of her? Honestly why her private members gym didn't prevent people like her from coming here in the first place she would never know. She was definitely going to have to have a word with the management and get them to stop this dreadful woman from harassing her. Yes that's what she would do. She'd speak to that fit young gym instructor and see if he could sort it out.

Yes, and perhaps he could sort her out too Cynthia wondered idly, after all, Will Kerr hadn't exactly proven himself in the bedroom. To be honest Will had been a bit of a disappointment. It seemed he was one of those men who was quite happy having a woman do all the work, surely he must realise that she had needs too! So far Will Kerr hadn't exactly been adept at filling them. She'd been left more than a little sexually frustrated. No, what she needed right now was a man who ensured she was gratified and who could meet her needs as well as his own. The only problem was her gym instructor was a little younger than she normally went for. But perhaps someone young and with plenty of energy was exactly what she needed right now……..

'Excuse me' she said smoothly to the blond haired blue eyed Adonis. 'I was just wondering if you could help me' Cynthia smiled coyly.

She watched his eyes flick over her body appreciatively and she was glad that she'd paid the extra hundred on her new figure hugging lycras.

'What can I do you for?' he quipped with a confidence that immediately told Cynthia he was a man who knew his own mind.

'Well I have a bit of an issue' she said playfully, 'and I was just wondering if maybe you'd be able to help me?' Cynthia preened.

'No problem' he said. 'If I can sort it for you I will.'

Cynthia then went on to explain to him how she was being stalked by the horrible woman in the fitness class.

'So' he said at last 'what exactly has she done to harass you, other than talk to you?' he asked.

'Isn't that enough' exclaimed Cynthia self-righteously. And she watched bemused as he threw his head back and laughed.

'Ok. I'll have a word. After all we wouldn't want to lose a valued customer like you just because someone doesn't know how to respect your personal space now would we?' he asked.

'That's it exactly', she said. I'm so relieved you understand how it feels to have your personal space invaded' she said flirtatiously.

'Well that depends really' he said meaningfully as his eyes locked on hers, 'whether it was someone I wanted to share my personal space with.'

'I can see you and I understand each other' said Cynthia. 'Obviously I'd really like to repay you for your kindness' she preened as she ran her hand over his muscular forearms.

'I don't normally get paid for my services' he grinned, 'normally the fact that a beautiful woman leaves satisfied is payment enough.'

Cynthia felt a little tremor of excitement run through her. Yes he would do she thought. He would do nicely.

'Well' said Cynthia 'I'm sure we can arrange something. How about I treat you to dinner at the Grand Hotel as a little token of my appreciation? Thursday night ok?'

'I'm working Thursday but I'm free on Friday if that suits you?' he grinned.

'Perfect. Why don't I just call here and collect you?' Cynthia asked.

'Sure thing' he said easily. 'I'm not working this Saturday so I don't mind a late night.'

'See you then' said Cynthia as she breezed past him into her top of the range BMW.

It never ceased to amaze Jeff just how keen these older women were to throw themselves at him. Ok so he knew she was probably only late-thirties but to him that was pretty old given the fact he'd just turned 21 the week before. He knew how this went. He had a regular supply of older women all too eager to please him, he would offer to pay but in the end she would happily foot the bill for everything, including the room he was certain they would end up staying in. He would get some uncomplicated, enthusiastic sex, a first-class meal, a ready supply of top of the range wine and his girlfriend would be none the wiser. Life as a gym instructor really was turning out to be one of the best decisions he had ever made. Who would have thought a council lad like him would end up staying in the best hotels money could buy all paid for by the likes of Cynthia Nixon. Now that's what he called having your cake and eating it.

Chapter 28

Brian meant it when he told Cynthia he had had enough. When he married Cynthia he had been so certain it would last forever. He never thought his marriage would go the way of so many of his friends. He hadn't intended to let his marriage fail. And yet he realised it was time for a reality check. His marriage was dead. He couldn't go on pretending just for the sake of his boys.

When he thought about the current state of his life he was shocked to discover just how unhappy he was. If he was being totally honest with himself he could see that things had been bad for a very long time and no amount of wishing things were different was going to change that.

The only problem was he knew he wouldn't be able to disengage himself from Cynthia without putting himself and the children to hell and back.

Cynthia would never agree to a divorce. She relished her role managing the medical practice and loved her title of 'business manager' almost as much as she loved reminding people that she was Mrs General Practitioner. The only positive thing was that she had no legal stake in the Medical Practice itself as he had established it shortly before Cynthia came on the scene and, despite her best efforts, he had never agreed to officially include her as a partner in the business.

So where did that leave him? The house was in their joint names. They had some savings and investments and a holiday home in Portugal. He would let her have the lot if it meant she would leave him and the boys in peace. But he knew Cynthia, and nothing he could offer her would ever be enough to cause her to loosen her grip on his life. However he had to start somewhere, which was why after much deliberating he finally decided to lift the phone and book an appointment with his solicitor.

No sooner had he put the phone down than Cynthia breezed in complaining as usual; this time about some 'moronic' woman who had been 'harassing' her in the gym. Brian had heard it all before. There was always a tirade about one poor soul or another. He had long since given up listening.

Now he had made up his mind that he wanted to be free from Cynthia for good it was all he could do not to pack a bag and leave. But he couldn't afford to do that. Cynthia was a master schemer and if he wanted to beat her at her own game then he would need to plan his next move very carefully. No, he resolved, he would bide his time, speak to his solicitor and then decide what to do.

Arriving at McCain and Co the following morning Brian realised things were already off to a less than desirable start. According to the secretary Mr McCain had retired six months previously. Apparently, they had sent all their existing clients a letter advising them of this and he should have received his some months previously.

Only he hadn't. And now he was waiting to see someone he had never dealt with before and who new nothing whatsoever about him or his business.

According to the somewhat biased secretary, Ms Kerry Ford was the best Family Law solicitor in the business and would be more than capable of handling his case.

The problem was, Brian was certain she would never have encountered someone like Cynthia before. He needed someone like old Mr McCain with a will of iron to handle this for him.

Brian's confidence was not greatly improved when he came face to face with Ms Ford. She was far too pretty and far too young to be as ruthless as he needed her to be. Brian was just about to make his apologies and leave when she fixed him with a steely gaze which, in light of her youth and attractiveness, took him completely unawares.

'I know what you're thinking Mr Nixon, and if you can't hide your emotions a bit better than that then your wife will walk all over you. Now would you like to take a seat or would you prefer to make an appointment with someone twice my age, who knows half as much, and watch me walk all over you when I represent your wife instead. Because believe me Mr Nixon she will know who the best divorce lawyer in the business is and will seek me out at the first opportunity. Unless of course, you are fortunate enough to retain me first. Now what's it to be?'

Brian was secretly more than a little impressed. Perhaps he had misjudged her, he thought taking a seat, she certainly didn't hold back and after all it wouldn't do any harm to at least listen to what she had to say.

'Now I understand that you intend to seek a divorce from your wife. Is that correct Mr Nixon?'

'Yes' said Brian, 'however, I have a feeling that she isn't going to make that easy.'

'How so?'

'Well she doesn't want a divorce at all and I want one as soon as possible.'

'Unfortunately, that does complicate matters Mr Nixon. You see the law must be satisfied that the marriage has irretrievably broken down and that can only be ascertained in one of five ways. If one party refuses to consent to a divorce then it may be that you have to prove the marriage has irretrievably broken down by living apart for five years.'

'Five years', interrupted Brian angrily. 'I can hardly bear to be in the same room as her for five minutes never mind be married to her for another five years!'

'If you allow me to finish Mr Nixon. There are other ways to obtain a divorce within a much quicker timescale. You appear to have already eliminated one further option which would involve waiting two years and then divorcing by mutual agreement. Are you absolutely certain that your wife will not consider a divorce?'

'It's not an option' said Brian dully.

'A third option is also out as it would involve your wife legally deserting you. So that only leaves us with the grounds of unreasonable behaviour or adultery.'

'Well then we have her', Brian said gleefully, 'no right minded person could possibly describe Cynthia's behaviour as reasonable. She's a nightmare to live with!'

'How so Mr Nixon? Is she verbally abusive to you?'

'Well no not really' admitted Brian

'Does she mentally or physically assault you?'

'Well no, but she's impossible to live with. She's constantly complaining about everything and everyone. She's never happy. She's scheming and conniving and one of the most selfish people I have ever met.'

'Ah but therein lies the problem Mr Nixon. You have not actually demonstrated that your wife's behaviour is unreasonable. Her solicitors would undoubtedly argue that while their client is by no means perfect her behaviour is just as acceptable as yours. The law makes allowances for the fact that couples cannot always see eye to eye. It may be that it drives a wife to distraction that her husband snores or leaves the toilet seat up or is never home on time but these would not be grounds for divorce and neither I'm afraid are any of the character failures which you have described in your wife.'

Brian felt defeated already. He held his head in both hands. This was turning out to be even worse than he'd imagined. He was never going to get rid of Cynthia. At least not for a full five years. How had he been foolish enough to believe he could actually just walk away from her?

'There is one other ground which we haven't yet considered Mr Nixon - Adultery. If you can prove adultery then you can have your divorce within a matter of months.'

Brian looked up. This really wasn't something he wanted to get into. He didn't like airing his dirty linen in public. Yes, he had his suspicions that Cynthia had been unfaithful but he really didn't want to involve Will Kerr. How could he do that to Laurie. Hadn't the poor woman suffered enough?

Kerry saw Brian hesitate. She could read this man like a book. He really was going to have to start and show some backbone if he wanted to deal with the likes of Cynthia Nixon and come out smelling of roses. At the same time Kerry felt sick to her stomach. Yes she had to do her job and yes she had to let him know that he could obtain divorce on the grounds of adultery, but what if Brian indicated that Cynthia had been unfaithful with Will. Kerry would have no alternative but to issue Will with a court summons and have him attend as a co-respondent. She wasn't sure if she could do that. Perhaps she should just tell Brian Nixon to go elsewhere. But then someone less sympathetic than her would end up hauling Will through the courts in a messy divorce trial, and in a town as small as this he would be crucified. Kerry held her breath and waited. Brian Nixon was mulling something over, of that she was certain. Finally after what felt like hours Brian shook his head and Kerry breathed a sigh of relief, if not for her case, at least for her friend.

'Perhaps I should leave you time to process the

particular difficulties of obtaining a divorce and we can discuss it further on your next visit. Right now, I really would like to make some assessment of your current financial situation.'

'I see that my former colleague, Mr McCain has been your legal advisor for a number of years. You have a medical practice which you hold in your sole name and that includes not only the land on which the building sits but the building itself and of course the goodwill of the business. You have also invested in a small apartment in Portugal which strangely appears to be held solely in your wife's name. Can you explain to me why you funded the purchase of this property and yet your name does not appear on the title deeds?'

Brian was stunned. 'But we own that property jointly Ms Ford. My wife was the one who put in the offer and attended with the Portuguese solicitors but I was the one who funded it and she was quite clear that we were - that we are - joint owners!'

'Except you are not Mr Nixon. This property is in your wife's sole name and the copy land certificate I have obtained confirms it. I see the money was paid for by direct bank transfer from your account to your wife's account in Portugal. Am I correct in saying that your wife then used the money in that account to pay for the property?'

'Yes I suppose she did' Brian said miserably.

'And did you at any time instruct the solicitors in Portugal to place the property in the joint names of you and your wife?'

'No Cynthia dealt with the solicitors. I was too tied up with work here and couldn't make the trip over. But she told me the apartment was in our joint names.'

'Well Mr Nixon it looks like your wife was only interested in looking after herself. Perhaps,' she said more sympathetically 'we should go through the rest of your finances to check that they are as you assume them to be.'

Brian nodded dully.

'Who manages the financial accounts of your business?'

Brian's face paled. 'Cynthia does' he croaked.

'Okay….. I'll come back to that in a moment Mr Nixon. I can see that you own the matrimonial home jointly. And that you own another property at 10 Rover Court in your sole name is that correct?'

'But she can't touch that surely' said Brian angrily. 'That was my mother's house. She left it to me in her Will.'

'I am afraid Mr Nixon that until I have a full breakdown of your finances and legally discover those of your wife then we cannot conclude that any assets either of you may hold as legally free from claim by the other party. In plain English Mr Nixon, everything either of you own is up for grabs. It is merely a matter of dividing the assets. Fortunately, I am here to protect your interests and assist you in getting the best deal possible.'

Kerry knew that the first meeting a client had with a solicitor to discuss divorce was almost always a very unpleasant reality check. People just assumed that it was simply a matter of applying for a quickie divorce which they would then get within a matter of months. It was often a massive shock to discover that only happens on TV. It certainly wasn't the way things were done in the North of Ireland, where marriage was still viewed as a lifelong commitment, especially when there were children involved. Now was clearly not the time to discuss residency of the children. Brian Nixon had already gone a deathly shade of white and was visibly shaking, whether it was with rage, or shock she couldn't actually determine.

'I would suggest that we have perhaps discussed enough for today. You've a lot to take in,' Kerry said sympathetically. 'Before we proceed further I will send a letter to your accountant and obtain a report from him on the financial position of the business and obtain an up to date financial picture from your bank. Perhaps you would see my secretary on the way out to sign the necessary consent forms. I know this has all come as a bit of a shock but I have handled worse believe me.'

Brian was barely aware of signing the forms and it wasn't until he got to his car that he realised he hadn't even got around to discussing custody of the boys.

Chapter 29

Kerry loved her job and she knew she was good at it but it was often difficult dealing with clients from a small town especially when everyone seemed to know everyone else's business. Today's meeting with Brian Nixon had been particularly stressful, not because of the work involved but because it was much too closely aligned with Kerry's own personal life for comfort. It seemed Cynthia Nixon's name was cropping up everywhere. First the way she harassed Laurie; then her fling with Will and now through her new client. No one seemed to have a good word to say about the woman and her actions certainly seemed to justify that reputation.

She would do her utmost to ensure that Brian Nixon got the best divorce settlement she could get him and to keep Will and Laurie out of things.

She had taken an instant liking to Brian though.

He was straightforward and decent, if a little too unassuming. She already knew from Laurie that Brian had been the one to suggest that his wife had spent the night with Will Kerr and yet he didn't seem to want to burden anyone else by involving them in messy divorce proceedings. Thank goodness it was him and not his wife who had come to see her first. Kerry knew she could never represent that woman after what she had put Laurie through. Poor Laurie, thought Kerry she really was having a horrendous time of it, she didn't need Will's name dragged through the courts, they were struggling to stay together as it was and she suspected a little courtroom drama might prove insurmountable.

Kerry was glad it was Friday night and was looking forward to relaxing in front of the telly with a glass of wine. The thought of Aidan coming over later was pretty delicious too. She had hardly seen him over the past week as she had so much work to catch up on after being off with the stomach bug. But things were going so well between them. Of course it probably helped that they had known each other most of their lives, and now that Michael seemed happy for his Dad to be dating, Kerry felt they had really taken a massive step forward in terms of commitment. She didn't want to get carried away, she knew it was early days and yet she already knew that she wanted to spend the rest of her life with him. She just needed to give him a bit of time to draw the same conclusion.

But maybe he already had? She was the happiest she had been in her whole life, a great job, great friends and the man of her dreams. Things really couldn't be any better.

Making a quick detour Kerry decided she had time to pop in and see how Laurie was doing on her way home. The answer was obvious as soon as Laurie answered the door. She looked as though she hadn't slept in days. 'Will's moved out' she whispered tearfully before falling into Kerry's arms.

'Hush now, hush don't cry Laurie. It'll be alright, really it will. We'll sort something out don't you worry. Why didn't you call me?' asked Kerry. 'You know I would have come straight over.'

'It's only just happened. We had a massive row, I couldn't get the image of him having sex with that woman out of my head and I just lost it. I told him I couldn't deal with it and that he had to leave.'

'What did he say Laurie?'

'He begged me to let him stay. Said it was all a terrible mistake and something that he would regret for the rest of his life. Told me he could never forgive himself for what he'd done to me and the kids and that he loved me more than life itself. All the usual things you'd expect from a lying, cheating, scumbag I suppose.' Laurie snorted scathingly. 'But I just couldn't bear to be in the same room as him anymore never mind the same bed. How could I even consider letting him make love to me again knowing he had been with that woman? I wouldn't be able to do it Kerry and if I can't even consider the possibility of sleeping with him again at some point then what's the point in staying together, torturing ourselves with what's happened. The sight of him was just making me more and more miserable.'

'I just can't believe Will's done this to you Laurie, what the hell was he thinking?'

'I can't believe it either Kerry but every time I look at him all I can think about is the pain he's put me through. I can't forgive him Kerry, I really can't. And it's not just the affair. It was the way he shouted at me after I accidentally bid at the auction. He was horrible Kerry, absolutely vile. I've never seen that side of him before,' she said shuddering.

'It's just so unlike Will to behave like that Laurie. Is he having some sort of mid-life crisis do you think? You know you do hear about things like this happening; men reaching a certain age and suddenly they snap and begin to question what the hell they're doing with their life and end up screwing up spectacularly as a result.'

'He has changed' said Laurie thoughtfully, 'but in hindsight the changes have happened so gradually I didn't even notice. Its only when I look back that I can see how much he's been distancing himself from me. He's away so much on business that I hardly ever get to spend quality time with him; but even when he's here he just wants to play with the kids - which I get, I really do - he hardly ever gets to see them but I need him too Kerry, I need his support, I need him to tell me I've been doing a good job. I don't need him teasing me about the state of the house or joking about how disorganised I am or telling me I'm scatty. I need him to help tidy the house, to tell me to sit down and put my feet up, to bring me a cup of tea or let me spend quality time with the children instead of always running round after everyone else like a blue-arsed fly.'

'Of course you do', said Kerry sympathetically. 'Everybody needs to feel appreciated and loved Laurie. You have a right to expect him to be there for you and not just take himself out of the equation.'

Laurie nodded slowly. 'Oh Kerry' she said at length, 'when I start to think about how nasty and vicious he was to me after the auction I realise just how little he respects me. Maybe he still loves me Kerry, I think he does in his own way, but he certainly doesn't respect me and that hurts almost as much as his fling with that woman.'

'I get that' said Kerry understandingly, 'but you know Laurie it's also important that you respect yourself. I hope you realise what a great job you do. You're a great mum and your kids are a real credit to you. I couldn't manage a day doing the job you do Laurie not to mention the fact you don't even get paid to do it. Being a mum is one of the hardest jobs in the world.'

'Thanks Kerry but the thing is it should be Will telling me that; it should be Will singing my praises and lending a helping hand. I need him to be there supporting me and I suddenly realised that he hasn't been there and he hasn't been supporting me for a long long time..'

'Oh Laurie, I'm so, so sorry this has happened to you. You don't deserve it, really you don't. You're a wonderful person and you deserve to be happy' Kerry soothed as Laurie sobbed inconsolably in her arms. 'Come on now Laurie you don't want the kids to see you like this. They'd be upset? What have you told them by the way?'

'Just that their Dad's had to go away on business. Sure he's away so often they'll hardly know the difference' Laurie sobbed.

'Ok, ok' she soothed, 'I think you need a little time to compose yourself Laurie. I'm worried the kids will catch on that something's wrong. Why don't you sneak upstairs and get in the bath and I'll entertain the wee ones til you come back down.'

'Thanks Kerry Laurie' said tearfully, 'oh and by the way they haven't had any supper yet....'

'No problem. I'll sort it' Kerry said pasting a smile on her face as Laurie headed off up the stairs.

She phoned Aidan. The glass of wine and night of passion would just have to wait.

Chapter 30

Cynthia was enjoying her date with Jeff. She had booked a secluded little table in the corner of the infamous Grand Hotel and had taken the liberty of reserving a suite upstairs, deciding that if things went well, she might as well make the most of it. And things were going well. Jeff couldn't take his eyes off her; he was drinking in her every word and seemed genuinely interested in hearing about her role as practice manager. He was so attentive, wanting to know where she went on holidays, what sort of jewellery she liked, where she liked to shop, and what kind of car she drove. He really was a breath of fresh air and was totally what she needed, especially after the week she'd had with Brian. There was just no pleasing him at the minute. She did everything for him; took care of the business; sorted out the staffing issues; managed the accounts; not to mention running the family home and making sure the kids wanted for nothing, and yet all he seemed to do was mop about in a mood, barely even speaking to her; and men claimed women were the complicated ones! Maybe that was what she liked about Jeff; he was so straightforward, not to mention handsome.

Cynthia realised she was already a little drunk, but she was enjoying the wine and the company, so she decided they deserved another bottle. Leaving Jeff to order with the waiter she nipped to the ladies' room. As she assessed herself critically in the mirror she decided she really only needed to top up her lippy, she was looking her best tonight. Her red low-cut Versace dress was classy and hung to all the right curves, not that she had any of the wrong curves, her regular gym attendance ensured she didn't have an ounce of spare fat anywhere. Her eyes were sparkling; probably a mixture of too much wine and the promise of what was to come.

On second thoughts she decided she would order a bottle of sparkling water from the bar rather than drink any more wine, she didn't want to pass from sexy and coquettish to drunk and needy, she liked to be in control in and out of the bedroom and the last thing she wanted was for Jeff to think she was some sort of drunken cougar. Returning to her table Cynthia smiled sexily at Jeff, 'so' she said 'it turns out I've had a little too much to drink to be able to get us home safely so I've booked a suite upstairs to stay over. There's room enough for two but if you prefer I can always call you a taxi?'

This was it. She'd laid her cards on the table, it was up to Jeff to decide what he wanted to do, she really couldn't be any clearer.

'Well I don't think I've ever stayed in a suite before' said Jeff grinning 'I'd quite like to see what it has to offer'

'Oh, I don't think you'll be disappointed' Cynthia purred 'like me it's got pretty much what any man could wish for.'

'Ah but does it come fully equipped with what every woman needs?' he quipped.

'Well obviously that's what I've got you for' Cynthia laughed delightedly.

'How do you know my equipment will be up to standard?' asked Jeff jokingly.

'Well, I suppose I'll just have to test it for myself.' Cynthia purred. 'Why don't we take this bottle of wine up to the room with us and finish it in comfort.

Jeff grabbed the bottle of wine and they headed to the lifts. Cynthia was desperate to touch him and as the lift pinged closed she ran her hand over his bulging biceps, unable to wait a moment longer.'

Chapter 31

Brian had been looking forward to his night out with his golfing buddies but when Chris Canton had called him a few hours earlier asking him to meet up to discuss something urgently he could hardly refuse. Canton Medical Global was one of the largest suppliers of Pharmaceutical products to the surgery and Chris had helped Brian out of a tight spot on more than one occasion. He was hoping however that whatever Chris wanted wouldn't take too long and he could still meet up with his mates at the golf club later. It wasn't that he didn't like Chris it was just that, after the week he had, he needed to let off some steam. The hotel bar was pretty crowded but fortunately Chris, who had arrived first, had managed to grab a table just before a crowd of rugby lads arrived.

Over a few pints, Chris outlined his plans to open up a Medical Devices research centre in

Belfast's Titanic Quarter which in addition to a state of the art research facility would have a full time production, sales and marketing team. For what it was worth Brian thought he was right on the money and told him so. As far as he was concerned GP's had been crying out for years for companies to invest and expand in the medical devices industry. The right products would definitely reduce the need for patients to visit GP's for routine testing most of which could instead be completed in the comfort of their own home with results being automatically emailed to GP surgeries for checking and further analysis. Brian was able to give him a couple of recommendations of people he knew who might be useful to add to his R&D and sales teams but it was pretty clear to Brian that Chris's marketing team had done their homework and there was little more he could contribute other than endorsing the project from a GP's perspective.

Not wanting to rush off straight away Brian got another round of drinks in and was just returning to his seat when he saw Cynthia coming out of the ladies room. His first thought was 'bloody Cynthia, I can't get away from her' but then he realised she'd told him she was meeting some old school friends at the Wine Bar, so why had she lied? Quickly ducking out of sight, he watched her place an order at the bar before retreating to the seats at the back of the restaurant. Now this was getting interesting Brian thought. Who was she here with? Was it really just her girlfriends?

Had they decided on a last minute change of venue or was she hiding something? As Brian returned to his table he positioned himself so he could see pretty much the whole of the downstairs bar and hotel lobby area. His mind was working overtime. If Cynthia was up to something he needed to be ready to catch her out. Grabbing his mobile phone, he turned the camera on and resolved to record whatever he could whether it was incriminating or not. If Chris thought Brian had been acting strangely on returning from the bar he was too polite to say but he must've noticed Brian's eyes constantly flicking round the lobby because he twisted round in his seat a few times to see what Brian was looking at.

Brian didn't have long to wait. Within five minutes he spotted her heading towards the lifts with a young blond man. Even at this distance he could tell she was in full flirt mode. Excusing himself, Brian made his way to the lobby and ducked behind a conveniently placed potted plant. It didn't hide him completely from view but he would just have to chance that Cynthia was so involved with the man she was with that she wouldn't see him. Hoping he'd remembered to press the record button on his camera phone Brian watched as his wife flirted outrageously with the man she was with. He couldn't believe what he was seeing and even though he really didn't give a damn about Cynthia anymore it was humiliating to watch her cheat on him like this.

As the lift pinged shut Brian replayed the recording. He was certain his solicitor could now help him get a divorce based on Cynthia's adultery. He noted the lift stopped on the top floor and realising those rooms were suites he thought angrily of the bill he would no doubt end up having to pay all because his wife wanted to sleep with another man. Brian was deeply hurt but he was also livid, he wondered briefly whether he should check for his wife's room number from the receptionist, but, did he really want to alert Cynthia that he knew what she was up to? That was something the old Brian would definitely have done but Cynthia had always managed to stay one move ahead of the old Brian. No he decided, he wouldn't alert her, he would speak to his solicitor as soon as possible, show her the recording and take it from there.

Chapter 32

Will had been in Edinburgh all week and it seemed that everywhere he went reminded him of Laurie. He walked past the students Union and an image of him and Laurie falling laughingly out of it flashed through his mind. He walked past the Castle and fondly remembered wandering around the grounds, frozen with cold, hand in hand with Laurie as she excitedly told him all her latest plans or bit of 'hot gossip.' He walked past the little chippy they used to frequent and remembered the two of them stuffing their mouths with piping hot fish and chips as they strolled down Princes Street on sleepy Sunday evenings.

He remembered the excitement in her voice in those days; she was always brimming with laughter. Happiness just seemed to radiate from her, her eyes would sparkle with mischief and she never, ever, stopped talking. It was as though she was failing the universe if she stopped to come up for air, and her constant chatter was like a soothing melody always playing in the background. He loved it. He loved her endearing Northern Irish accent and her infectious laughter, he loved that she was always buzzing with excitement. She was his therapy really. Even if he had the worst possible day, ten minutes with Laurie would have him hooting with laughter and ease the stress away. Not to mention how she made him feel in bed. Other girls he had been with always seemed to hold something back. It was as if sex was something they felt they should offer but then they forgot to enjoy it. It wasn't like that with Laurie. Laurie treated sex with the same passion she treated everything else; she was relaxed, spontaneous and generous with her body. She savoured sex and her simple enjoyment of it made him feel invincible.

Will still couldn't believe she'd kicked him out. He had been certain they would be able to work through this. He had never seen Laurie so beaten and to think that he was the cause of it made him sick to his stomach. To say he wanted her back was the understatement of the century. He couldn't function without her. Yes, he knew he could go through the motions of going to work and talking to people as though he was alright, but inside he was completely broken.

He was regretting agreeing to meet Ben now. He knew the subject of Laurie would inevitably come up and he wasn't sure he could manage to talk about it. He hadn't seen Ben since his last trip to Edinburgh six months previously, but as it was an unspoken rule that the two of them would try to meet as often as his business trips across to Edinburgh allowed, Will had contacted him as normal. Ben was a good guy. They had both studied Business and Management at Uni, only Ben had gone on to start up his own Company, whilst Will was still a mere employee.

The restaurant Ben had booked was a good choice as far as Will was concerned, not too posh and not full of students either.

'You look like shit man' said Ben easily. 'What the hell have you been doing to yourself?'

'Thanks Ben. Don't hold back now will you? Any other insults you want to add?' Asked Will scathingly.

'Well you do' said Ben 'and what's with the beard? In fact it's not so much a beard as a mangy looking lump of fuzz which has somehow managed to attach itself to your chin.'

Will groaned. In truth he hadn't bothered shaving since Laurie kicked him out. He had no desire to make himself look presentable. It was all he could do to keep putting one foot in front of the other and get through the day.

'Pint?' asked Ben

'Double vodka and coke' ordered Will.

Ben raised his eyebrows but declined to comment. Something wasn't right. Will looked like a train wreck and he rarely ordered spirits never mind doubles.

Ben placed the drinks order and hungrily scanned the menu. 'I could eat a scabby horse' he said 'I'm so hungry my stomach thinks my throats cut.'

'Not much new there then' said Will. Ben's vociferous appetite was a long standing joke between them; he ate them out of house and home in their student days and could still eat double what Will could in a single sitting.

After placing their orders Ben chanced another look at Will. He really did look ill. 'So, want to talk about it?' Ben asked questioningly

'Not really' groaned Will although suddenly he felt like he might want to after all. 'It's Laurie' he blurted shamefully, 'She's kicked me out'.

'Shisshhhh' whistled Ben. 'Wasn't expecting that! What happened?'

'Awh usual crap' said Will despairingly and catching Ben raise his eyebrow questioningly he began to outline what had happened between him and Cynthia Nixon.

'Sounds like a ball breaker to me' said Ben. 'You know I always could tell one of those a mile off and it always took you about three months to catch on.

Doesn't surprise me she managed to get you into bed.'

'Gee thanks for the vote of confidence.' Will mumbled.

'What? Are you going to tell me you wanted to sleep with her and went to bed with her knowing you'd be cheating on Laurie?'

'Of course not!' shouted Will defensively. 'I hadn't a bloody clue what I was doing. I was completely and utterly wasted. I don't think I've ever had so much to drink. Must have been my guilty conscience.' Will cringed remembering how he had torn strips off Laurie after bidding at the auction and then getting totally hammered to block out what he'd done.

'Do you remember the night Angus McIntyre ruined his five-year relationship with Marie Kirkpatrick?' Ben asked.

'It'd be a bit difficult to forget that night in a hurry' said Will wondering just where Ben was going with this. He remembered the night well though because it was the faculty ball and was held in one of the nearby hotels. Angus and Marie had swanned in looking like loves young dream. They'd been together since they were fifteen and were so in tune with one another it was sometimes difficult to figure out where one ended and the other began.

Anyway, at some point during the evening, Marie lost track of Angus's whereabouts and deciding he must have went up to their hotel room she headed upstairs to check he was alright. When she found him she got a lot more than she bargained for. He was being ridden ragged by Carla Ferguson who Marie swears had been after him for weeks. Marie who couldn't stand Carla Ferguson told Angus he was welcome to her and if he thought she would ever want him back after he had slept - not the word she actually used - with that slut then he was sorely mistaken.

'Well I bumped into Angus a few years back and we got talking.' Ben continued. 'It turns out Carla planned the whole thing. Apparently, she'd been pestering Angus for weeks trying to turn him on, you know the usual ball breaker tricks, accidentally rubbing up against him, flashing a bit too much cleavage, bending over right in front of him with a too short, too tight skirt on. But he was having none of it, he was a one-woman man, the only one he was interested in was Marie. Then the night of the ball he had a fair amount to drink, well actually he was pretty damned plastered, and he already had a thumping headache so he decided to head up to the room for a bit and lie down. He says he can't really remember what happened next, just that when he woke Carla was sitting astride him absolutely naked. Well, before he had a chance to react to what she was up to Marie walked in.'

'He always swore that he never let Carla into the room but of course Marie didn't believe him. It wasn't until several months later that an ex-mate of Carla's told him that Carla had planned the whole thing. She had followed him up to the room earlier and then returned to reception saying she'd lost her room key. The hotel receptionist checked her name and saying she was Marie Kirkpatrick the receptionist gave her a duplicate key. Then all she did was keep an eye on Marie who was pretty much asking everyone if they'd seen Angus and once she heard her say she was going to check her room Carla got her mate to delay her for five minutes while she high-tailed it to the room to make sure she was 'in position' before Marie arrived - and the rest as they say is history.'

'Wow, unbelievable' said Will, 'are women really that devious?'

'Just the ball breakers' said Ben, 'and the sad thing is Angus and Marie never did get back together. She's married to some Canadian bloke now and Angus said he never met anyone he liked as much as Marie. So what I'm saying Will is, if you can't remember sleeping with this woman, how can you be sure you did?'

Shit thought Will, he's right. Will remembered going back to Cynthia's hotel room to ask her about the auction and he vaguely remembered someone helping him into bed just before he passed out drunk but the next thing he remembered was being woken in the morning by someone whom he had believed to be Laurie. As soon as he realised it wasn't, he had pushed her off him. Ok so there where bits in that scenario he really didn't want to think about in detail but he had definitely never knowingly allowed that woman access to his body and he had definitely pushed her off before anything had actually happened. Technically, that meant unless he had slept with her when he'd been passed out drunk he hadn't actually had sex with her, even though she led him to believe he had.

'The conniving scheming bitch' he said venomously.

'So, you think you might be in the clear then?' said Ben

'I think Laurie will never believe me anyway' groaned Will.

'Well you'll just have to convince her then won't you mate?' said Ben

'I don't think she'll buy it' said Will desperately. But at least now he believed there was a good chance he hadn't actually slept with Cynthia. There was a possibility he could convince Laurie. After all, could he really be blamed for what had happened any more than Angus could?

Just then the food arrived and Ben and Will talked about other things for the rest of the evening.

'I really hope you and Laurie work it out Will' said Ben as they were leaving. 'I think you'd look a long time before you found someone half as lovely as Laurie.'

'I know I would' Will admitted. 'I think I've been so busy feeling sorry for myself I forgot to try and hold onto her.'

'Ah mate don't end up like Angus, he's bloody miserable. He never got over losing Marie. And you've got kids to think about. Get it sorted Will. Whatever it takes - just bloody well get it sorted.'

After his night out with Ben, Will had been doing some serious thinking. For obvious reasons, he didn't want to have to tell Laurie exactly what had happened in the hotel room with Cynthia Nixon. There were still so many things about waking up in the morning in Cynthia's hotel room that would be too difficult to explain. Not least how he managed to get himself into that situation in the first place. At the same time, he couldn't see how he could convince Laurie that this wasn't all his fault without telling her the whole story.

The one thing he did know was that he wasn't going to give her up without a fight. He'd been a bloody fool. He'd been taking her for granted for months now. Just being in Edinburgh had reminded him so much of how Laurie used to be he suddenly realised how dejected she'd become. Where had the vivacious, fun loving, woman of those heady Uni days gone to? Of course no-one gets married, gets a job, has kids and a whopping great mortgage and remains unchanged, but he still thought the old Laurie was in there somewhere desperate to be given a chance to get her sparkle back. And suddenly that was what he wanted more than anything, just to see her relaxed and happy with a smile on her face, to hear her chatting away without a care in the world. He was her husband. He loved her. He wanted to bring the old Laurie back to life, to make her happy again even if that meant letting her go.

He thought back sadly to all the times over the last eighteen months or so when Laurie had said they needed to 'talk' and how he had dodged her efforts like a speeding bullet. He hadn't wanted to listen. Life was complicated enough, he didn't want her to tell him he had to be at home more, or help out with the kids more, or stop taking her for granted. But Will realised if he already knew those were the things she would say to him; didn't he already know those were the things she was struggling with? He had seen it. He just hadn't wanted to make more of an effort because he was being a selfish git.

There were going to be some changes Will resolved and he knew just where to begin. Maybe he couldn't win Laurie back but he could begin to make her life more enjoyable. As Will lifted the phone he was filled with hope for the first time in weeks.

Chapter 33

Laurie didn't know how she'd managed to get through the last few weeks. Her heart was literally breaking. She missed Will so much it was like a physical pain and yet she still felt that she had done the right thing in asking him to leave. She needed time to think things through. Strangely, she was relieved that she felt Will's loss so deeply. A secret part of her had often wondered whether she and Will had drifted apart to the extent that she wouldn't care whether he was still a part of her life or not. It was almost a relief in some ways to realise that she still loved him and that she missed having him around. It was one thing Will being away with work on a weekly basis it was entirely different realising he wasn't coming home. The kids missed him too. The younger ones accepted that he was away on business but Shane knew something wasn't right. He was constantly asking where his Dad was and she was tired of trying to dodge his questions.

She made sure the kids Skyped their Dad every night and she left it to Will to explain where he was and why he hadn't been home. The kids were bursting with news to tell their Dad but as soon as the call ended they deflated quicker than a burst balloon. There was no doubt about it, they were all missing him. The only problem was Laurie didn't feel ready to have him back. Kerry suggested that she and Will meet up and try and talk things through but she couldn't bring herself to do that. She didn't know if she was ready to open herself up to all the pain that would bring. She didn't want to ask herself whether she could ever forgive him.

Today was the first time in weeks that she would see Will. He was calling to take the kids out so he could spend some proper time with them. When the doorbell rang she heard Charlotte and Shane race to open it.

'Daddy, why did you ring the doorbell?' Charlotte asked giggling. 'Did you want to pretend you were a surprise visitor?'

'Course I did' she heard Will say hesitantly. 'I wanted to see if you were ready for our big day out together.'

'Yesss!' exclaimed Charlotte clapping her hands with glee.

'Well son', he said to Shane 'what have you been up to?'

'Not much' said Shane sullenly 'Where have you been Dad? You've been away an awfully long time 'on business" he said sceptically.

'Yeah I know I have son' said Will 'Sorry about that, it was just one of those things'

'Are you home for good now then?' asked Shane accusingly

'Well….' said Will falteringly 'I'm not sure really. We'll see.'

'We'll see always means no' said Charlotte despairingly. 'When adults say 'we'll see' it just means they want to find a way of stopping you go on and on about it when the answer is really no and they don't want to tell you.'

Laurie realised they would have to find a way of telling the kids what was happening. She couldn't go on pretending that Will was away on business and for that reason alone she and Will would need to sit down and discuss what exactly to tell the children.

'Where's Mum?' asked Will deftly changing the subject.

As Laurie stepped into the hall she caught Will's eye and Will told Charlotte and Shane to get their shoes and round up the others as he was taking them out for a treat.

'Yippee' cried Charlotte excitedly 'Where are we going Dad?' she asked.

'You'll see' said Will

'Is Mum coming too?' asked Shane astutely.

'If she wants to' said Will chancing a longing look at Laurie.

'I think I'll let Daddy treat you kids today,' said Laurie pasting a smile on her face. 'I'm really looking forward to having the place to myself for a change' she said smoothly. 'Why don't you go and get the twins sorted Shane. I think their changing bag is on the kitchen table but you'll need to help find their coats and hats.'

'Ok' said Shane sullenly stomping off towards the kitchen.

'Laurie' said Will pleadingly 'We really need to talk'

Laurie nodded silently. 'Ok' she said. 'Tonight after you bring the kids home we'll put them to bed and then have a bit of a chat, but Will' she said 'I only want to talk about the kids. I'm not ready for anything else.'

'Ok' said Will sadly. 'Whatever you want.'

Twenty minutes later and Laurie found herself nursing a cup of tea in a completely silent house. It was strange how she always longed to have the house to herself and then on the rare occasions she did she found the silence too distressingly eerie to enjoy it.

She wanted to give herself some time to plan out exactly what she needed to say to Will and how exactly they could break the news of their separation to the kids. She knew Shane would be devastated and Charlotte would no doubt tell the whole world in about five seconds flat. She didn't know if she could face the sympathetic faces of the other mums at the school gates. The very thought of it made her cringe, was her marriage really over? Was this what the sum of their years together had been reduced to? In another month or two would she be sending the kids off to stay with their Dad at the weekends? In another year or two would she be watching Will and a new partner play Dad and step-mum to their children? Laurie shivered involuntarily, the thought of it made her feel sick to her core, but sadly these things were now very real possibilities and if she couldn't bring herself to forgive Will then that was the way things would probably turn out.

Chapter 34

Will loved spending time with the kids. It was a bit of a struggle though to find something that would keep them all occupied as they were all at such different stages. He opted to visit the local indoor soft play area. He had been there often enough on the kids' birthdays to know that they had a great area for toddlers as well as free fall slides and an indoor basketball court to keep the older ones occupied.

'Daddy' said Tom 'I really really really realleeeeeeeeeeeeeeee missed you.'

'Not as much as I missed you' said Will grabbing him around the waist and tickling him 'til he squealed.

Tom's laugh had always been highly infectious and soon the two of them were wrestling and laughing. Charlotte not wanting to be left out attached herself to his left leg so he couldn't move without dragging her with him while Shane jumped on his back and the twins squealed delightedly at all the commotion.

Finally Will managed to shake them all off and chased them to the bottom of the climbing ropes which they shimmied up as fast as monkeys at a zoo. Returning to the twins, Will grabbed one in each arm and swung them upside down, listening to their delighted squeals as they swung from side to side.

Two hours later Will reckoned the kids had burned off enough energy to be able to merit a McDonalds. Five happy meals and a big mac later and they were all sitting contentedly when Charlotte suddenly stood up and let rip with the loudest fart imaginable. 'Charlotte' Will cried despairingly, 'what do you think you're doing?'

'Tom told me you should always stand up to fart otherwise it might get stuck' she said proudly.

Will glared accusingly at Tom while trying to avoid eye contact with the numerous glowering parents shooting daggers in their direction.

He heard the little boy at the next table say excitedly to his mother 'Mum did you hear how loud that girl farted? Did you Mum? How come you always tell me that's rude when I do it?' he whined.

'It is rude' said the mother crossly. 'Only very ill-mannered children do that Ollie.'

Will wished the ground would open up and

swallow him.

'I wouldn't worry about it mate', said the man at the next table laughingly. 'I've two of my own and they'd let you down a bagful every time.'

'Fart, fart' said the twins delightedly, 'fart, fart'

'Awh Charlotte' said Tom flapping his hand in front of his nose 'your farts really stink!'

'Stink, stink' shouted the twins excitedly, 'fartie fart, stink, stink'

'MYsoluti FARTS DO NOT STINK!' shouted Charlotte indignantly. 'Tell him Dad, tell him my farts do not stink!'

Will felt his face burning with embarrassment, he felt sure he could feel the tips of his ears pulsating with heat. He didn't know where to look, by this time all eyes in the restaurant were focused on him and the scene his kids were making. All he wanted to do was bury his head in his hands and weep with shame.

'You are such a loser Charlotte' ribbed Shane 'I can't believe you fell for that one. Did you really think your farts would get stuck if you didn't stand up to let them out? Everybody knows your farts come out twice as loud if you stand. That's the only reason Tom told you to do that. High five bro', said Shane and as he and Tom high fived each other delightedly Charlotte burst into angry tears.

'I hate you both' she sobbed angrily, 'I really,

really HATE YOU!'

'Fart, fart' continued the twins delightedly.

'For goodness sake keep quiet, all of you!' hissed Will angrily. But the kids were all now so caught up in themselves they didn't even register the angry tone in Will's voice. Short of shouting at them at the top of his voice, which would only result in more angry stares from nearby customers, Will was at a loss to know what to do. How had they got out of control so quickly? Charlotte was alternating between sobbing and screaming; the twins were giggling and shouting out their new-found words and the boys were laughing uproariously at Charlotte's expense.

The woman at the next table had obviously had enough she grabbed her son by the hand and pulled him and his half-eaten McDonalds towards the door. She glared at Will as if he was some sort of monster before directing her final insult towards their table. 'Now that's what happens Ollie if parents get divorced. Dads take their kids to McDonalds for want of something better to do and let them wreak havoc on everyone else!'

The whole restaurant went eerily silent. Embarrassed diners looked steadfastly down at their meals on the table in front of them. No one was willing to make eye contact with a shamed Will. Shane's mouth dropped open in disgust. 'I knew it' he said tearfully. 'I knew you and Mum were getting a divorce' he cried.

'Divorce?' shouted Charlotte. 'You and mummy can't get a divorce!' She pleaded.

'What's a divorce?' asked Tom cautiously.

'It's when your Mum and Dad can't stand each other anymore so they live apart and you only get to see your Dad every other weekend' Shane shouted accusingly.

'Nooooooooooooooo' wailed Charlotte 'Nooooo' she wept. 'Please Daddy, please, please, don't get a divorce' she cried.

Even the twins picked up on the change of atmosphere and stared silently up at Will in wide eyed innocence.

'Let's go' said Will miserably as he gathered up their things and ushered them towards the door. 'We'll talk about this when we get home.'

Laurie was definitely going to kill him.

Chapter 35

'Mum, Mum' squealed Charlotte running into the house. 'Dad says you're going to get a DIVORCE!'

'Charlotte' Will shouted angrily. 'You know fine well I didn't say any such thing'

'What's going on Will?' asked Laurie hugging Charlotte to her.

'Nothing' said Will 'it was just a stupid comment some woman made in McDonalds and it upset them that's all. She thought I was a single parent and Shane got the idea into his head that we're getting divorced.'

'Are you Mum?' asked Tom tearfully. 'Are you and Dad getting a divorce?' Will we only get to see Dad every other weekend? Will Dad be moving out?'

Will watched the colour drain from Laurie's face. He thought she was going to pass out, he caught her by the shoulders and guided her to the nearest chair making her put her head between her knees. 'Shane' he said urgently go and get your Mum a glass of water.

As Shane ran to the kitchen Charlotte and Tom stood tearfully by Laurie's side.

'Laurie' said Will gently 'Are you ok?'

Laurie lifted her head gingerly and glared at Will. If looks could kill he knew he'd be six feet under. 'How could you be so irresponsible Will?' She hissed angrily. 'I can't trust you to do anything right. You only had them for a couple of hours and look at the state of them. Were you trying to upset them?'

'But Laurie, I didn't …….' Will began 'it isn't my fault.'

'No Will it never is!' Laurie hissed angrily. 'It never bloody well is! Just go' she pleaded angrily, 'just go'

'But what about the kids Laurie, we can't leave things like this? We need to talk about this.'

'Haven't you done enough damage for one day?' She hissed furiously. 'I'll talk to them Will, I should never have agreed to let you take them out today without explaining things to them beforehand. All you've done Will is make things ten times worse. Now for the last time, leave us in peace.'

As Will gingerly made his way towards the door he was conscious of six pairs of eyes cautiously watching him. He called out a subdued goodbye but got no answering response. He was a shit Dad and an even shittier husband. No wonder Laurie wanted nothing more to do with him he thought glumly as he made it to his car. All he seemed to do was make things worse for everyone. They'd all be better off without him.

As Laurie gathered her little tearful brood around, her mind struggled desperately to find the right thing to say to them. The problem was she couldn't lie to them. She couldn't reassure Charlotte that they weren't getting a divorce because she didn't know whether that might turn out to be the case; she couldn't tell them everything would be alright because she didn't even know herself whether it would be. In the end, she opted it would be best to tell them as little as possible.

'Look kids' she said soothingly 'I know you have had a really bad day but I don't want you to be upset. Daddy and I both love you very, very, much. Please don't cry.'

'But' sobbed Charlotte 'I don't want you and Daddy to get a divorce. I want things to stay the way they are. I love daddy!'

'I know you do sweetheart and Daddy loves you too. We both love you all very much and just want you all to be happy.'

'Don't get a divorce then,' said Shane angrily

'I don't know where all this talk about divorce has started but Daddy and I have never even talked about getting a divorce.'

'You haven't?' asked Shane hopefully

'No' said Laurie shaking her head.

'Does that mean you aren't getting a divorce?' asked Tom.

'No stupid' said Shane, 'it just means they haven't decided yet'.

'Please, please, don't get a divorce Mummy' pleaded Charlotte. 'Promise Mummy, please please, please, promise you won't.'

The kids knew that Laurie never agreed to make a promise unless she could keep it. She had drilled it into them since they were babies that if you promised something then you absolutely one hundred per cent had to keep your promise. There was no way she could promise them that she and Will wouldn't get a divorce. They would hate her forever if she promised them that and then broke it.

'Do you know that marriage is like a promise?' said Laurie at last. 'When two people decide to get married they make a special promise to one another called a Vow and that means that they promise each other to stay married forever. Your Dad and I made that promise to each other when we got married and you know that we both really believe that you should never ever break a promise, don't you?'

Three little heads nodded solemnly.

'Well your dad and I sometimes have to work a little harder at keeping that promise to each other and now is one of those times. We are working really, really, hard to keep our promise. It's just that sometimes people can work harder at keeping their promise if they think about it on their own. So Daddy and I have decided that he will move out for a little while so that he can think about how to keep his promise to me and I can have a little bit of thinking time on my own so I can work hard at keeping my promise to him. Does that make sense?'

'And then will you be happy again?' asked Charlotte.

'Well that's what we're hoping' said Laurie hugging her daughter's small frightened body to her. 'We're hoping that once we get a little bit of time on our own that we will be able to keep our promise to each other. You know that Daddy and I would never break a promise to each other unless we just really, really, couldn't keep that promise any more don't you?'

'But you won't break your promise to each other will you Mummy?' asked Tom.

'Well I hope not' said Laurie carefully. 'Just remember that Daddy and I have kept our promise to each other for a very, very, long time already and it is very hard to keep a promise forever but we are going to try our very best. Now what about some of my special hot chocolate and marshmallows and we'll all cuddle up on the sofa and watch a DVD?'

'Yes please Mummy' said Charlotte and Tom at once.

'What about you Shane?' asked Laurie

'S'pose so' said Shane grudgingly.

Oh dear thought Laurie she really wasn't sure whether she had handled things well or not. She could only hope that somehow she and Will could sort things out and she wouldn't have to put the kids through any more confusion and upset. She had told them she would try her best to keep her promise and she knew she owed it to them to do just that but, right now, when she thought about Will all she wanted to do was throttle him.

Chapter 36

Brian managed to get the last available appointment with his solicitor and was now looking at her hopefully having just shown her his video evidence of Cynthia with the man in the lift.

'I know you probably think that this is indisputable evidence of an affair Mr Nixon' she said at length, 'but I'm afraid it's not.'

'What do you mean it's not? It has to be!' said Brian disbelievingly. 'Look at the state of the two of them, it's obvious what they have in mind.'

'To some extent I agree with you' said Kerry. 'Logically it would appear that your wife booked a hotel suite and was seen entering a lift with an unknown man in a state of … well let's just say 'excitement.' The intention seems to be that they were going to spend the night together. Unfortunately, if your wife is half as devious as you think she is she will have a very convincing explanation to justify all of this.'

'What possible alternative explanation could there be?' Asked Brian. 'She booked a room, she entered the lift with a man, she didn't come home that night and I certainly didn't see either her or him leave the hotel while I was there.'

'Unfortunately, the law requires very specific proof of adultery Mr Nixon.'

'Like what?' asked Brian disbelievingly.

'Adultery can be evidenced if a spouse is caught *in flagrante delicto* or in non-Latin terms caught in the act of having sex with someone else. Other indisputable evidence of adultery would be a pregnancy which a person other than the spouse has been responsible for. Adultery can also be evidenced by a written admission duly sworn by the party or parties who committed adultery.'

'I can't believe it's so difficult to prove' said Brian dejectedly. 'I just assumed that if you suspected your wife of having an affair and had some fairly convincing evidence to that effect then you'd get your divorce.'

'Unfortunately, a judge only accepts indisputable evidence of adultery,' explained Kerry, 'especially if the spouse in question denies committing adultery. Do you think your wife will deny committing adultery when confronted with your video evidence Mr Nixon?'

'If Cynthia thinks there's any possibility at all of wriggling out of this then she will definitely deny it' said Brian glumly.

'In my opinion Mr Nixon your wife will claim that the man is merely a business acquaintance or a friend who was ensuring that she got safely to her room but who left almost immediately afterwards. She will claim that she had to book a hotel room as she had too much to drink and couldn't be bothered getting a taxi and unfortunately Mr Nixon, without absolute proof to the contrary the judge will opt to believe her and will deny you your divorce.'

'I thought I had her this time,' said Brian despondently.

'In some cases I have known clients to hire private detectives - at considerable expense might I add - to gain similar incriminatory evidence, only to have a judge throw the entire case out of court. At least you haven't expended thousands of pounds on private detective fees Mr Nixon.'

'No I suppose not but it's so frustrating. I know she was going to have sex with that man. And if that isn't humiliating enough now I find I still can't even divorce her because of it.'

'I sympathise Mr Nixon, I really do but you

wouldn't be the first person to pass through these doors only to discover that Charles Dickens was absolutely right when he said, 'the law is an ass.' On a more positive note I have now heard back from your accountant and I am happy to say that your Practice seems to be on firm financial footing and furthermore that whilst your wife may regard herself as your business partner there is no reason to suggest either financially or legally that she has any right to claim that title. Did you know that you pay your wife a wage for her work as your business manager Mr Nixon?'

'Yes, I know she takes a small wage; I told the accountant that I had no objection as she does help manage the place.'

'I would hardly term it a 'small' wage Mr Nixon' said Kerry showing him a figure which made him blanch.

'I had no idea it was that much. When she first started working at the practice we agreed a figure but that has risen considerably since then.'

'On the plus side Mr Nixon, the fact that she is not a legal or financial partner in the business, but is merely an employee, does mean that she will be unlikely to justify a claim in a share of the practice itself. Of course it also means that in due course you will be free to 'restructure' the Practice meaning that her services may no longer be required and a new employee on a less substantial salary might be justifiable. I know it's early days but I think we should eventually push for her to accept a one-off lump sum payment rather than a continuing financial encumbrance against you.'

'Cynthia will never agree to that,' said Brian miserably. 'She will want her pound of flesh.'

'You leave that to me Mr Nixon. I have a few tricks up my sleeve which will make her think she is getting a much better deal by accepting a one-off payment rather than a continuing claim for maintenance. Your accountant and I had a very interesting phone call earlier today and there are a few legal loopholes which, with the correct financial planning, will undoubtedly protect most of your business assets from any potential maintenance claims. You have no idea how fortunate you are that your wife is not your legal business partner Mr Nixon. If she were you would have stood to lose everything but the shirt on your back.'

'Well at least that's something' mumbled Brian.

'Mr Nixon what I need now is a little time to allow your accountant and I to make some changes to your finances. There will be a few matters he will need to discuss with you and a few documents for you to sign but once that process is complete I see no reason to delay sending a letter to your wife indicating that you are Petitioning for divorce. If you are forced to wait five years the sooner we get the process started the better.'

'Once again Ms Ford you've given me a lot to think about. Thank you for your time.'

'No problem Mr Nixon. If anything significant occurs in the meantime please don't hesitate to contact me.'

As they shook hands Brian left the office feeling a strange mix of disappointment and relief. He was glad his solicitor seemed confident in sorting out the financials but bitterly disappointed that he couldn't get his divorce on the grounds of adultery. He had been so certain the evidence he had gathered would be enough.

Chapter 37

Kerry was glad Brian Nixon was her last appointment and she could finish for the day. She was meeting Franco to get her highlights done and then they were heading out to La Bamba afterwards for a meal and cocktails. She'd been looking forward to it all week. Since she and Aidan had got together she felt she'd hardly seen any of her friends. WhatsApp was fine for a quick catch up but she missed her evenings out. When she'd worked in Belfast Centre she and Franco would have met up most nights after work and being part of the buzz of city life, flitting from one bar to the next, was one of the things she missed most about moving away from the city.

'Good to see you Kerry' said Franco. 'The usual I presume' he asked while whipping out a gown swivelling her into a chair and turning her to face the mirror.

'Yes please' said Kerry.

As Franco set to work with his colours Kerry got a chance to give her friend the once over. 'You're looking good Franco. Have you been working out?'

'Si Kerry I have gotten into new exercise and it suits me well I think.'

'You?' 'Exercise!?' feigned Kerry in mock horror. 'What has happened to the Franco I know and love whose only form of exercise is of the carnal knowledge variety?'

'Ah well you see my dear I discovered that age does not suit me. I have a typical male problem around zi middle and I decided to do somethink about it.'

'Well it suits you' said Kerry 'I don't think I've ever seen you so toned. Are you going to the gym?'

'I am doing a class there si. You've heard of Piloxing?' he sighed 'I think zat I am becoming a little bit in love with it. It is like - how do you say - an addiction! Yes I think zat I am now a Piloxing addict.'

'So what is it then, this Piloxing?'

'What! You never heard of ze Piloxing! It is all ze rage in the city, you really have become a little country girl haven't you?' he taunted. 'Piloxing iz a how you say mash-mish of Pilates and boxing it is vunderful you know. Gives great little booty don't you think?' he said turning and shaking his highly toned tush in

Kerry's face. Kerry reached out and gave it a little squeeze but there was nothing to squeeze, his butt was solid muscle.

'My, my, my,' said Kerry 'I have to say Franco I am most impressed. I never would have put you down for being an exercise fanatic and yet I saw you a couple of months ago and you didn't say a thing.

'I just start it notta so long ago but I love it so much I go to classes maybe five times in ze week. Is marvellous yes?' He asked lifting his T shirt to reveal a highly toned torso.

'Well if those are the sort of results you get where do I sign?' asked Kerry

'You cannot sign' he tutted. 'It is full all of ze time. Never any space. I am lucky because I friends with ze owner and he let me book ze classes in advance, but you my dear, must sadly stay in your pre-piloxing state of little bit of saggy bum - yes?

'No!' wailed Kerry 'I do not have flabby bum Franco and you know it!'

Franco chuckled. 'I know, I know Kerry I tease you- yes? You look fabulousa my darling. You have little love glow do you not?'

Kerry blushed. 'Well maybe just a little.'

'I knew it. Franco he says to himself when you come in 'now zere is a woman in love'. But how my dear? When did zis happen?'

'Well do you remember my friend Laurie. I brought her to see you the last time we were in Belfast?'

'Ah but of course smiled Franco. Ze beautiful woman with ze sad smile and ze terrible hair. But Franco make her smile again. Her hair was great success si?'

'Oh yes she loved her hair unfortunately things have went a little downhill since you saw her last.'

'How so?' Asked Franco

'I'll tell you over dinner but let's just say all is not well at home.'

'Oh zat is so sad. But, how does zis explain about your new lover?'

'Well Aidan is Laurie's brother. I've known him all my life but when Laurie and I got home from Belfast that was the night when we finally got together.'

'But zat is marvellossa!' Franco exclaimed. 'And is he good enough for you my bella? Does he look out for you?'

'Yes he looks after me' said Kerry. 'Oh Franco he's lovely' she said grinning like a loon.

'And are you in ze love with him?'

'Well…..' Kerry hesitated. 'It is early days you know. We've only been together eight weeks but yes

I'm in love with him and I'm pretty sure he feels the same way.'

'He not tell you zat he loves you yet bella?'

'No,no not yet. But that's normal right?'

'Of course, of course' said Franco gently. 'He willa tell you wen he is ready si?'

'Do you think that I should tell him first?' Asked Kerry.

'I think zat you could tell him zat yes Kerry but then you will always be wondering why he did not say it first. It eat you up like how you say - a giant worry wart!' He finished proudly.

'I will ignore that pathetic use of simile' Kerry scorned 'but yes you're right I suppose' sighed Kerry. 'I need him to tell me first. He's been hurt before so I think that might be what's holding him back but I guess it's still early days in a relationship isn't it?'

'Si of course it is. Would you like zat I meet him? You wanta me to check him out?' Asked Franco puffing out his chest.

'I think maybe Franco I need to wait a while before I let you loose on him' laughed Kerry.' I don't want to give him the jitters.'

'Zee 'jitters', wat is ze 'jitters' you are mocking me now I think' Franco said eyebrows raised.

'Come off it Franco. I've known you too long to

be fooled by the 'mi English is notta so good I am from Italy si?' act. In fact you can drop the accent altogether if you like I think everyone else has gone home.'

'Alright, alright' mumbled Franco 'since it's only you here. Really Kerry you forget sometimes that I have a reputation to maintain.'

'Yeah, yeah Franco and you forget I've known you way before you re-invented your Italian roots. Now have you nearly finished? I am starving hungry?'

'Finito' said Franco 'sorry, sorry force of habit – all finished' he said, showing her a mirror.

'Gorgeous as usual' grinned Kerry, 'now let's get out of here.'

Thirty minutes later and Franco and Kerry were sitting in a lovely little booth at La Bamba waiting to get served.

'So' said Kerry 'I know you've been champing at the bit to tell me all about him.'

'About who?' asked Franco innocently.

'Don't play the innocent with me Franco. I saw the gorgeous model-like bloke who works here shooting you massive puppy dog eyes when we arrived.'

Franco's eyes lit up with excitement. 'He's a very, very bad boy that one!' said Franco. 'Very demanding you know' he sighed. 'I met him at Piloxing class.'

'Thus, the real reason you started going five times a week' laughed Kerry.

'Ok, Ok maybe that was a tiny part of it' said Franco, eyes glinting mischievously.

'So are you and he an item then?' Asked Kerry.

'It's casual' said Franco. 'He's a very moody boy - gets very jealous unless he has my attention all of the time. It's a little draining if I'm honest. But he has such a hot body I just can't seem to say no.'

'Oh poor you,' mocked Kerry.

'George doesn't approve' said Franco carefully.

'No, well what business is it of his anyway?' asked Kerry. 'He can't leave you high and dry and then expect you just to sit in pining for him now can he?'

'I think he's jealous' said Franco.

'What? You think he wants to get back with you?'

'I don't know' said Franco. 'I can't second guess George. I thought we were fine. Lifelong partners the whole shebang and then he dumps me the night after our 10 year anniversary. No reason, no explanation, nothing other than an 'I can't do this anymore' and that's it! Ten years together and it was over just like that!'

Kerry could see tears glistening in Franco's eyes. Eighteen months on and Franco still hadn't come to terms with what George had done.

'You still love him don't you?' said Kerry.

'That's not the point' said Franco angrily. 'The point is he finished with me and then he takes the hump when I start seeing somebody else!' Said Franco incredulously.

'But isn't that normal?' asked Kerry. 'Don't people always want what they can't have? And the fact that you are looking so hot and have a real stud muffin drooling all over you is bound to leave George questioning whether he did the right thing.'

Franco threw his head back and laughed 'Stud muffin, did you really just say 'stud muffin'?', roared Franco with tears running down his cheeks. 'Oh Kerry, my love we really do need to get you back to the city, your street cred has just hit rock bottom.'

Kerry felt her face glowing red. 'What exactly is wrong with the term 'stud muffin'' she wailed indignantly?

'There's just nothing right about it,' laughed Franco 'but of course it's part of the reason I love you' he grinned.

'Anyway, stop trying to change the subject. Do you want to get back with George?'

Franco played with the box of matches in front

of him and studiously avoided making eye contact with Kerry. 'It's hard Kerry,' he said at length. 'I can't just turn off the feelings I've always had for him but he hurt me so badly I don't think I'll ever be able to forgive him. Besides I didn't say he wanted to get back with me I just said he didn't approve of my 'stud muffin" he said grinning.

Kerry walloped him good naturedly around the arm. 'Do you know what I think?' she asked.

Franco shook his head.

'I think you deserve to have some fun in your life. You're looking better than I've ever seen you. You're obviously having fun with stud muffin so forget about George, have fun and if he does want you back there'll be time enough to think about it then.'

'You're right as usual,' grinned Franco 'and on that note let's have some fun. I think we've time for some cocktails before our meal so let's start as we mean to go on. A couple of Cosmopolitans, I think?'.

'Now' he said turning to face Kerry 'tell me all about this new man of yours ....'

Chapter 38

Kerry had the worst possible hangover. Of course that was only to be expected after a night out with Franco. They had made a fantastic night of it, drinking cocktails til the wee small hours before Kerry finally caught a taxi home. Nonetheless she was definitely getting older, either that or her body had gotten out of the routine of a heavy nights drinking and was letting her know it! Oh good thought Kerry chancing a look at the bedside clock. It was only 11.00; she could easily lie in for a couple more hours, hopefully the room will have stopped spinning by then.

She forced her eyes closed trying to forget about the niggling pain in her bladder but soon realised she wasn't going to get any sleep until she paid a visit to the bathroom. The trouble was that getting there and back was going to make her feel a hell of a lot worse. Gingerly she slid her legs over the side of the bed and sat for a moment waiting for her head to stop pounding. Reluctantly she realised that wasn't going to happen anytime soon. As soon as her feet hit the floor she felt the bile rise up the back of her throat and she bolted to the toilet just in time to empty the entire contents of her stomach down the bowl. As she rested her forehead against the cold ceramic seat she vowed she was never, ever going out drinking with Franco again.

Thinking a long hot shower might help bring her round Kerry undressed and slipped under the hot water, which was fine until she felt herself go light headed and realised she was in danger of passing out. Soaking wet she grabbed a towel and crawled back into bed closing her eyes as tightly as she could in a vain attempt to stop the room spiralling. At some point she must have fallen asleep again because the next time she woke it was 2.10pm and she was feeling slightly more human. Slipping her dressing gown on she made her way downstairs for some much needed tea and toast together with the obligatory paracetamol. 'Franco you git' she texted 'hope you are feeling as bloody miserable as I am this morning'

Almost immediately the text pinged back 'Ur out of practice country girl! Mite b ur morn but sum of us bin at wrk 6 hrs already! xx'

'Gd -hope ur sufferin – goin back to bed!'

'No girl– u going to gym -remember???'

'Oh no' groaned Kerry she did vaguely remember something about a contact of Franco's friend starting up a new gym class – she hadn't signed up to it or anything as stupid as that had she?

?????? she texted back

As Kerry's phone buzzed with an incoming call from Franco she reluctantly pressed answer.

'Now you listen here girl. I did not, NOT! put my reputation on the line for you just so you could destroy it in one fell swoop. I hope you appreciate how many strings I had to pull to get you into the one and only Piloxing class in your area last night! Don't you dare let me down,' he said furiously 'do you hear me!!!'

'Franco I'm ill,' she wailed miserably 'please don't make me go! Please! I will embarrass you by vomiting all over the lovely instructor in his lovely new shiny gym.'

'Kerry,' warned Franco, his voice dangerously low. 'I don't care how ill you are. You make it to that gym for 3pm or I swear I will never ever cut your hair for you again. EVER. You can find yourself another hairdresser.'

'Shit' thought Kerry, it wasn't worth pissing Franco off, it would take her months to get a new hairdresser, never mind the fact she'd have to grovel to him for months on end to get him to forgive her.

'Ok' she mumbled. 'I'll be there'.

'Good girl' said Franco. 'You'll love it. Chao.'

As Kerry hung up she wondered how the hell she was going to survive a Piloxing class when she could barely even see straight never mind balance on one leg. As she pulled on her gym clothes and stuck her hair back in a ponytail she grabbed her car keys and prayed she wasn't still over the alcohol limit from the night before. That would be all she'd bloody well need to lose her licence and her practising certificate in one fell swoop.

The class was packed. That was a good sign, hopefully she could bluff her way through, standing at the back going through the motions, then she'd say a quick hello to Franco's friend of a friend at the end and tell him how wonderful he was whilst secretly planning never to return. There was no way Kerry could follow the instructor, she could hardly even see him! She resolved just to vaguely follow what everyone else in front of her was doing.

Fifteen minutes in Kerry felt like her lungs were going to explode. Her stomach heaved every time she moved and the threat of being sick all over the lovely new dance studio was a real possibility. Thirty minutes in and Kerry who had been doing as little as humanly possible for the last thirty minutes still thought she was going to die.

At the end of the forty five minutes Kerry

thought she could actually smell the alcohol soaking from her sweaty pores but amazingly she had survived and even more amazingly her hangover had eased slightly. Now all she needed to do was lie down in a darkened room for twenty four hours and perhaps she would pull through after all.

As Kerry waited to speak to the instructor at the end of the class she found she could see him properly for the first time, he was quite good looking actually, if she hadn't already been with Aidan she might have been interested. There was also something vaguely familiar about him, she wondered if she'd met him before. He definitely wasn't one of her clients, she would have remembered someone as good looking as him, perhaps she'd met him on a night out with Franco. She normally had a very good memory for names and faces.

And then suddenly the penny dropped as she saw Cynthia Nixon make her way over to him and pull him to one side. He was the man on the video clip Brian Nixon had shown her. 'Oh no' thought Kerry cringing this was all she needed. As Kerry ducked her head pretending to tie her shoe lace, she watched the two of them out of the corner of her eye. They were definitely flirting with each other but nothing more than that. It was probably more than his job was worth to be caught fraternising with the customers thought Kerry.

Kerry quickly gathered up her stuff and left;

there was no way she was going over to introduce herself to him now. She liked the fact that so far neither Cynthia nor the gym instructor knew who she was and she certainly wasn't going to draw attention to herself, especially not when it was more than likely that she and Cynthia Nixon would be meeting across the courtroom in the near future. She spoke to the receptionist on the way out and asked her the name of the Piloxing Instructor and then asked her to pass on to Jeff how much she had enjoyed the class. That should keep Franco happy at any rate.

Thankfully the rest of Kerry's weekend was pretty uneventful. Aidan called round with a bottle of wine and a takeaway on Sunday evening and it went someway to showing Aidan the delicate nature of her stomach when she refused to have even so much as a glass.

'Your Franco sounds like a bit of a character' said Aidan, 'I'd like to meet him sometime.'

'Franco takes a bit of getting used to' said Kerry grinning. 'He speaks before he thinks most of the time and you need the hide of a rhino not to take offence at some of the things he comes out with. Let's just say he's direct. He'll tell you exactly what he thinks whether you want to hear it or not.'

'Well you two seem pretty close' said Aidan.

'Yeah we are', said Kerry 'we go back a long way Franco and I, he's kind of like the big brother I never had. I can tell him anything and know that he'll either help me through it or tell me to wind my neck in and quit whinging. Did you know that the only reason I actually qualified as a solicitor is because of Franco?'

'What do you mean?' asked Aidan.

'Half way through my second year at Law School I decided I had had enough. I was sick to death with all the study and student life had lost its appeal. I was living in a pokey little flat just off the Donegal Road with two other girls. I didn't even know them that well when they asked me to move in with them, but the rent was dirt cheap and I thought 'what the hell' how bad could it be? Unfortunately it wasn't the smartest move I ever made. They turned out to be using drugs in a big way. Their dealer was round at the house every other night and if they couldn't pay for their drugs he let them off as long as they agreed to entertain his 'friends."

'What are you talking about here Kerry? Do you mean they agreed to have sex with someone just so they could feed their drug habit?'

'Yep, you got it in one' said Kerry. 'Of course I was a bit green behind the ears and it took me a good few months to figure out what was going on. I just thought they were very promiscuous and when I asked them if they would mind not bringing a different man back to the house every night of the week they just laughed at me. Asked me how the hell else did I expect them to pay for their weed. I couldn't believe it. I said I was moving out, and I did for a while but I got fed up living on other people's sofas and of course none of the flats I stayed at temporarily were really conducive to studying. It's kind of impossible to have a good night's kip on the sofa when there's a party going on in the same room' she grinned.

'What did you do?' asked Aidan.

'I tried to join in of course' she laughed but Aidan could see the shadow pass over her face and pulled her to him.

'My grades hadn't been great before but at that point I started failing miserably. I looked ill, I hardly ever got any sleep. I survived on pot noodles, tomato soup and toast and was totally miserable. Eventually I went back to the flat. Barricaded myself in my room at night and tried to ignore what was happening in the room beside me but in the few weeks I'd moved out things at the flat had gotten worse. My flatmates were entertaining well into the night and the number of dodgy looking blokes coming and going into our flat over the course of the week was scary.'

'Why the hell didn't you just go home to your Mum and Dad?' asked Aidan.

'I couldn't. They were going through divorce and I couldn't bear to see them tearing strips off each other. Every time I went home they ended up telling me just how bad the other one was and I felt like I was being torn in two. It was actually less painful to stay at the flat.'

Aidan hugged Kerry closer to him. 'What happened?' he asked.

'Well one night I got up to pee and as I was coming out of the bathroom one of Caitlin's male 'friends' grabbed me and pushed me back inside. I was terrified. He asked me why I hadn't joined in the party and did I want what he had to offer. He shook a little packet of white powder in my face and when I told him I didn't do drugs he accused me of thinking I was better than him. He told me he would show me a thing or two and before I knew it he had his hands all over me. He was so strong' Kerry sobbed, reliving the most terrifying moment of her life all over again.

'Oh Kerry I'm so sorry,' said Aidan. 'You should never have had to go through something like that. I want to kill him. Did he ….. did he hurt you?'

'No' sobbed Kerry 'I was lucky. I started screaming at the top of my lungs and thankfully Caitlin heard. She started hammering on the bathroom door and told him if he didn't let me go she was calling the police. I don't know whether she would have or not but he was so angry that she would even dare suggest it he swung open the door and punched her straight in the face. As she fell back she banged her head on something and knocked herself out cold. He thought she was dead started shouting at his mate to get the hell out and within minutes they scarpered.'

'What happened your flatmate?'

'Thankfully she was alright. Spent a night in hospital with concussion but was back home the next day. It gave us all a wakeup call. She and Briony cut back on the drugs and the men at least for a while and I was lucky enough to meet Franco. He only had a small salon at that time but he was cheap and did a good job. I was pouring out my woes to him one day while getting my hair cut and he offered to let me live in the small room above the salon. It was only a one room bedsit but it had a little kitchen area and a pull out bed and it was clean and it was safe. I took it. He never even asked me for rent, which was just as well as I hadn't a penny to my name. When I told him I couldn't pay he just told me I could pay him back when I got my law degree and started making some real money. So that's what I did. I started working hard at my degree course because I knew I didn't want to keep on living the way I had been and I wanted to pay Franco back. If it wasn't for him I really don't know what I would have done. Somewhere along the line we became the best of friends.'

'Wow, now I really want to meet the guy.'

'Yeah Franco's great. A bit unconventional you

know but a real gem.'

'I just keep thinking how things could have been so different for both of us if only I'd plucked up the courage to ask you out when we were younger' Aidan said miserably.

'I often think that too but you know maybe the timing just wasn't right for us. We've certainly both done a lot of growing up since then and maybe it's better that we waited a while. Maybe something would have come along to burst our bubble and we wouldn't have been mature enough to deal with it.'

'No point in looking back with regrets I suppose' sighed Aidan. 'I'm just glad I have you now' he grinned as he cupped her chin in his hands and drew his lips down upon hers kissing away their shared regrets.

Chapter 39

It was now several weeks since Cynthia had her first date with Jeff and things were working out just the way she'd hoped. He was just what she needed. He jumped when she called and was always more than happy to take her out for dinner or stay overnight with her. Of course it was a bit inconvenient that he had a girlfriend. It would have been much handier if she could have popped round to his house whenever she fancied a bit of fun, but as he never complained about her husband, she could hardly complain about the little mouse he shared a house with. She was confident that it was only a matter of time before Jeff realised what a dull little waif his girlfriend was and gave her the boot and what better way to help him realise that than by showing him what a good time he could have without her.

Cynthia had been very careful to take him to the best restaurants and entertain him with the best that money could buy. She had sported him a few expensive gifts as well, not too much, just enough to make him restless for more. Anyway, he had more than earned his Cartier watch and new Bose sound system. He was a fast learner and had quickly realised the benefits of having a little no-strings attached fun with her.

Cynthia realised a large part of the fun for both of them was the meeting up in secret and taking risks. Plus he knew what he was doing and had no difficulty sending pleasure to all the right areas.

Tonight she had agreed to collect him from the gym as it was his night to lock up. She really couldn't understand what was keeping him though; she'd been waiting in the car for twenty minutes and hadn't seen anyone other than the receptionist leave in all that time.

Finally breathing a sigh of frustration Cynthia gave up and decided to go looking for him.

As she rattled the doors of the gym she caught sight of him on his phone inside. It didn't take a genius to work out that his insecure little girlfriend was checking up on him yet again.

Catching sight of her at the door Jeff's face broke into a wide smile and as he opened the doors to let her in he raised a finger to his lips indicating she should be quiet. Cynthia didn't appreciate being put on hold, especially not for someone so unworthy of

Jeff's attention.

Checking the doors were locked behind her Cynthia decided it was time to have a little fun. She wordlessly began rubbing her hand over Jeff's crotch; it gave her a little thrill watching him squirm while he was trying to concentrate on what he was saying.

'Yes honey I know I've had to work late a lot recently'

'but you know how short staffed this place is .....'

Jeff was struggling not to let the moan escape from his lips and the more he fought it the more Cynthia wanted to make him lose control.

Suddenly he froze and Cynthia caught his stare as he nodded towards the CCTV camera in the foyer. He hastily grabbed her hand and strode purposefully to the rear of the gym where there were no cameras in sight.

Cynthia slowly pushed him down onto the bench press and gave her mouth free reign over his body. With a sense of victory, she was aware of him making his excuses and ending the call. As Jeff hastily pulled her body onto his, Cynthia gave herself up to the pleasure. Nothing, she concluded, ever tasted better than forbidden fruit.

Chapter 40

Maggie set the receiver down she caught the flicker of concern in her own eyes, reflected in the mirror above the phone table. She had suspected that something wasn't right between Will and Laurie and she'd been worried about them for weeks. Every time she'd tried to talk to Laurie about it she had carefully avoided her. Of course the children had told her that Dad had been away 'for the longest time ever' and she knew they were missing him. At least Will's phone call explained a few things, although she was certain there was still a lot he wasn't telling her. That suited Maggie just fine. She didn't hold with airing your dirty linen in public the way some of these young ones liked to do nowadays.

She was more than happy to agree to Will's suggestion. Why sure she'd been telling Laurie for months now that she needed to take things a bit easier and make some time for herself, but since

Laurie had become a Mum herself she seemed to think that Maggie was a frail old lady. Ok so she might be a Grandma but she liked to think that she was a very fresh 72 year old, and since Joe had died, her one joy in life was being a part of the lives of her children and grandchildren. Maggie knew how lucky she was to have all her grandchildren living so close by. She lived in fear of being like her dear friend Betty who had one daughter living in Australia and the other in England and she only got to see her five grandchildren once in a blue moon. The days were long when you had no one calling in to see you or when you didn't get caught up to date on all the latest comings and goings at the school or how the wee ones were doing with their homework or their sports.

Michael was a great one for lifting Maggie's spirits. She loved all her grandchildren dearly but she had to admit to having a special place in her heart for Michael. Maybe it was because she and Aidan had practically reared him between them or maybe it was because she was devastated that the poor wee soul had been abandoned by his mother when he was just a baby. Michael was more like a son to her than a grandson in many ways. With grandchildren you always had to hand them back to their mothers but with Michael she was his 'surrogate' Mum and luckily that meant she didn't have to hand him back.

Of course that didn't mean she wouldn't have preferred the wee soul to have his own mother, it wasn't easy for Michael knowing he was different from the other boys and girls in his class; to send his Granny a Mother's Day card instead of his real Mum; to miss out on having his Mum make his birthday cake and plan his birthday parties; to not have his Mum run his bath and tuck him into bed at night. But they all did what they could and she liked to think that between them she and Aidan had done a pretty good job of raising him. He had a great sense of humour Michael, which definitely helped him cope with it all, but at times she sensed he was lonely too.

Kerry was a lovely sensible girl and Maggie was glad Aidan and she had started going out together. Of course it was a great source of amusement to Michael who loved to embarrass his Dad by making great gushing kissing noises when he saw the two of them together or tease them about holding hands in public, but, at least he was secretly pleased about it. And she couldn't blame him. She'd known Kerry ever since she was at Primary school with Laurie and if it turned out Aidan and she got married, well she couldn't want for a nicer daughter-in-law. She knew she was getting ahead of herself, they'd only been together a short time but already they seemed to be very much in love and they were well suited, of that she was certain. Her only fear was that Aidan would end up having his heart broken all over again. Mind you she supposed it wasn't so much that he was heartbroken when Angela left him, more that he was devastated she had abandoned Michael.

She and Joe had urged Aidan not to marry the girl in the first place. She was a silly, flighty little thing, not at all suited to Aidan and if it hadn't been for her bible bashing parents insisting Aidan do the decent thing she knew she and Joe could have persuaded Aidan just to be the best Dad he could to little Michael, not to tie himself down to someone he didn't even love. Oh, but nothing would do but Aidan had to marry her just to please her parents. After the wedding, her parents still refused to have anything to do with them anyway so it was all for nothing. Let's hope his luck with women has changed she thought optimistically. It could hardly be more of a disaster than getting a girl pregnant after they'd only been dating a few weeks she thought pityingly.

Chapter 41

As Laurie took delivery of the bouquet of flowers her forehead wrinkled in confusion. Where these from Will? If so wasn't it a bit of cliché? Man has an affair, sends wife a bunch of flowers and low and behold everything's forgiven. What the hell did he think he was playing at? They hadn't even spoken to one another since the last disastrous occasion when he'd taken the children out. Over the course of the last number of weeks she'd all but given up hope of them ever getting back together. Sending flowers was about as much use as pissing on a forest fire. Eventually she found the note and opened it. It was from Will.

'I know, I know! Sending you flowers is about as pointless as pissing on a forest fire!'

That made her smile. He'd always been able to

tell exactly what she'd been thinking.

'You're thinking this is the ultimate cliché and maybe you're right but I don't know what else to do. It seems every time I open my mouth I make things worse! So, I thought I'd show you how much I love you rather than tell you. I won't ever give up on you Laurie. Expect the first of your gifts later on today. It's certainly not the most romantic gift ever but hopefully it'll be more useful than I've ever been.

Will x'

What did he mean the first of her gifts? She really did hope he didn't think he could buy his way back into her affections. No. He knew her better than that. Didn't he? He would know she'd hate anything smarmy and insincere, as if forgiveness could be bought instead of earned.

What could he mean – more useful than I've ever been – that left things pretty open ended, she mused bitterly, considering he'd been next to useless over the past few years. Maybe it's a new vacuum cleaner she thought drily, but considering he'd never used the old one she very much doubted he'd even realise it needed replaced.

Grudgingly Laurie admitted to herself that he'd

sparked her curiosity but she knew better than to get overexcited. After all, this was Will, and the only inspiring thing he'd ever done for her was propose and that was so long ago it didn't really count.

'Oh Mummy!' cried Charlotte delightedly 'What beautiful flowers. Are they from Daddy?'

'Yes sweetheart they're from your Daddy.'

'Are they for you Mummy? Daddy must love you very, very, very much Mummy don't you think so? They must have cost about a million pounds Mummy, don't you think so Mummy?'

'Flowers don't cost a million pounds you dumbo,' said Shane scathingly.

'Oh but they're so pretty' said Charlotte delightedly, 'don't you think Daddy must love Mummy very much?' she asked her brother wide eyed with delight.

Shane glanced at Laurie but her face gave nothing away. He shrugged; grunted and turned away leaving Laurie to wonder just what was going through his head.

'Shall I put them in a vase Mummy?' continued Charlotte.

Well so much for dumping them straight in the bin thought Laurie. If Will saw them on display he'd think she was softening and nothing could be further from the truth.

'Shall I Mummy? Will I put them in your lovely pink vase Mummy? You know the one with the white swirls on it?'

Given that Laurie only had the one vase there was little chance she didn't know it.

'I'll just go and fetch it and then we'll be able to look at the lovely flowers Daddy sent you, won't that be nice Mummy?' said Charlotte earnestly.

Laurie knew that her daughter was just anxious that Will get back in her good books. Her heart melted for what they were putting their children through. There was no way she could destroy Charlotte's hopes so she pasted a smile on her face and told Charlotte to go get the vase.

Laurie had just about put Will's note out of her head when later that day a pink van drove into the driveway and a middle aged woman with a bright pink T-shirt hopped out.

'Hi!' she said amiably. 'I'm Molly. Did your husband let you now we were coming she asked?'

'Ummh no, not exactly' said Laurie, 'who are you again?'

'I'm Molly from Sparkle and Shine. We're a cleaning company.' she said pointing to the now obvious writing on the side of the van. 'Your husband has employed us to clean your house twice a week Mondays and Thursdays 3 hours at a time. Is it ok if we go ahead and get started?' She asked. 'Only we pride ourselves in giving value for money and the longer I stand here chatting the less work we get done.'

Laurie was gob-smacked. 'How many of you are here?' she asked hesitatingly.

'Oh just me and Freya', said Molly 'so we won't get in your way too much. We bring all our own materials so you just need to show us the layout and we'll get stuck in.'

'But...but.. I didn't know you were coming' Laurie stammered, 'the house is a complete mess.'

Molly threw her head back and laughed. 'Well that's the general idea' she said. 'You've no idea how many of our clients clean for the cleaners coming. Sounds pretty pointless if you ask me. Your husband was very clear that he wanted a company that would do everything and anything. Generally we use the first few weeks to get to know the place and give it a really deep clean and then we review everything with you to make sure you're happy and see if there are any particular jobs you want done. Some people like us to clean out the fridge, others like us to wash the windows and frames or maybe wash down the doors and skirting boards. Basically Mrs Kerr we aim to please. We're happy to do whatever you need us to.'

'But you won't even be able to see my floors' said Laurie mortified. 'The children's toys and clothes and well 'stuff' is lying everywhere.'

'No problem Mrs Kerr. If it's alright with you we'll provide plastic storage boxes and load everything into those. That way we can make the most of our time and get to the essential cleaning areas. It's up to you to decide whether in future weeks you would like us to take some time to organise your household objects into specific storage areas. We're happy to provide that as part of our service, or whether you prefer to put things away yourself. I tell you what Mrs Kerr why don't we start in the kitchen. That way you can have a cup of tea while we clean and we can tell you a bit more about the service we provide at the same time.'

Three hours later Laurie was stunned by the amount of work Molly and Freya had done. Everything was stacked neatly into boxes. Her floors were clean, her furniture was polished to within an inch of its life, the bathrooms were gleaming, her kitchen tiles shone, as did her work surfaces and she hadn't had to raise a finger. Molly insisted that she sat down and relaxed - apparently as per Will's very specific instructions - while they got on with cleaning her house.

Everything looked brighter, cleaner, better. Even the children were in a kind of awed wonderment. Tom called Molly and Freya the 'magic fairies' and the name had struck a chord. That's exactly what they were like thought Laurie delightedly, little magic fairies who came in and swept and cleaned everywhere and left you feeling about a million per cent better. She always thought that she would hate to have people in cleaning her house. The very thought that they'd be secretly disgusted by the state of her house had her shrivelling in shame but with Molly and Freya, nothing could be further from the truth. They were lovely; chatty and friendly, they'd even given the twins little dusters and she had looked on fondly as they toddled around after Molly polishing everything after her. Will could not have given a more perfect gift or found a more perfect company. At last thought Laurie with an almost smile – he's managed to do something right.

Two days later a thick embossed card addressed to Mrs Laurie Kerr popped through Laurie's letterbox. It was hand made. Inside was a painting of a fire which looked as though it had been made from the painted fingers of a child's hand. As she read on she understood that this was not the painted imprint of one child's finger but of five children. Below the little painted fire she read;

'A Poem for our Mummy

"Your love is our fire

Cheerful and bright

Warm and casts out night

Unites us with light"

By Shane, Charlotte, Tom (Cassie and Ellie only helped with the fingerprints Mummy as they can not rite poettary yet – dad says they are two little).'

'Laurie as you can see our children have their Dad's poetic talent and are not the wonderful English scholar that there Mum is! I dare not hope to rekindle our love but for the sake of our beautiful children I hope to rekindle your flame. I would give anything for them to know the Laurie I know. The wonderful woman whose smile can light up a room! The one whose eyes actually do sparkle with excitement! The only woman I know who can laugh with such utter abandonment the whole world laughs with her.

If I could add my line to their poem it would be

'I'm sorry I stamped your fire out'.

(You see what I mean about their fathers poetic talent!)

From now on Wednesdays are to be Laurie days. Your Mum is minding the children so as soon as the older ones are dropped off at school you are to spend a day doing something just for you. Just in case you find yourself struggling to think of something….. the children and I have enclosed a voucher for a massage and afternoon tea.

All my love

Will xx

(P.S Your Mum says yes she IS SURE she can manage our beautiful children one day a week and that she's looking forward to having them and she's tired of you trying to hog them all the time anyway!)'

Laurie wasn't sure whether to laugh or cry at this second lovely gift that Will had given her so for the next hour she spent her time re-reading the card and doing a little bit of both. She could hardly take it in. First the cleaners, now, a whole day to herself every week. She had to admit that a month ago she would have refused both but now she was weary to the core. She was fed up even thinking about the disastrous state of her marriage. Her brain had mulled it over and was still no wiser in bringing a solution. She just knew she was desperately unhappy and some 'time out' was exactly what she needed. She lifted the phone and booked herself in for her massage in two days' time. She was going to make the most of it, after the past few months she'd had, she felt as though she deserved it.

Chapter 42

Will wasn't sure what Laurie's reactions had been to his gifts but he wasn't going to give up on his hope of winning her back. He was aching to see her but he was missing his kids almost as much. He appreciated with frightening clarity that he didn't want to be a divorced father seeing his kids only briefly from one week to the next.

Already he no longer felt part of a family, it seemed to him that Laurie and the kids coped quite easily without him, but he felt stilted, abandoned and alone. Selfishly he admitted that even though he knew it was his own fault he still resented the fact that he couldn't simply slot back into his old life. It was a shock to his system to suddenly realise what his life would be like without them. They completed him. Without them he didn't feel whole.

Unsurprisingly Will wasn't in a good place when

he took the phone call from Chris Canton at Canton Global Medical asking him to meet. It didn't help that Chris Canton was decidedly vague on the purpose of the meeting but as he had mentioned that Brian Nixon had recommended him as a contact Will felt obliged to attend. As the meeting drew closer he felt more than a little curious to find out what it was about.

As the receptionist showed Will into the office Chris greeted him warmly.

'Will! Great to see you again.' said Chris rising to shake his hand. 'Thanks for coming in especially since I gave you so little information about what it's about.'

'It's great to be here' said Will smoothly. 'I hadn't realised just what a fantastic setup you have. I'm very impressed.'

'Well I hope you'll be even more impressed when I show you our laboratories, which as you know is where all the action is. I just keep things ticking over.' said Chris humbly. 'We have a great staff here and thankfully at last we are making some really exciting progress in the medical devices area. I'm sure you know a fair bit about that already?' asked Chris.

'I do indeed' said Will. 'I've been watching that market develop with interest for a few years now. I think it's safe to say my boss would love to get his hands on the sort of technology you guys are developing here. It would be great for us to be able to offer our clients not just the best pharmaceuticals that money can buy but also introduce them to medical devices that can link patients more directly to hospitals and surgeries. I don't think it's quite dawned on the 'powers that be' just how much time and money they could save.'

'I'd better watch you' said Chris laughingly. 'I had heard that you could sell snow to the eskimos, but I think that you might have misunderstood why I called you here. I wasn't thinking of linking in with Worldwide Pharmaceuticals. We've worked too hard on developing the products to lose out on the profit in selling them' he smiled. 'I'm not interested in doing any sort of deal with the company you work for Will. I'm interested in you.'

'What do you mean?' asked Will.

'I mean I'd like to offer you the opportunity to join our team.'

'But my background is sales not science' said Will.

'You're misunderstanding me Will. I don't want you to switch from sales to product development. I'd like to offer you a job selling our products. Of course I appreciate that it would be a bit of a risk for you. Unfortunately I can't offer any guarantees on what the projected sales forecast will be like. I can only let you see our products and hope that their innovation speaks for itself. If you can see the benefit for GP surgeries, hospitals and clinics then I know you'll be able to sell them. All I ask is that you keep an open mind and let me show you what we've produced to date and what we hope to sell before you turn me down.'

'I'd love to see them' said Will enthusiastically. 'Unfortunately I have to warn you from the outset that my personal circumstances are such that right now I don't know if I can afford to risk changing my job.'

'Ah I thought that might be the case,' said Chris knowingly. 'But I also have it on very good authority that your wife would like you to travel less.'

Will's mouth dropped open in surprise. How the hell did Chris Canton know anything about his private life?

'I can see you're confused' said Chris 'but you should know that I like to do my homework before I go handing out job offers. Just in case you're wondering, it was your wife who informed me that you travelled far too much for her liking. You might remember I was seated beside her at the Charity Dinner?'

'Yes,' said Will 'I do, but I had no idea she'd mention something like that to you.'

'It was just a passing comment' said Chris 'but I take it that it's true?' He asked.

'Well a bit less travel would be good' said Will 'but right now its more important that I can keep bringing in a steady wage.'

'The wage will be good' said Chris easily. 'I'll match what you are on currently but I'll also give you a 15% profit share in everything that you sell in your first year; I'd review that annually of course; I can also personally guarantee that you will travel a lot less, definitely no more than two or three nights a month.'

'But why me?' asked Will. 'You hardly know anything about me. How do you know I'd be any good?' he asked.

'Like I say, I do my homework' said Chris 'and I trust the person who recommended you implicitly. Now would you like to see our products?' He asked.

Two hours later and Will was all but sold on the idea of a change of job. Canton Medical was a professional company and he could see them making a vast profit with their medical devices range. More than that though was the knowledge that if he and Laurie ended up getting a divorce his current job required him to travel so much that he would hardly ever get to see his kids. Being a divorced parent was hard enough without also being an absent one. That fact alone was enough to make Will accept the job.

Chapter 43

Much to her surprise Kerry had decided to keep up with the Piloxing class and, even more surprisingly, she loved it. It was by far the best exercise she'd ever tried, the mixture of boxing and Pilates challenged her body and although she ached in places she never thought possible she could tell she was already starting to firm up.

The other benefit of course was that she could keep an eye on Cynthia Nixon, and until Brian issued his divorce proceedings, she could do so while remaining completely anonymous. Brian was right about one thing, the woman was definitely having an affair with Jeff the gym instructor. They were both very subtle about it, they only shared the odd glance here and there and were never openly flirty with each other during the class but Cynthia tended to hang back after class to have a private word with him and the little touches of physical contact between them were blindingly obvious if you were intent on looking for them.

'What do you think of her?' asked Linda after class one evening nodding her head in Cynthia's direction.

'I don't really know her' replied Kerry cautiously. Linda seemed like a nice enough girl but Kerry had only started to get friendly with her the last couple of weeks and she wasn't about to blow her cover.

'She's a nasty piece of work' said Linda authoritatively. 'The first few weeks I came here I tried to be friendly to her. I thought she was a little frosty but you know it's kind of hard to tell when you're just asking if she enjoyed the class and making polite conversation. Well I'd only spoken to her a couple of times and then one day I thought I'd wait for her and see if she wanted to grab a coffee after the class had finished. What a mistake that was.'

'What happened?' asked Kerry knowing from what she had already learned from Laurie that it wouldn't be pretty.

'Well she looked me up and down with utter disgust and asked me if I really thought she would be seen dead going for a coffee with someone who was three stone overweight, had no style, no looks and obviously no taste in clothes.'

'Ohhh that was downright nasty.' replied Kerry

sympathetically. 'What did you do?'

'I'm ashamed to say I didn't do anything. I was so shocked I couldn't think of a single thing to say in response. My face went the colour of a beetroot. I felt so stupid. The truth is I only buy my gym clothes from Primark so she was right.'

'Well snap' said Kerry gamely 'and she was not right. You are easily twice as attractive as her and have gorgeous curves. Anyway not of all us want to spend hundreds of pounds on Louis Vuitton wear for the gym.'

'I'm afraid I wouldn't know the difference between Louis Vuitton and Primark.' said Linda smiling shyly.

'Who the hell cares anyway' replied Kerry 'it's a gym for flip sake not a fashion show. Anyway given that I'm a fellow Primark Fashion guru do you fancy joining me for a coffee?'

'Oh that would be great' said Linda 'but would you mind if it was just in the gym's coffee shop, only my friend Lisa works here as a receptionist and said she'd try and meet me there on her break.'

'Perfect' said Kerry. 'I only have time for a quick one so it will save me driving into town.'

As they sat down with their coffees waiting for Lisa to join them Linda explained that she and Lisa had met at Uni and been friends ever since. 'Really it's only because Lisa works here that I managed to get into the Piloxing class at all. Did you know that there's a six month waiting list for the classes?' asked Linda.

'Gosh I knew the classes here were popular but I didn't realise the waiting list was that long! I have a confession to make. I only got in because my friend Franco called in a few favours with a contact of his.'

'It seems like everybody in the class has called in favours from someone' laughed Linda.

'What's this about favours?' asked Lisa joining them.

'Oh nothing really,' said Linda 'we were just saying that we can't understand why other gyms haven't caught on to how popular Piloxing is. It must be a real money spinner.'

'Oh they've caught on alright. The problem is they can't get enough instructors qualified to take the classes. The waiting list to gain the training is as long as the wait list for the classes so the instructors are few and far between. That's what makes Jeff so indispensable.' she said grudgingly.

'Don't mind Lisa' said Linda shooting Kerry a friendly look. 'She's just hacked off because her friend Charlotte has been living with the guy for two years and Lisa's convinced he's doing the dirty on her.'

'Oh poor girl' said Kerry sympathetically. 'Do

you think he's been seeing someone from the gym?' She asked innocently.

'I don't think it,' Lisa said. 'I know it.'

'Really?' Asked Linda 'I thought you said you didn't know who it was.'

'Well I didn't until today' said Lisa miserably.

'Ok, so spill the beans,' said Linda edging forward on her seat. 'Is it that twenty year old brunette he hangs around sometimes?'

'No' said Lisa glancing warily at Kerry. 'It's not her. I don't know if I should say really. I don't want to get into any trouble.'

'I promise you I would never repeat a word' said Kerry gravely. 'Anyway I have a fair idea who it might be.'

'Really?' asked Linda

'Unfortunately I think it might be the person we were discussing after the class' she grimaced.

'NO!' screamed Linda. 'Not bloody Cynthia Nixon.'

'Shhhh keep your voice down,' hushed Lisa. 'I don't want to get into any trouble.'

'Well is she right though?' Asked Linda.

'Afraid so' said Lisa miserably. 'What the hell do I do? I really think Charlotte has a right to know but she's so in love with the guy I don't think she'd believe me if I told her. She probably wouldn't believe it unless she saw the proof for herself?'

'What do you mean saw the proof?' asked Kerry astutely.

Lisa's face turned a deep shade of red. 'Nothing… I shouldn't have said anything. Bloody Jeff. If I showed anyone I'd probably be the one to end up losing my job while that two timing wanker gets to keep his.'

'Showed anyone what?' asked Kerry.

'Well' she said hesitatingly, 'he only bloody well got caught on CCTV camera shagging that dirty bitch in the gym after work the other night. The managers are furious. Went on and on about health and safety; abuse of trust; inappropriate behaviour. They all wanted to sack him on the spot and they would have done except Jeff reminded them just how difficult he would be to replace and how popular his Piloxing classes were. He swore that if they sacked him he'd go straight to Gym'n'Slim and take all his clients with him. In the end they had to back down and content themselves with giving him a written warning when everyone in the room knew it should have been instant dismissal.'

'How do you know all this?' asked Linda

'Unfortunately, I was the one to discover it in the

first place' she grimaced. 'One of our clients reportedly hurt his back on the bench press yesterday and the Management asked me to review the CCTV footage to check whether he'd used the equipment properly. I just left the footage running after I viewed the incident and that's when I saw what Jeff was up to. If you had seen what I saw....' she shuddered involuntarily 'you'd bloody well wonder how Jeff still has his job.'

'What they actually had sex, right there on the bench press?' asked Linda incredulously.

'Eugghh please I don't want to relive it' said Lisa. 'It makes me want to throw up. Let's just say there's nothing that woman wouldn't do. When I think about what she and Jeff were up to while poor Charlotte has no idea what a two-timing cheat he is ...well it makes me feel sick to my stomach. She deserves to know. I just don't want to be the one to tell her she said miserably. The problem is I thought Jeff would get the sack and then all I'd have to do would be to tell Charlotte why. I think she would have believed me. She'd have known it had to be something serious for him to lose his job over it and I don't think she would have accused me of making it up. But of course he's managed to wriggle out of it and now I don't think she'd believe me unless I showed her the actual proof and I couldn't do that to her. I can't get the images out of my head so I couldn't put her through that. It would just be cruel.'

'Lisa, I have an idea' said Kerry cautiously, 'and if it works you'd be doing more than Charlotte a favour. Listen...................' as Kerry outlined her grand plan both Lisa and Linda's eyes widened in astonishment. So many lives could be changed but would Lisa trust her enough to go through with her plan. After all she hardly even knew her.......

Chapter 44

As Brian Nixon entered the office of Kerry Ford he hoped that this time she would have better news for him.

'So' said Kerry, 'how have things been?'

'Just the same I'm afraid' said Brian despondently, 'I've been wondering if you thought we could send the letter to get the divorce proceedings started yet?'

'Well things might be looking up on that front but it all depends on how desperate you are to get a quick divorce.'

'I thought you said a quickie divorce was unlikely since I couldn't prove adultery? I presumed I would be waiting the full five years' said Brian glumly.

Kerry looked at Brian Nixon sizing him up. She was taking a definite gamble if she went through with her plan. However she knew Laurie spoke highly of him and from what she had witnessed of his wife, this man needed all the help he could get. She only hoped that underneath that pleasant exterior he had an iron backbone.

'Ok' she said at length. 'I've decided to take a chance on you Mr Nixon, just don't let me down.'

Brian looked up questioningly.

'It just so happens that quite by chance I have stumbled upon some fairly incriminating evidence against your wife which I have no doubt would prove her adultery.'

'What!' said Brian amazed. 'But how ….? When……?'

'You don't need to concern yourself with that. In fact I'd really rather that you didn't ask me too many questions about it' she stated eyeing him intently. 'You see I'm taking a bit of a risk confiding in you at all. Let's just say that it may not be entirely within the accepted protocol of my professional code of conduct. I need to know if I can trust you?' she asked.

'Yes' he said simply 'You can. Believe me I know what it's like to risk stepping over professional boundaries. If you're willing to trust me I promise I'll stick within the parameters of whatever you tell me'.

Kerry let the silence which followed stretch between them. Her gut told her she could trust him albeit it was contrary to her professional judgement.

'Ok' she said at last. 'Here's the deal. You don't ask me any questions; you don't breathe a word of our conversation to anyone and you do exactly as I say. Do you understand?'

'Yes' he said solemnly.

Kerry could practically see the questions bubbling up in him but to his credit he held his tongue.

'I want you to imagine if you will that I have an acquaintance who is very concerned about her friend. She knows for a fact that her friend's partner is cheating on her with a married woman. Are you following me so far?' she asked.

Brian nodded and waited for her to continue.

'Well let's just say that my acquaintance stumbled upon some very graphic video evidence proving that her fears were correct. Unfortunately the nature of that footage is so graphic that she couldn't allow her friend to view it. At the same time she knows her friend is so in love with the guy she's with that if she just went to her and told her what she knew her friend wouldn't believe her. By all accounts her friend's partner isn't just a two-timing cheat but also a very convincing liar. She also fears that it would be a case of 'shoot the messenger' and she would end up losing her best friend. Do you get the picture?' She asked him.

'Yes' said Brian, 'I think I follow you. I just don't know what it's all got to do with me?'

'The married woman is your wife Mr Nixon. The man she's having an affair with is the same one you saw her enter the hotel lift with a few weeks back. Do you still have the camera footage of that?' Kerry asked.

Brian nodded.

'Well the deal is that I will be given a copy of the video evidence which proves your wife's adultery if you can persuade this man's partner that he is in fact having an affair.'

'What? You mean I'd have to approach a complete stranger and try and persuade her that her partner has been carrying on with my wife?'

'I'm afraid so' said Kerry.

'But…..' stumbled Brian. 'Why would she believe me any more than her friend?' He asked

'I would imagine there would be a couple of reasons' said Kerry. 'Firstly you have as much to lose as she does. Surely in theory it would be as difficult for you to believe your wife capable of having an affair as it would be for her to believe her partner was capable of it. Secondly what reason would you have to make it up? You don't stand to gain anything by it. And thirdly you can explain that you saw them together at the hotel, you can convince her that they spent the night together and you can show her the less graphic video evidence of them in the lift together. Your little video clip may not have been enough to persuade a judge on a point of law but it should be more than enough to persuade a girlfriend.'

Brian held his head in his hands.

At length he spoke 'So if I do this? If I go up to a complete stranger and tell her that her partner is having an affair with my wife and if I can persuade her to dump her boyfriend then your... 'acquaintance' will release the actual video evidence to you which will prove adultery?' He asked.

'You got it' said Kerry. 'Of course, the decision is entirely up to you. No one is forcing you to do this.'

'I need to think about it' he said at last. 'Unlike my wife I really don't enjoy wrecking people's lives.'

'I understand' said Kerry. 'Just ask yourself one question though. If you were in the girlfriend's shoes wouldn't you prefer to know that your partner was cheating on you rather than being played for a fool?'

Brian nodded silently; he knew only too well what it was like to be played for a fool. 'Is this the only way to get the video footage released?' he asked.

'I'm afraid so' said Kerry. 'My acquaintance is risking a lot by releasing it at all. If the source of the evidence was ever traced back to her she would lose her job. She really cares about her friend or she wouldn't be risking giving me a copy of the recording at all.'

Kerry handed Brian a piece of paper with a name and address on it. 'Her name is Charlotte' she said, 'and this is where you'll find her. If you don't want to go ahead with it just tear it up. Oh and by the way we never had this conversation. Got it?'

'Yes' said Brian. 'Thanks', then hesitatingly he asked 'Why are you doing this for me? You don't stand to gain anything by it. You'll get paid regardless.'

'Let's just say you seem like a nice guy and sometimes the law needs a helping hand to come to the right decision.'

As Brian left the office his hands were trembling but he was resolved to do what he had to do.

Chapter 45

Kerry was blissfully happy. She and Aidan had decided to take their first ever mini-break together and were heading to the Fermanagh Lakes for the weekend. Michael was also happy as he was spending the weekend with his cousins and couldn't wait to teach the twins some more new words. Kerry and Aidan had a laugh at that one. Laurie was only just beginning to get over the shock of her toddlers unusual choice of first words which Michael had so proudly taught them.

As they arrived at the beautiful resort on the shores of Lough Erne, Kerry was delighted to see that it had a swimming pool and spa. She'd been so busy at work recently she hadn't had a minute to herself and it was wonderful to let Aidan take control of the booking. It was lovely not to have to stress over where to go but just to let someone else sort it all out. Being relatively single for the last few years Kerry had forgotten what it felt like not to have to make all of the decisions, all of the time, and she found it liberating just to be able to relax and enjoy.

'This is gorgeous,' she said to Aidan smiling at the view from their bedroom window. 'Look there's even a little balcony where we can sit and look out over the lake and have a few drinks.'

'You're gorgeous' said Aidan coming up behind her and wrapping his arms around her. 'You've no idea how much I've been looking forward to getting you on your own' he said gently nuzzling her ear.

'Two whole nights' said Kerry dreamily. 'Two whole days without having to think about work.'

'If I'm honest,' said Aidan grinning 'I was thinking more along the lines of two whole days and nights making love to you.'

'Oh, were you now?' said Kerry laughingly. 'And what makes you think I'm that kind of girl?'

'Just chancing my arm' said Aidan running his hands up and down her thighs and over her bum making her let out a little involuntary moan.

'I can see we're not going to get much time in the Spa this weekend' she said turning to face him and raising her lips to meet his.

'Oh I don't know' he said while kissing her hungrily. 'I think I'm rather looking forward to seeing you in your bikini.'

'You obviously haven't seen my swimsuit' said Kerry. 'It's about as sexy as a Granny in a onesie.'

Aidan burst out laughing.

'Of course I like you best when you're wearing nothing at all,' he grinned, unzipping her jeans and pushing her backwards onto the bed.

Kerry let out a little shriek of surprise.

'Oh, what do we have here?' he asked seeing her lacy pink La Perla underwear for the first time. 'Not too shabby for a woman who claims to look like a Granny in a onesie.' he said teasingly. 'I can't take my eyes off you Kerry. Did I tell you I think you're gorgeous?' He asked.

'Ummmhhh you may have mentioned it' said Kerry whose eyes were sparkling with anticipation.

'Maybe I better check you believe me' he said playfully, 'I mean they do say actions speak louder than words' he said playfully.

'Maybe you'd better' said Kerry pulling his body on top of hers. 'In fact I think maybe you'd better show me over and over and over again.'

'You may be right after all' said Aidan. 'I'm not sure we will have time to visit the spa……'

Hours later, and only when Kerry had finally confessed that Aidan really had shown her that she was gorgeous, did they finally make it to the restaurant.

It was just as well that Aidan had thought to book them a table in advance as they would never have got one otherwise. The restaurant was packed with locals and tourists alike all keen to sample the culinary delights the hotel was famous for.

'You know Kerry' said Aidan over dessert. 'I really am glad you agreed to go out with me. I'm totally happy' he said grinning. 'Until I met you I didn't think I was any good at relationships.'

'The feeling's mutual' said Kerry. 'I just can't believe that we're together at last. I just keep waiting for something to come along and spoil it.'

'I know what you mean' said Aidan 'it doesn't really seem ….real....too perfect maybe?' he said taking her hand and staring tenderly into her eyes.

'Do you think it's possible for two people to stay this happy?' she asked. 'I don't really have the best view of relationships given the fact that most relationships I deal with end up in divorce she said with a sigh.'

'I don't know' said Aidan. 'I guess when you think about it the chances of staying blissfully happy with one person for the rest of your life are pretty slim but that doesn't mean to say it isn't possible' he said wistfully. 'My Mum and Dad were pretty happy I think. I never thought Mum would get over losing him. They were so much in love their whole life. I'm not saying they never disagreed or anything like that but they were like two people fused into one. They got each other. They looked out for each other and they never ever lost that bit of romance that only the best relationships seem to keep their whole life through. I used to think I'd never find someone like that Kerry. Someone who I wanted to spend the rest of my life with' he said looking at her earnestly.

'And now?' asked Kerry.

'I think I'm getting there' he said grinning. 'I guess I just need to get over some old war wounds. Appreciate that not every relationship I have needs to end in disaster.'

'I think we all carry scars from previous relationships' said Kerry thoughtfully. 'I'm not saying I was ever as hurt in a relationship as you've been but I do know what it's like to have your heart trampled on. I suppose every relationship carries a risk of getting hurt' she said 'but I guess some risks are still worth taking.'

'I think you might be right' he agreed giving her hand another little squeeze.

The rest of the weekend passed in a blur. By the time Aidan dropped Kerry home on Sunday night she was so tired she felt she needed a weekend to recover from Aidan's relentless efforts to prove to her she was beautiful. She allowed herself a small smile at the thought before kissing him a long goodbye and letting herself into her house which felt doubly lonely and quiet without him.

Chapter 46

It was now almost three months since Will had moved out and Laurie was beginning to realise what life was really like without him. Grudgingly she had to admit that not having him around was becoming harder and harder to endure. It wasn't the fact that he could help out with the kids or even put petrol in the car or put the bin out; it was simply the reality of not having someone around to share your day with.

When it came right down to it her family and her friends had their own lives, their own families and their own interests. She was beginning to realise that only a parent could share a funny story about the kids and laugh unrestrainedly. Only a parent felt the true delight in their child's achievements and didn't have to care about whether they were boasting or not. Only parents shared worries about the little things other people wouldn't even know upset their child.

She would find herself thinking - I must tell Will that Shane scored an A in his Maths test or wanting to have a laugh about the twins first words and suddenly remembering he wasn't there to tell.

It was lonely.

A house full of kids and noise and banter and she was still lonely.

She missed him.

She missed curling into him at night; she missed the warmth of his body next to hers; she missed knowing he was there to get up in the night and double check she had locked the doors.

But she also missed what they used to have. The old thrill of spending time together, just the two of them. Being free to think only of themselves and not all their shared responsibilities. How had life got so complicated? How had they drifted so far apart? When had they stopped making time for each other? And most of - all were did they go from here?

The sad thing was that while she knew she could forgive him a lot, she couldn't forgive him for cheating on her. She couldn't set aside her own self-respect and self-worth in favour of forgiveness. Was she too proud she wondered? Would other people forgive and forget and move on? He was drunk after all. Ironically after she told Kerry that being drunk was no excuse and made no difference she had started to question whether, perhaps it actually did. She knew he wouldn't have had sex with someone else under normal circumstances. If he had set out to betray her and had sneakily went behind her back, like some devious little creep, she knew without a shadow of a doubt that their relationship would have been over. She knew she would have closed the door once and for all on what they had and moved on.

But despite his shortcomings, if there was one thing she knew about Will, it was that he was honest. He didn't have a devious bone in his body. The other thing she knew was that Cynthia Nixon played hard ball and if she had set out to get Will then in his inebriated state he would have been easy pickings. But sadly the fact remained that they did have sex and that act couldn't be undone no matter how much she wanted it.

She was stuck. She couldn't move on beyond his infidelity and yet she didn't want to spend the rest of her life without him. She had tried for weeks now to come to a decision and yet she was no closer to reaching one.

The one good thing about Wills 'gifts' was that it was helping her to see that he was trying. He couldn't make things right but she could see that he was at least trying to make her happier. The cleaners were continuing to come twice a week and Laurie couldn't believe what a difference that one act was having on her stress levels. She had also been faithfully making use of her precious Wednesdays to treat herself. Sometimes she just took herself of for a walk or had a leisurely browse around the shops or went for a quiet cup of coffee; but it was making a difference. Just slowing down for a day and taking a step back was helping her rediscover her identity. She was beginning to see that having five babies in such close succession meant that she had been forced to put her hopes and dreams on hold. Unfortunately they had gradually disappeared altogether.

She was also realising that she had resented Will for not having to do that. The fact he had shouted her down after accidentally bidding at the auction just epitomised how superior he now believed himself to be. She returned to that night often, picking away at it like a dirty scab refusing to heal. He had belittled her and publicly ridiculed her. He had obviously long since stopped treating her as his equal and now treated her like his inferior. Did being a full time Mum demean her so much that her husband now considered her unworthy of respect? It had damaged her confidence and made her doubt her self-worth. She had always hoped Will appreciated what she did for him and the kids but now she wondered if he was secretly scornful of her? All-in-all he had acted like a complete prick and if that was really what he thought of his wife and mother of his children then she was beginning to see that she deserved better.

And yet would she really have changed anything?

She loved being a Mum. It was without doubt the best job in the world and the most important one too.

She couldn't have managed a job and five kids and the truth was she wouldn't have wanted to try. She loved being at home with her kids, she didn't want anyone else to be the one to see their first tooth cutting through; to see them take their first step; to hear them utter their first word; to take them to their first day at school; to watch them win their first sports day race. Laurie knew those moments were irreplaceable and for that reason alone it was inconceivable to her that she should miss them. That being said she had also reached a few conclusions. Firstly although she loved being a Mum, she'd been foolish not to have taken a bit of time for herself; secondly she needed to try and maintain her identity and not spend the next twenty years living vicariously through her children; thirdly she loved Will and wanted him back. The only problem was, in her book, love didn't equal forgiveness and as she couldn't forgive him she couldn't see that ever happening.

Chapter 47

Brian had done it. But quite simply it was the worst thing he'd ever had to do in his life. As he had relayed his fears that her partner was having an affair with his wife he had watched the poor girl dissolve into tears. To make matters worse she had invited him in and insisted on plying him with sympathy for his loss. He felt like a fraud. The truth was it was no loss to him how Cynthia spent her time and with whom, but he could see that Jeff meant the world to that poor girl. He had done his best to explain that his wife was likely to have been the instigator but Charlotte had insisted that at the end of the day Jeff seemed only too happy to oblige.

She had insisted on seeing the video clip of them entering the lift together and admitted that he hadn't come home the night Brian had seen them at the hotel. She confessed that he had been sleeping at a 'mate's house' on a number of occasions over the past few weeks and admitted that she'd been getting suspicious that he was cheating on her. To make matters worse she ended up thanking Brian for telling her and said while she knew her relationship with Jeff was now over she really hoped he and his wife would make a go of things for the sake of their children.

Brian had struggled to tell himself that she had a right to know her partner was cheating and that it was all for the best, but it didn't stop him feeling like a no good selfish swindler.

True to her word Ms Ford confirmed that she had received a copy of the CCTV footage from her acquaintance and that if he was ready she would write to his wife indicating that she had been retained on his behalf. Brian had confirmed that she could go ahead and issue divorce proceedings on the grounds of his wife's adultery. He wasn't sure if there would ever be a good time to commence divorce proceedings but he concluded it would be better just to get it over and done with rather than prolonging the agony.

As the letter was due to arrive by first class post Cynthia was likely to receive it in the morning. He had arranged for the kids to have sleepovers at friends' houses as there was no way he wanted them to be there when she received the letter. Was he doing the right thing by his children he wondered? Should he be trying to stick with his marriage for their sake? She was still their mother at the end of the day and even though she was hardly the warm and loving type it was still going to be hard for his boys to see their parents split up. To hell with it he thought bitterly. Cynthia had ruined enough lives already. He was damn sure she wasn't going to ruin his any longer. He hadn't put himself through all this to back down now. Let battle commence he thought assiduously. He was more than ready for the onslaught.

Chapter 48

Brian heard Cynthia collect the post from the mat and braced himself. It didn't take long for her to round on him like the demon possessed psycho that she was.

'You devious, lying, cheating, duplicitous, coward' she roared. 'How dare you do this to me?' she raged.

'Apparently Cynthia it's you who's the 'lying, cheating, duplicitous coward,' Brian said calmly.

'Don't try and develop a sense of humour now Brian I'm too used to you being a depressed, insignificant, little worm entirely lacking in either humour or charisma. What the hell do you think you're playing at?' she bellowed.

'What does it look like Cynthia? I'm divorcing you' he said evenly.

'No chance' said Cynthia angrily. 'Hell will freeze over before I ever agree to a divorce you good for nothing son of a bitch.'

'Cynthia if you think I'm such a 'good for nothing son of a bitch' perhaps the question you should be asking yourself is why you'd want to stay married to me?' he replied coolly.

'Because' she screamed, 'I have my reputation to think off. Do you think I'm going to be a divorcee? A scorned, discarded, woman that everyone looks down on. No!' she shrieked 'you may be a complete waste of space but you're my husband and you will remain so until I decide otherwise'.

'And why the hell do you think I'd agree to stay married to someone like you?' Brian replied scathingly. 'The biggest mistake I ever made was making you my wife. You've ruined my life with your pompous, egotistical condescending bitchiness. You're a haughty narcissistic affront to the rest of womankind. You alienate everyone around you Cynthia. No one likes you. Those pretentious, high-class people you think are your friends, know as well as I do that you're a nobody, you come from nothing, a poverty stricken tart who played me like the fool I am and snared me into a marriage which I have regretted every day since.'

'How dare you speak to me like that!' she replied venomously. 'I made you what you are. Without me you'd be a no good loser more interested in playing golf than making a living. You wouldn't have a career if it wasn't for me. You lack ambition Brian, always have, always will. You'd be nothing without me.'

'Cynthia' said Brian bitterly. 'You didn't do anything for me that I wouldn't have achieved on my own. In fact the only thing you helped me do was work longer hours than I ever wanted to simply so I'd have to spend as little time as possible with the money grabbing bitch I foolishly made my wife.'

'How dare you?' screamed Cynthia. 'I made that business what it is. You obviously don't appreciate the amount of work I put in as Practice Manager. You have no idea what I have to put up with. Your receptionist is nothing but a numbskull of a girl and you'd be ripped off by every pharmaceutical company that came through the door if it wasn't for me. I'm as much responsible for the profits of the business as you are' she yelled angrily.

'You?' Brian laughed mockingly. 'Cynthia the amount of money you receive for doing that job more than redresses any possible profit the business could hope to make from your so called 'skills'. The reason we've lost so many suppliers over the years is that you've insulted and alienated every one of them. The products we have now are more expensive than the ones we used to have and of a poorer quality but we're left with no alternative but to accept them because no one else is willing to deal with you. You've almost brought my business to its knees.'

'You're talking through your arse Brian. You don't know the first thing about our finances. Like everything else in your sorry good for nothing life I sort out everything for you. You have no idea of the financial state of the Practice. I'm the one who deals with the accountant; I'm the one who balances the books she shouted angrily.'

'Not anymore' said Brian steadily.

'What the hell do you mean by that?' she asked wildly.

'I mean that I've spoken to the accountant and it turns out I can no longer afford to employ a Practice manager. Unfortunately, my dear I have no alternative but to make the post redundant.' he said unable to prevent a small smile of satisfaction grace his lips.

'You conniving, scheming odious little man' Cynthia screamed. 'You can't do this. I own half of that Practice. Do you think I'm just going to walk away from it?' She laughed haughtily.

'I think you'll find you don't have a choice' said Brian confidently. 'Thankfully Cynthia I never made you a partner in the business. You're nothing but an employee and an expensive one at that. Of course I'll give you four weeks' pay in lieu of notice. Oh and don't make the mistake of turning up in my Practice on Monday morning or I'll have you forcibly evicted' he stated decisively.

For the first time in his marriage Brian felt empowered. He could see Cynthia was stunned. Whether it was because he was actually standing up to her for a change, or because for once he was a step ahead of her, he didn't know but she was definitely rattled and struggling to find a way to regain her superiority. Brian on the other hand was feeling quite euphoric. Fifteen years of vitriol seemed to be spewing out of him at an irrepressible rate and he was delighted to be finally giving Cynthia a taste of her own medicine.

Cynthia decided to change tack. She'd never seen Brian like this before and she needed to buy herself some time to figure things out. She'd let him have his little moment in the limelight but she was damned sure she would be back as Practice Manager before anyone ever noticed her absence. 'Oh Brian' she said scathingly 'you really have no idea what I'm capable of –do you? I can assure you that you'll regret the day you ever tried to gain the upper hand over me. I will take everything you own and I will crush it. I will destroy you as easily as everyone else who has ever tried to stand in my way.'

'Do your worst Cynthia. I'm more than ready for you this time. You see I've had enough! Enough of your power games, enough of your endless mind games, enough of being cuckolded, I don't care what I have to do anymore as long as I am free of you at last.'

'Hahahhahahhaha' laughed Cynthia hysterically. 'You will never ever be rid of me Brian. Ever! I really meant the 'til death do us part' clause in our wedding vows. That's the only possibility you have of ever leaving me and maybe that's what it'll take' she laughed evilly. 'I might be prepared to be a widow Brian. In fact the more I think about it the more attractive that possibility becomes.' she cackled. 'But divorce on the grounds of adultery?' she asked scathingly. 'Never! You will never ever prove adultery. What makes you think I'd ever cheat on you - poor baby' she said fake smoothly running her hand across his cheek. 'And if I did what makes you think I'd ever be stupid enough to get caught?' she mocked.

Brian didn't respond. His solicitor had warned him that the less he said about the evidence they had obtained the better and he wasn't about to be drawn in by Cynthia's attempts to taunt him into telling what he knew.

'Who do you think I'm having an affair with?' she asked

Brian remained resolutely silent. His face gave nothing away.

'Answer me or are you deaf as well as stupid?'

'Hahaha' she mocked again. 'You think you've got me? Oh you really are indisputably guileless.' she said scathingly. 'This is about seeing Will Kerr leaving my hotel room isn't it?' she taunted.

Brian remained stony faced but he was interested to see where Cynthia was going with this.

'Well let me tell you Brian you're wrong. I know what you think happened between me and Will Kerr but nothing could be further from the truth. The man wasn't capable of having sex' she laughed scornfully.

Brian couldn't help but react. He had wanted to know exactly what had gone on between her and Will Kerr ever since the night of the charity ball but for Laurie's sake more than his own. He didn't want to shoot himself in the foot but as Cynthia clearly had no idea that she'd been caught on camera red handed or perhaps more fittingly bare arsed he couldn't see any reason not to get as much information out of her as possible.

'Oh come on Cynthia' he said amusedly. 'You can't argue yourself out of this one. Laurie and Will have split up over it so don't try and tell me there was nothing going on between the two of you. In fact I'm sure I'd be doing Laurie a favour if I called Will to court to testify, after all I may as well help her get her divorce at the same time I get mine.'

'That's it?' Cynthia said disbelievingly. 'That's all you've got?' She asked

Brian noted the fleeting look of relief cross

Cynthia's face. How right his solicitor had been. If he'd tried to pursue her for adultery with only the merest evidence Cynthia would have laughed at him all the way to court.

'Oh Brian I might have known you'd get yourself into a state about nothing' she said derisively. 'Trust you to read more into it than there was' she said smoothly. 'This is all just one big misunderstanding. You can tell your Solicitor he might as well drop the divorce proceedings now. You won't succeed' she said definitively.

'Oh but I think I will' said Brian confidently. 'You see Cynthia I'm sure Will Kerr isn't nearly as devious as you are and I can't see him lying under oath.'

'It'll be as easy getting this thrown out of court as it would be swatting a fly' laughed Cynthia amusedly. 'He'd be lying under oath if he said we did have sex. You haven't a hope of succeeding Brian. I might have known you'd try and pull a stunt like this you've been as moody as a menopausal woman recently. Maybe you should see a Doctor', she said scathingly.

'Oh I think I'll take my chances,' said Brian. 'I don't see that I've got much to lose.'

'How many times do I have to tell you Brian nothing happened between me and Will Kerr. It wasn't even remotely possible.'

'Cynthia I have it on good authority that he and Laurie split up because he spent the night with you so don't try and bluff your way out of this one.'

'Oh alright then' said Cynthia placating him. 'He did spend the night in my hotel room but only because he was too drunk to go home. I don't know how the man could possibly believe himself capable of anything remotely sexual given the state he was in. It's hardly my fault he jumped to the wrong conclusion.'

'You mean you didn't have sex with him?' asked Brian.

'No darling of course I didn't', she said flakily.

Brian knew she was a lying conniving bitch so there was always the distinct possibility that she was lying to save her own skin but given the fact that more than one person had commented on how drunk Will Kerr had been there was a chance that she was in fact telling the truth.

'Now that we've cleared up this little misunderstanding,' said Cynthia smoothly 'you can tell your solicitor to drop it. You're not going to get rid of me that easily she said.'

'I was afraid of that' he said evenly.

Cynthia allowed herself a long slow smile of victory.

'Nevertheless,' said Brian 'I'd suggest you go and

see your solicitor. This isn't going to go away as easily as you think.'

'Really Brian this is a needless waste of time and resource. You haven't thought things through' she said purring. 'Think how much worse off you'd be financially' she said. 'You do know what's yours is mine.'

'I know nothing of the sort' said Brian angrily. 'I've worked hard for everything I've earned. I've given you the very best of everything and you still insist on treating me like dirt. You came from nothing Cynthia and I intend to see that you leave with nothing.'

Cynthia threw her head back and laughed unreservedly. 'You really are a simple little man Brian' she said. 'I made you what you are. You have as much ambition in your whole body as I have in my little finger. If it wasn't for me you'd have nothing. Any judge in his right mind will see that I deserve the lion's share of everything you own.'

'I think you'll find that you're the mediocre one,' said Brian angrily. 'What skills do you have Cynthia other than being a conniving, duplicitous, scheming tart who whores herself out for pleasure?' he asked bitterly.

'Don't you ever call me a whore!' shrieked Cynthia incandescent with rage.

'Why does it remind you of your mother?' he taunted mercilessly. He regretted saying the words as soon as they were out of his mouth but he couldn't take them back. He didn't even see Cynthia's slap coming until he felt the fiery sting on his cheek.

'How dare you!' she raged. 'How dare you imply I'm like that whore!'

Cynthia had only ever referred to her mother once in the whole course of their relationship and that was in the very early days of their marriage when Brian had quizzed her relentlessly. She told him that her mother was a no good drunk who prostituted herself for money and was usually so drunk she didn't care who she slept with. She'd begged Brian never to mention her again. Brian had been true to his word and never raised the issue again, until now.

So this is what it feels like to start divorce proceedings Brian thought miserably as Cynthia stormed out of the house. He may have temporarily gained the upper hand but it brought him no joy. If only Cynthia could see that it was in her best interests to simply agree to the divorce, but Cynthia was as unrelenting and stubborn as they come, and if she had made up her mind to fight him all the way he would have no option but to show the video clip in open court to prove her adultery. He wanted a divorce alright but was he really prepared to demean the mother of his children to that extent?

Chapter 49

Thank goodness the weekend had finally arrived. Kerry was totally exhausted and if it wasn't for the fact that she'd arranged for Franco to call round she'd have quite happily jumped into her PJ's and had an early night. Unfortunately Franco didn't know the meaning of a quiet night in and she knew he'd drag her out to the local pub for a few bevvies at the earliest opportunity. She'd be lucky if she could talk him out of going to a club she thought despairingly.

She'd told Franco she would cook but she simply didn't have the energy so she called in at the local Chinese on the way home and got a selection of their favourite dishes. She'd bung it in the microwave when he arrived and hope he didn't complain too much about the horrors of consuming too much MSG.

She barely had time to shower and change before Franco showed up looking a million dollars. Kerry's heart sank as she realised he wasn't intending sitting in her house all night in that garb, a night on the tiles was definitely on his agenda.

'Kerry darling' he sang. 'It's so good to see you my love I would say you're looking gorgeous but I'd be lying', he said holding her at arm's length and taking in her pale face, soaking wet hair and tatty dressing gown. 'Seriously he said what have you been doing to yourself? You look terrible.'

'Don't hold back now Franco why don't you tell me what you really think?' Kerry laughed kissing him on both cheeks before ushering him into the house.

'You want me to style your hair for you bella?' he asked kindly.

'Oh Franco would you. I'm so knackered I can't even be bothered drying it. I was just going to let it dry naturally.'

'Ok my love you sit down and I'll get us some wine. We can have a drink and a chat while I work my magic' he said cheerfully.

'Sounds great' said Kerry plunking herself down on her favourite armchair while Franco made himself useful locating a bottle opener and some wine glasses.

'Chinese?' he asked questioningly wrinkling his brow in disapproval.

'Fraid so,' said Kerry. 'Sorry Franco I just didn't have the energy to cook anything. I'm only in the door five minutes.'

'You work too hard bella. Even I don't work past 7.00 on a Friday night.'

Kerry gave a small shrug. 'What can I do?' she asked. 'People expect their cases to be dealt with. Being too tired is no excuse.'

Franco poured two large glasses of red wine and set about styling Kerry's hair

'So how are things going with lover boy?' he asked.

Kerry's face broke into a wide grin. 'Brilliant!' she said cheerfully. 'We get on so well Franco. We had a fantastic weekend in Lough Erne' she said 'absolutely glorious.'

'Lots of wonderful sex?' asked Franco who was always keen for all the juicy details.

'Like you wouldn't believe' said Kerry happily. 'I can't wait for you to meet him Franco. You'll love him' she said. 'In fact next time we get together I'm bringing Aidan. It's definitely time for my two favourite men to meet up and talk about how wonderful I am she said mischievously.'

'What if I don't like him bella? What if he's not good enough for you?'

'There's no chance of that' said Kerry confidently. 'You are so going to love him Franco.

Almost as much as I do' she said wistfully.

'Have you told him that yet?' asked Franco.

'No' she said 'I'm still waiting for him to tell me first.'

'Ummh' said Franco noncommittedly.

'Honestly Franco he really is lovely. I think he came close to telling me he loved me on our weekend away. I think he's just frightened that if he says those three little words then everything will change. That it'll get all complicated and serious.'

'Isn't it about time that he admitted that it is serious?' Franco asked. 'I don't want to see you get hurt Kerry. You're already head over heels in love with the guy. It's time he made up his mind if he feels the same way.' said Franco disapprovingly.

Catching the fleeting look of self-doubt pass across Kerry's face Franco decided to change the subject. He didn't want to be the one to ruin Kerry's hopes of a happy ever after but if Aidan didn't make some sort of commitment to Kerry before too long she'd end up with a seriously broken heart.

'Ta da' said Franco. 'All finished. Now what about some food he said already pulling the Chinese from their containers. Kerry there's enough food her to feed ten people never mind two. I hope you're hungry' he said.

'Not really actually. I don't seem to have had

much of an appetite lately. I think my system hasn't fully recovered from that bug I had a while back.'

'Maybe you're pregnant' joked Franco.

'Thankfully I've got everything covered in that department said Kerry. Can you imagine how Aidan would react if I was pregnant she said in horror. His only other serious relationship resulted in his girlfriend getting pregnant within a few months of them getting together and that didn't exactly turn out well. He'd run for the hills if the same thing happened to me.' said Kerry.

'Are you sure there's no chance you could be pregnant?' asked Franco. 'Have you done a test?'

'I don't need to Franco. I had a new coil fitted six months before I met Aidan and they're full proof.'

'Nothing's full proof Kerry' said Franco.

'Well I never had any problems with the last one' said Kerry 'and it did me four years.'

'Is Aidan the first bloke you've slept with since you had the new one fitted?' asked Franco.

'Yes! You know he is' said Kerry defensively. 'Unlike some people I don't make a habit of sleeping around' she exclaimed giving Franco a knowing nod.

'Ok, ok don't get your knickers in a twist. I was only asking. It's just,' he said hesitatingly, 'you look done in, you're off your food and you haven't touched the wine I poured for you'.

'I just don't feel like it' said Kerry.

'Exactly!' said Franco. 'That's why I'm suspicious. Since when has Kerry Ford ever turned down a glass of red wine?'

'Well if it keeps you happy I'll have some then,' said Kerry taking a large swig from her wine glass. 'Now how about we get stuck into that Chinese. I think maybe I just found my appetite.'

'There is such a thing as trying too hard you know Kerry. You don't have to prove anything to me. I just want you to be sure that's all.'

'I am sure' said Kerry. 'There's no chance I'm pregnant Franco. Honestly.'

'Ok then' said Franco, 'I'll drop it.'

But Kerry was rattled. Could she be pregnant? She had been feeling pretty rotten recently and Franco was right she hadn't touched a glass of wine in weeks or coffee either for that matter. Why was that she asked herself? Actually, she already knew the answer - she couldn't even stand the smell of coffee at the minute never mind the taste of it, so either she'd undergone a mysterious taste bud transplant or......

'Franco' she said carefully as she pushed her Chinese food round and round her plate. 'Do you really think I should do a pregnancy test?'

'Well what harm can it do Kerry? You're already pretty convinced you can't be pregnant so why not just make sure. Do you want me to pop out to the chemist for you bella?'

Kerry nodded slowly and Franco lost no time in grabbing his car keys and heading to the late night chemist.

While he was gone Kerry's mind replayed her recent symptoms over and over again. Why hadn't she noticed until Franco pointed it out? Her new found aversion to coffee and alcohol; feeling tired all the time, loss of appetite, and if she admitted it, feeling a little bit nauseous. But there could be a million different explanations for that she thought. She probably had a viral thing that was upsetting her system. There was no reason to think she was pregnant. The coil was fool proof after all. She'd just take the test to make sure and then she really was going to make an appointment with her Doctor and get him to run some blood tests just to be sure it wasn't anything sinister.

Franco returned bearing four pregnancy kits. 'Just to be sure' he said catching Kerry's incredulous look.

'Ok' said Kerry 'I'll do a test but Franco I really don't think there's any need. I've been doing some thinking while you've been gone and I really do think it's much more likely to be a viral thing than a .. preg

…..than anything else' she said.

'I agree' said Franco putting his arms around her, tilting her chin and forcing her to make eye contact. 'Kerry, I agree, I really do but wouldn't it be better just to make sure?'

Kerry nodded silently.

'Ok,' said Franco at length, 'enough stalling, let's just get it over with. The sooner you do it the sooner you'll put your mind at ease, and Kerry' he said, 'just so you know, no matter what it is, we'll deal with it together, we'll sort it out, it really will turn out ok.' he whispered lovingly.

'Thanks Franco' said Kerry falteringly giving him a little squeeze. 'You're right I'd better just get it over with,' she said making her way to the upstairs bathroom her legs physically shaking. She'd never felt so nervous. Her heart was hammering so hard she thought it was going to jump right out of her chest, she actually felt sick at the thought of what she was about to do. She forced herself to slow down and think rationally, there was no way she could be pregnant, the coil was one of the best contraceptive devices ever.

As Kerry took the test she could barely wait for the two minutes to tick by but at the same time she didn't want to look at the result. It'll be fine she recited over and over, it'll be fine, but as the two blue lines appeared on the test stick Kerry felt her whole world tilt on its axis. She had only taken the test to prove to Franco she wasn't pregnant, not to find out that she was!

She couldn't be! This couldn't be happening, the test was wrong she thought irrationally …..but what about all the other symptoms she'd failed to acknowledge until tonight? Please no she begged please don't let me pregnant. This was all wrong, please don't let this be happening - it would be a disaster she thought miserably. She felt sick; her brain felt muddled, confused. She actually felt a bit light headed, she grasped the sink for support, but the feeling that her head was floating away from her body wouldn't go away, she heard the swoosh, swoosh, swoosh of the blood hammering in her ears, she was clammy and dizzy and suddenly everything seemed very far away, noise was distant and muffled and as her last coherent thought slipped away she was vaguely aware she was falling.

When she came too she was lying on the bathroom floor shivering uncontrollably; her skin was clammy and worst of all there was blood smeared across the corner of the bath. Guessing she must have hit her head on the way down she gingerly checked her head for cuts and found a raised bump just behind her right ear. When she pulled her hand away her fingers were sticky with blood. Slowly she grasped the toilet bowl and hauled herself up to sitting position; whether it was the effort of moving or the bump to her head she didn't know, but she felt her stomach heave and she vomited violently into the toilet bowl which she was still gripping for support. She felt disorientated; the room was spinning, she'd always wondered how that must feel, now she knew and wished she didn't; her vision wasn't quite right either, little black dots kept jumping out at her from behind her eyelids; she felt her head go all fussy again, floating, disconnected from her body but this time she had the good sense to realise she was going to faint and managed to lie down on her side in the recovery position; she heard the swoosh, swoosh, swoosh of the blood in her ears but thankfully this time she managed to remain on the right side of consciousness. She was too frightened to move in case she tipped her body over the edge. 'Franco' she bleated. 'Franco help me...' she called a little louder before she was once again lost in a fuzzy cloud of uncertainty.

On waking for the second time she found Franco kneeling over her. His face was pasty white; his eyes overflowing with concern as he gently bathed her face with a cold flannel. 'Welcome back' he said softly. Kerry gave a small smile and tried to raise herself up into sitting position but the effort started the pounding in her head again and Franco's gentle admonishment to lie still had her sinking back down onto the bathroom floor. Now that she was conscious she realised her body was shivering uncontrollably;

she was so, so cold, but her skin still felt clammy and sweaty.

'You're freezing' said Franco 'we need to get you warmed up, don't try and move' he warned as he left the bathroom. He returned a few minutes later with her duvet and pillow. 'Ok' he said gently 'I'm just going to lift your head slightly to put this pillow underneath ok?' he asked.

Kerry couldn't answer, the effort was too much, and besides her teeth were chattering so hard she didn't think she'd be able to get the words out.

As Franco eased the pillow under her head his hand grazed her bloody ear and Kerry winced in pain.

'Kerry I don't want to alarm you but did you know you're bleeding?' he asked. Kerry nodded slowly but even the slight movement made her feel queasy again.

'Ok Kerry I think we need to call an ambulance. You've had a nasty bump to the head; you've been sick and you've lost consciousness. We need to get you checked out.'

'No' Kerry managed to breathe squeezing his hand as hard as she could.

'I know sweetie, I know you don't want a fuss, but this could be serious Kerry, don't you see? You've had a head injury and at the very least you're suffering from concussion. I don't know what to do and I'm not sure I should move you. I promise I will stay with you the whole time but we need to get you to a hospital,' he said, already pulling his phone from his pocket and dialling 999.

Kerry couldn't believe this was happening she'd never fainted in her life before yet somehow she'd managed to pass out twice in a row, banging her head in the process. She was pretty sure this was not the normal response when someone found out they were pregnant.

Pregnant! Was she really pregnant? Her brain rushed uncontrollably from one dreadful repercussion to the next; she wanted to scream at the top of her lungs, but as she couldn't even speak for fear of passing out again all she could do was lie motionless on the floor while her mind tumbled out one devastating scenario after another.

Ironically her main thought was not for herself, or her successful career, or of being a single mother, but for Aidan. Trapped once already by an unwanted pregnancy there was no way he would ever accept that this was an accident. She had seen for herself that he was only just beginning to recover from the wreckage of an unplanned pregnancy the first time around. They hadn't even talked about kids but she knew that he had been so scarred by what had happened in his life that there was a very real possibility that he would never want more children. EVER! They'd only been going out a few months and it so mirrored what had happened with Angela that Kerry knew this pregnancy had doomed their relationship to failure. It wouldn't matter that Kerry loved him; it wouldn't matter that this was the last thing she wanted for either of them. The fact was he would see her in the same light as he saw Angela, incapable of sorting out contraception, expecting him to play the hero and ride in to rescue her. She didn't understand how this could have happened but the fact was - it had happened and it was a complete disaster. As Kerry felt her life unravel one thread at a time the tears rolled freely down her face.

'Oh babes,' said Franco 'please don't cry. It'll be alright. I promise you it'll be alright. I won't leave you,' he said lovingly. 'I promise I'll take care of you, you don't have to go through this on your own.' If only it was Aidan saying those words thought Kerry miserably but once he knew about the baby there'd be little chance of that.

Ten minutes later the ambulance arrived and after giving Kerry the once over they fitted a neck brace, loaded her onto a stretcher, and carted her off. She was still feeling lousy; sick, dizzy and disorientated; it didn't help that they kept on asking her questions. All she wanted to do was sleep. Didn't they realise how tired she was. What was with the questions? Seriously, didn't they realise she couldn't answer them? How would she know how long she'd lost consciousness for – she was unconscious at the time for heaven's sake. Thank goodness Franco was there, she could hear him rattling off her name, age, date of birth, next of kin. She was so glad she had him, he would sort it all out she thought woozily.

She thought it would be better when they got to the hospital but it just meant more people asking more questions. Her brain was so muddled now she couldn't even work out what they were asking her. It was just like a cacophony of voices all distorted and jumbled. Why wouldn't they just let her sleep? She was so, so tired. Every time she nodded off they started shouting her name and poking her and prodding her until she woke up again.

And why did they need all these lights? They were making her feel dizzy and they were so bright; they were hurting her head. Why was there so much noise? She felt like her head was going to explode. Oh the noise was deafening! Please let it stop she begged silently; please just let me sleep.

Where had Franco gone? She couldn't see him now, all she could see were people in white coats; Franco must have got her into a really good hospital, they were making a real fuss, buzzing around her like little bees. Her head hurt; she really did just want to sleep, if only she could sleep she'd be fine when she woke up. Really she couldn't keep her eyes open any longer no matter what they said. Ah that was better; she felt her head floating again and this time she didn't try and fight it; she really was getting good at this fainting malarkey; in fact once you got used to it, it was quite relaxing, like floating off on a little cloud; at long last the noise was getting fainter and fainter and the lights were fading, she knew all along that all she needed was a bit of peace and quiet and a good long rest.

Chapter 50

When Kerry woke up the drilling had stopped but her head felt as though someone had taken out her brain and filled it with a ton of bricks. It was so heavy she thought that if she tried to move it left or right it would just topple off her body. Good job she had this neck brace thing on she thought or her head might roll off and go tumbling along the floor. She allowed herself a small smile at the thought; mind you she didn't feel she had much to smile about.

Franco was lying sleeping in a chair at the side of the bed. He'd been true to his word she thought lovingly, he hadn't left her. But really she would have been just fine at home. He really was a fuss pot, calling an ambulance. She would never tell him because he had meant well and everything but if he had tucked her up in her own bed with a nice hot water bottle she would have recovered without all this drama. Moving her had just made things worse; the questions; the light; the drilling noise. Mind you Franco always did love a bit of drama she thought fondly.

Franco's eyes glazed open. It took him a minute to realise Kerry was awake but when he did his face split into a wide grin.

'Hey honey,' he said lovingly 'welcome back – again.' How are you feeling?'

'Grruur phanx' what the hell was she saying?

'Grruurr phanx' she tried again more determinedly. She knew she wasn't saying it right but she couldn't seem to get her words out. She started to panic her eyes alight with fear. She tried again desperately to speak 'phanno' she said pleadingly 'phanno.'

Franco's face displayed the shock Kerry was feeling. She could see him search desperately for some way to help her but it was clear he was just as shocked as her. 'Kerry' he said pretending to remain calm, 'I'm just going to see if I can get a doctor ok honey? Don't panic I'll be right back'

'nnnno pheas nnno lllo mi' she cried desperately but whether he didn't understand her desperate plea for him not to leave her or simply chose to ignore it she didn't know.

Minutes later he was back with a doctor and nurse in tow.

Kerry do you know where you are asked the doctor?

'sspitll' attempted Kerry miserably.

Sounds like hospital to me said Franco loyally.

'Ok Kerry, I don't want you to try and speak and I don't want you to nod your head but can you give me a thumbs up if the answer is yes to some questions and thumbs down if the answer is no.'

'sss' attempted Kerry again and then remembering she wasn't supposed to speak gave him a thumbs up.

'Do you know your name?' he asked.

Thumbs up

'Do you know who this gentleman here is?' He asked nodding at Franco

Again thumbs up

'Do you remember what happened?'

Again thumbs up but unfortunately for Kerry remembering what happened also made her remember the two blue lines on the pregnancy test 'nnnooo foorr rremmm' she cried desperately panic once again taking over.

'Kerry listen to me' said the doctor. 'I'm going to give you something to make you sleep again. Your brain has suffered a trauma and it needs to rest so it can recover. If you tire yourself out it could make things worse.' He turned and spoke to the nurse and minutes later she appeared with the biggest needle Kerry had ever seen. As if she wasn't feeling faint enough already Kerry thought miserably.

'She doesn't like needles' said Franco understandingly squeezing her hand. 'Don't look at it Kerry – look at me,' he said fixing her with his eyes. He really did have lovely eyes thought Kerry dreamily. She felt the sharp prick of the needle but kept her eyes focused on Franco. She could hear him lovingly repeat that everything was going to be alright and that she just needed to rest. Finally, the effects of the drugs took their toll and she passed into oblivion for what felt like the tenth time in as many hours.

'What the hell is wrong with her?' asked Franco desperately, 'has she had a stroke?'

'No I don't think so. The CT scan didn't show any bleeding on the brain. It's more likely that the trauma to her brain has caused it to swell and put pressure on the neurological pathways the brain normally relies on to produce speech', explained the Doctor.

'Well what the hell does that mean?' asked Franco 'will she be left like this not being able to communicate?'.

'I don't know' said the Doctor.

'Well get me someone who does know', said Franco angrily.

'You misunderstand me', said the Doctor. 'In some cases speech returns within a few hours or even days; in other cases it can take months; unfortunately in a few rare cases it never fully returns to what it was pre-injury. There is no way of knowing for certain how long this will last. As you know we've already ran extensive tests but I think we'll arrange to do a second CT scan later today just to rule out the possibility that the brain has started to bleed internally, or at least see if there is any change to the amount of swelling caused by the injury.'

'Oh shit,' said Franco. 'So what happens in the meantime?'

'Well the good news is that most patients make a full recovery. The other really important factor is that she recognises you and remembers what happened and is aware of her surroundings, so her memory doesn't seem to be affected – just her speech. But I'm afraid it's a matter of waiting. I'll be happy to answer some more questions as things progress but right now I have other patients to see so you will have to excuse me,' he said turning and walking out of the ward.

Franco was quite literally devastated. It looked as though Kerry's head injury was more serious than anyone had thought possible. He didn't know what to do for the best. He knew Kerry wouldn't want a fuss but there were people who needed to know that this was happening. He'd wait a few more hours he decided and then he'd phone Aidan and Laurie. There was no point adding to their panic by phoning them at 5am. He didn't want to alarm them but he couldn't handle this on his own.

Chapter 51

When Laurie got the call from Franco to say that Kerry had been in an accident and was in the hospital her first instinct was to leap into the car and go straight there. But of course having five children meant you just couldn't do that. Her Mum was visiting her friend in Newry and wouldn't be able to mind the children and there was no one else that Laurie could ask at such short notice. Her only alternative was to contact Will. She hadn't spoken to him for weeks. The children had seen him of course and he'd been spending some time at the house with them but Laurie was always careful to be ready to walk out the door as soon as he arrived and on the few occasions he had attempted to speak with her she had resolutely ignored him. But these were desperate times. It sounded as though Kerry was seriously injured. She owed it to her friend to be there for her. She had no alternative but to get in touch with Will.

'Laurie I'm so glad you've called me' Will said delightedly.

'Don't get your hopes up Will I'm only calling because I've got no other choice. Kerry's been in an accident and I need you to come and mind the children.'

'What sort of accident?' asked Will, 'Is she going to be alright?'

'I don't know said Laurie. Just get here a.s.a.p.' she said and hung up.

Franco had said it would be a good idea to bring Kerry some bits and pieces from home so as soon as Will arrived she headed over to Kerry's house. Letting herself in with the spare key she quickly gathered up some toiletries and spare pyjamas and headed straight for the hospital. She bumped into an ashen faced Aidan in the car park and gave him a quick hug.

'Franco called you too then' said Aidan miserably.

Laurie nodded.

'I just don't understand what happened said Aidan. I spoke to her last night around 6 o'clock last night and she seemed fine.'

'Franco thinks she bumped her head on the bath' said Kerry. 'He doesn't know what happened but it was pretty clear from the state of the bathroom that she hit her head pretty hard. There was a fair amount of blood in there' said Laurie shivering involuntarily.

'Why were you at Kerry's?' Asked Aidan confused.

Laurie waggled the bag at him by way of explanation.

'Will they let us both in to see her do you think?' asked Aidan.

'Franco said they'll only let you in if you're immediate family' replied Laurie. 'Apparently, he had to tell the staff he was her husband,' she said smiling briefly at her brother.

'Trust Kerry to have a gay husband' joked Aidan but his heart wasn't in it.

'I think we may have to be a bit economical with the truth ourselves' said Laurie. 'Franco recommended that we say we're her brother and sister. He reckons it's the only way they'll let us anywhere near her.'

'I'm game if you are' said Aidan. 'If it's the only way I get to see her I'm more than happy to follow Franco's lead and stretch the truth.'

Franco met Laurie and Aidan in reception and Laurie quickly made the introductions. Laurie had only met Franco once before and on that occasion he'd been brimming with joie de vivre today he looked wrung out.

'Kerry's told me a lot about you' said Aidan warmly. 'I've been looking forward to meeting you. I'm just sorry that we have to meet like this. How is she?' he asked.

Franco sank down into a nearby chair, pale and ashen faced. 'Last night was the worst night of my life' he said desperately. 'I don't really know what happened' he said hesitating 'but I think maybe she fainted and cracked her head on the edge of the bath on the way down, by the time I reached her she was out cold, she'd split her head open and she'd been vomiting. She'd come around by the time the ambulance crew reached us but by the time we got to the hospital she was drifting in and out of consciousness and then all hell broke loose. Within minutes there were six doctors and as many nurses swarming round her; I couldn't get to her he sobbed and I promised her I wouldn't leave her he cried. They took her off for scans and tests and I couldn't find her. It was two hours before anyone would tell me what was going on and even then I had to lie and tell them I was her husband. Sorry mate.' he said looking shame faced at Aidan.

'You did the right thing,' said Aidan 'but why didn't you call me sooner?'

'I would have,' said Franco miserably 'but I don't even know your surname and I didn't get hold of Kerry's mobile until after she was brought into intensive care.'

'She's in Intensive care!' exclaimed Laurie desperately. 'Just how serious is this she asked?'

'I'm not going to lie to you,' said Franco. 'Last night I was sure she was going to die.' he broke off sobbing. Laurie reached her arms around him while Aidan looked on helplessly.

Finally Franco regained control of himself and clutched Laurie's hand gratefully. He took a deep shuddering breath before continuing. 'The good news he said mock brightly is that the CT scan was clear.'

'So does that mean she's going to be alright?' asked Aidan hopefully.

'Well it's definitely a step in the right direction', said Franco not quite able to meet their gaze.

'But if the CT scan is clear surely that means she'll make a full recovery?' stated Aidan.

'Well,' said Franco hesitatingly. 'That's what I hope. But apparently the brain is a lot more complicated than that. I can't think of any easy way to tell you this,' said Franco despondently. 'she came round for a short while in the early hours of this morning but her speech was incoherent.' He looked at them sadly. 'She was trying desperately to be understood but nothing she said made any sense. It was all just gobbledy gook.'

Laurie and Aidan looked at Franco stunned. He knew they were both in shock. He had lived through this for 12 hours and his mind still couldn't take it all in so heaven only knew how Laurie and Aidan were feeling.

'Is…is… will she be …I mean …is she going to be alright?' asked Aidan hesitatingly.

Franco filled them in on what the doctor had told him.

'I need to see her,' said Aidan purposefully. 'I need to be with her.'

'Ok,' said Franco 'I'll take you both to her. I don't know if they'll let all three of us in but let's just look as if we have a right to be there and go for it.'

Five minutes later and the three of them had convinced the nurse in ICU that they were all immediate family and she grudgingly agreed to let them in. They had been warned not to disturb the other patients and were all standing around Kerry's bed as quiet as mice.

Laurie was horrified by all the tubes, drips and monitors attached to her friend. 'Oh, poor Kerry,' Laurie whispered at length. 'I can't believe she's hooked up to so many machines.'

'The doctor told me it was touch and go as to whether they would have to intubate her. If she had slipped into a deeper loss of consciousness they wouldn't have had a choice.' said Franco.

'How long will it be before they wake her up?'

asked Aidan.

'I'm not sure,' said Franco. 'I think maybe they intend to keep her sedated for a while but they didn't say how long.'

'Did the doctor say when he'd be back round to see her?' asked Laurie.

'No, but it is ICU so I guess they'll keep a fairly close eye on her.'

Aidan couldn't believe that this was happening. What the hell had happened? She'd seem fine when he spoke to her yesterday. Was it really possible she might never speak again? How would she deal with that? Her job, her life depended upon her being a good communicator. Had she really worked so hard to achieve all that only to have it taken away from her so unexpectedly? How would he feel about having a girlfriend who might now be radically different from the one he had fallen in love with? The thought jarred him out of his reverie. Was he really in love with her?

'Here comes the Doctor' said Franco, 'perhaps he'll be able to give us an update' he suggested hopefully.

'Mr Ford?' asked the Doctor. It took all three of them a moment to catch on that he was addressing himself to Franco.

'Oh yes' stumbled Franco guiltily.

'I'm Mr Boyd. I'll be your wife's Consultant

Neurologist while she's with us here at the Royal Victoria. You were speaking to a colleague of mine earlier I believe?'

'Yes,' said Franco. 'Can you tell us what's happening?'

'I've had a detailed look at your wife's CT scan and I'm pleased to tell you that everything looks well. Obviously, there is still a considerable amount of swelling behind your wife's right ear but it seems fairly consistent with an impact of this nature and I can't see any evidence of a secondary haemorrhage.'

'Will her speech come back?' Asked Laurie.

'Yes hopefully it will he answered but we would really like to do another CT scan of Mrs Ford's brain just to be sure she hasn't had a bleed subsequent to the last scan. Are you relatives of Mrs Ford?' he asked.

'Yes' said Franco seeing Laurie's face flush red. 'This is her brother Aidan and sister Laurie.'

'Would you like them to leave Mr Ford? There are a couple of questions I need to ask you which you might prefer to be done in private.'

'No, no it's fine' answered Franco guiltily, knowing they had as much right to be there as he had which was basically none at all.

'Ok' said the Consultant warily. 'In that case could you tell me how far advanced your wife's pregnancy is?'

'Pregnancy?' gasped Aidan. 'No, there must be some mistake'

'I'm sorry' said the Consultant 'there's no mistake. I take it you and your wife hadn't told the extended family the good news then he said smiling. I did ask you if you wanted them to leave' he said defensively seeing the shocked look on Franco's face. 'You did know your wife is pregnant?' he asked.

'Yes' squeaked Franco guiltily. 'Well .... I mean I thought she might be...... I think she'd just found out herself' he said eyeing Aidan steadily. 'I found this on the bathroom floor when I reached her' he said pulling the pregnancy stick from his back pocket. 'In fact I'm convinced that it was the shock of finding out that caused her to faint and bang her head.'

'Why didn't you tell us you suspected your wife was pregnant?' asked Mr Boyd.

'I...I ......I'm not sure stammered Franco. I was too busy worrying about her head injury. The possibility of her being pregnant seemed a bit irrelevant at the time.'

'Was the pregnancy a bit of a surprise to you both then?' he asked

'Yes' stammered Franco 'very much so. It wasn't planned at all.' he said looking intently at Aidan.

The Doctor looked at Franco clearly wondering

what sort of family set up this was. It almost looked as though the husband was seeking the brothers forgiveness for getting his own wife pregnant and the brother looked more shocked about the pregnancy than the husband.

'Thankfully we always do a test for pregnancy along with the other blood tests so we knew very early on that she was pregnant. Unfortunately as a result of your wife's pregnancy we haven't been able to carry out the normal range of tests we would usually complete when a person presents with a brain injury. Some of the drugs we would normally use pose a slight risk to the foetus so obviously we seek to use alternative safe drugs as much as possible. The reason I'm telling you this is that a second CT scan, while largely safe, obviously possesses a slightly increased risk to the foetus. In light of the fact that your wife is unable to provide her own consent I need you to sign the necessary forms to enable us to carry out a second scan.'

'Oh, oh I see' whimpered Franco. 'I… I … can I have a little time to think about it?' he asked the doctor at last.

'Very well' said the Doctor with a sigh. 'I'll do the rest of my rounds and come back in an hour. In the meantime I'll put your wife's name down on today's wait list for the scan or she may miss the opportunity altogether. You can still pull her out of it if you decide not to consent but really the risks to the baby are very minimal and I really do think it would be in your wife's best interests to allow us to carry out a second scan.'

With the doctor gone no one spoke. Aidan was shaking uncontrollably. His head a mixture of emotions; confusion, fear, doubt.

'Aidan,' Franco said at last. 'She really, really wouldn't have wanted you to find out like this you know?'

'Did she tell you?' asked Aidan angrily

'No' said Franco defensively. 'I honestly believe she'd just found out herself.'

'If she was even remotely suspicious she was pregnant why didn't she tell me?' asked Aidan bewildered. 'Did she plan this?' he asked angrily. 'Did she want a baby and I was the fall guy? I'm such an idiot. Why do I never learn?' he asked loudly. 'I trusted her. I believed her when she said she was taking precautions. I should have known better than to ever trust a woman with contraception.' he blazed angrily.

'Aidan' said Laurie softly. 'Keep your voice down. We're in ICU and you're going to get us kicked out of here.'

'I don't bloody well care' shouted Aidan angrily. 'How could she do this to me? I thought I could trust her but she's no better than bloody Angela.'

'Aidan that's not true' said Laurie quietly. 'She's nothing like Angela. No contraception is full proof. There's no way Kerry would ever have planned this. She didn't do this on purpose.'

'Aidan' hissed Franco 'I know you're shocked but right now this isn't about you. This is about Kerry and your baby. I need to know if you want her to have this scan.'

'I don't bloody well care' he answered angrily. 'I've had enough. I'm out of here' he shouted and with that he turned and stormed out of the ward.

'Should I go after him?' Asked Laurie clearly torn between running after her brother and staying with her friend.

'I think he needs some time to cool off' said Franco angrily. 'I can't believe he just stormed off, abandoned Kerry and his own baby. Your brother is a total arse.' he said furiously.

Laurie couldn't agree more. This wasn't like Aidan, what the hell had gotten into him. He wasn't the sort to just shirk his responsibilities.

By the time Aidan reached the carpark he was already beginning to cool off. What the hell was he doing? He couldn't turn his back on Kerry. She was critically ill. Taking some deep breaths to calm himself he spent the next thirty minutes walking around the car park trying to calm down and gain some perspective. He knew he had to go back in there. He couldn't leave Laurie and Franco to deal with this. It didn't matter how much he wanted to run away and pretend none of this was happening the truth was it was happening and he had to find a way to deal with it. He was just so shocked. He hadn't had time to sort out how he felt about any of it. But Franco was right, this wasn't about him. He had to focus on Kerry. He could sort out what his feelings for her were later. Right now he had a duty to be there for her. It wasn't fair to leave Franco and Laurie to deal with this.

'I'm sorry said Aidan contritely. I was out of line,' he said miserably as he returned to Kerry's bedside.

'Damn right you were' said Franco angrily. 'I'm only glad that Kerry wasn't awake to witness what an arse you are.'

'It won't happen again' said Aidan. 'I don't walk away from my responsibilities.'

'That's all she is to you?' asked Franco angrily. 'A burden to be dealt with?' he asked disgusted.

'Franco go easy' pleaded Laurie. 'He's had a lot to take in. Give him some time. Please.' She begged.

Franco looked at Aidan and wanted to punch the guy so hard he'd be the one needing a bed in ICU to recover. But he had to think of Kerry, what would she want? 'Ok' he said at last. 'I'll let it go for now but you better have yourself sorted out by the time Kerry comes round. She has enough to deal with right now without realising what a no good waste of space her boyfriend has turned out to be.'

Aidan had the good grace to feel ashamed but that didn't change the fact that he still didn't know how the hell he was going to sort out this mess.

'Right' said Franco decisively; 'much as I can't even stand to look at you right now I think you need to make the call about the second CT scan' he told Aidan resentfully.

'I don't think there's any choice,' said Aidan. 'Kerry's health has to come first and the Doctor said the risk to the… the…ba…baby was very small.' Just saying those words made it seem so real. Kerry was carrying his baby. He kept thinking he'd wake up and someone would tell him this was all a dream. It had all happened so fast. It seemed like everything was so normal one minute and the next Kerry was critically ill and carrying his baby.

'Franco' said Laurie 'Aren't you scared the hospital will find out you're not even Kerry's relative, never mind her husband and report you to the police for some kind of… I don't know.. fraud or something.'

'The thought had crossed my mind' said Franco. 'But what the hell can I do about it now? He asked.' I suppose Kerry's next of kin would be her Mum and Dad but since one of them lives in Spain and the other's six foot under what else can I do?' he said miserably. 'Besides I know a good lawyer and when she makes a full recovery she'll keep me right.' he said giving a little half-hearted smile.

'It should be me' said Aidan. 'I'm the one who should be sticking my neck out for her not you' said Aidan miserably. 'I'm sorry Franco. If you want to come clean I'm happy to take responsibility for her.'

'It won't work like that,' said Franco scathingly. 'All that will achieve is to get us all kicked out of here and then the hospital will have to contact Kerry's mum in Spain and that will just mean an even longer delay before Kerry gets her scan. I'm not risking Kerry's health over some bullshit bureaucracy' he stated adamantly. 'Agreed?' He asked them.

They both nodded in agreement.

Two hours later and Kerry was wheeled off for her second CT scan.

'Let's just pray its good news' said Aidan miserably.

Chapter 52

Brian decided that he should do the decent thing and pay Laurie Kerr a visit to let her know what he'd found out. It wasn't fair that her marriage had been jeopardised because of his wife's remorseless ability to manipulate people.

He was very much surprised to have Will Kerr open the door to him. He thought Will had moved out.

'I was looking for Laurie,' said Brian amiably shaking Will's hand by way of greeting. 'Is she about?'

'Come in come in' said Will good-naturedly. 'As long as you don't mind the chaos' he laughed.

'I'll stick the kettle on' said Will. 'You look like you could use a good strong cup of coffee. Rough morning?' He asked.

'You could say that' said Brian. 'You may as well

know' he said after a pause, 'I've started divorce proceedings.'

'Ouch!' said Will. 'I think you'll be needing something stronger than coffee' he replied sympathetically.

'No,no' said Brian seating himself at the kitchen table, 'coffee will be just fine thanks.'

'I'm sorry about your marriage' said Will.

'Don't be,' said Brian raising a small smile. 'It's been on the cards a long time and it's a bit of a relief to be finally doing something about it.'

'I can't say I'm a big fan of your wife,' said Will. 'but I'm sorry you have to go through a separation. I wouldn't wish it on anyone' he said miserably.

Brian silently assessed Will Kerr. He had certainly lost a lot of his cocky charm that was for sure. He was still friendly but didn't have that swagger that Brian usually associated with him. 'Forgive me if I'm speaking out of turn' he said at length 'but I assume that since you're living back at home that you and Laurie have sorted out your own difficulties?'

Will groaned and held his head in his hands. 'I wish we had' he said 'but no, I'm only here minding the kids as Laurie got called away on an emergency. We aren't back together and I'm beginning to think we never will be.' He said despondently. 'I've been a complete idiot' he admitted freely. 'Took Laurie completely for granted and acted like a drunken teenager instead of a fully-grown man. It's no wonder she won't even speak to me. I've hurt her so badly I don't think she'll ever forgive me. In fact, I don't deserve her forgiveness. I can't believe what I've put her through, shouting her down after accidentally bidding at that charity auction and then getting so drunk I ended up ....' he trailed off, suddenly remembering who he was talking to and an embarrassed silence lay between the two men.

'You ended up spending the night with my wife' said Brian calmly, fixing Will with a steady glare.

Will's face flushed as the penny suddenly dropped. Brian had clearly found out about Cynthia and him spending the night together and that was the reason they were getting a divorce. Brian had obviously come round to tell Laurie about his divorce and let her know the reason why. 'I…ummhh…… I ……..I don't really know what to say' said Will. 'I really was incredibly drunk' he mumbled apologetically.

Brian wasn't a nasty man by nature but he had to admit he was rather enjoying watching Will Kerr squirm. It wouldn't do him any harm to feel the full consequences of his actions. 'Perhaps you want to tell me what happened?' said Brian at last.

'Not really' answered Will

'Don't you think you owe me that at least' said

Brian.

Will hesitated. What the hell did he have to lose, he thought at last. His marriage was as good as over anyway. Brian Nixon obviously already knew what had happened so what difference did it make. If he had to apologise to this guy it was the least he could do. If the man wanted to beat him to a pulp, well, to be honest he deserved it.

'I can't really remember much about it to be honest. Like I said I really was off my face drunk. The last thing I remember was passing out in your.......your wife's hotel room. When I woke in the morning I was pretty horrified to be honest. I couldn't believe I'd ummmmhhhh you know but well ......ummh it turns out I must have at least that's what Cyn........what she said. To this day I really don't know if I did or not, for a while there I became convinced she was making the whole thing up, but I guess nobody can be that cruel and if you two are divorcing over it well it really must be true' he said ashamedly. 'All I can say is that I'm really truly sorry. If I could undo what happened that night I'd do it in a heartbeat.'

Brian let the silence stretch between them until Will could stand it no more. 'Is that why you're here?' he blurted. 'To tell Laurie what a no good lousy two timing rat I really am? If it is I rather think you're wasting your breath – she already knows.' he said miserably.

'I did come around to tell Laurie about the divorce,' he said 'and I am asking the court to grant me a divorce on the grounds of adultery.'

Wills heart sank.

'My wife thinks I'm being entirely ridiculous. She swears that nothing happened between the two of you and that you were too drunk to be capable of anything more than passing out on her bed. She was really rather adamant that if you were called to testify you would be entirely unable to confirm that you'd had sex because it simply hadn't happened. And for once I'm inclined to believe her.'

Will looked up confused.

'I'm here to tell Laurie that I don't think anything happened between you and my wife.'

'What?' asked Will disbelievingly.

'I think she made the whole thing up simply because she enjoys manipulating people. Oh believe me I think that she wanted it to happen and she had targeted you to be the one who would make it happen but she didn't count on you getting yourself so drunk that you wouldn't be capable.'

'But, but..' stammered Will. 'She led me to believe that we had….'

'I have no difficulty believing she would do something like that' said Brian. 'My wife likes to have power over people and if she can't physically control them then her next weapon of choice is mind control.'

Will was stunned. He felt as if a giant weight had been lifted off his shoulders. 'You know' he said at last 'I don't think I ever fully believed that I had sex with her. In all the years I've been with Laurie I've never, ever, cheated on her and believe me I have had plenty of opportunity - so I couldn't understand why I would suddenly cave in and have sex with a woman who I didn't even really like. I just put it down to being too drunk to know better. Are you really going to tell Laurie what Cynthia told you?'

'Yes,' said Brian 'I am. Do you think you could pass on the message that I want to see her?' he said smiling.

'Yes' said Will. 'I don't think I'll have any problem doing that. Thanks.' he said. 'You may just have saved my marriage.'

'You know it's quite possible that my wife will pay you a visit to make sure you're both singing from the same hymn sheet. She may well want you to provide a statement of some sort swearing that you did not in fact commit adultery with her. She's very determined that I don't divorce her.'

'But if I give her the statement won't that mean you won't be able to get your divorce?' asked Will confused.

'I don't want you to worry about that' said Brian. 'Just leave that to me. In fact I've just had an idea that might turn out to be very advantageous to you and Laurie.' As Brian laid out his plan to Will a genuine smile passed over Will's face for the first time in months. He was more than willing to do what Brian Nixon wanted him to do.

By the time Laurie returned home that night she was seven shades of exhausted. She'd spent all day watching her best friend being treated to a plethora of scans, tests, bloods and injections. She couldn't shift her underlying worry that Kerry would be left with permanent brain damage and of course the atmosphere between Aidan and Franco hadn't helped either.

Franco was still acting like a lioness protecting his cub and Aidan was clearly struggling to get his head round the fact that Kerry was pregnant never mind the fact that she was seriously ill.

The good news was that the doctors were happy with the second CT scan. Kerry was now 'critical but stable' and they had taken her off the Propofol injections which kept her sedated. They expected her to regain consciousness towards the early hours of the morning. Of course that had led to another fight between Aidan and Franco as only one visitor was allowed to stay overnight with her in the ICU. Aidan had stood his ground and insisted that he be the one to stay. His determination coupled with the fact that

Franco hadn't had any sleep the night before and was totally exhausted led him to eventually agree to go home and get a couple of hours sleep. He had made it clear he didn't trust Aidan to do the right thing by Kerry and was determined to be back in the hospital at the crack of dawn when Kerry was due to wake up.

Thankfully all the kids were in bed by the time Laurie got home. Will must have sensed she was exhausted because other than making enquiries after Kerry he didn't pester her about their current marital situation and for that she was extremely grateful. He'd passed on a message to her that Brian Nixon had called round and wanted to see her and asked if she would pop into the surgery during normal hours. Laurie had no idea what it was about but she was too exhausted and overwrought with worry about Kerry to give it much thought. Will had promised to be back first thing in the morning to look after the kids and let her get back to the hospital.

As Laurie crawled into bed that night she prayed for the first time in years. She prayed Kerry would be alright, that she didn't have brain damage and that Aidan would somehow find the strength to deal with the hand fate had dealt him.

Chapter 53

The hospital was a different place at night; eerily silent other than the constant beep, beep, beep of machines. For the first time Aidan actually noticed the other patients in the ICU whose loved ones also sat anxiously in chairs by bedsides praying for the change that would herald the road to recovery. Absently he wondered if his own face was etched with the same fear he could see on those around him.

As he watched the rhythmic rise and fall of Kerry's breathing he realised how fortunate he was that she was still alive. The doctors had cautioned that if Kerry had banged her head an inch lower, the impact against her temple would almost certainly have killed her.

He'd almost lost her.

As the night wore on interminably his mind replayed the last few months he'd spent with her. He couldn't ever remember feeling so close to anyone before. Until he started dating Kerry he always felt he was walking on eggshells around girlfriends. He was never really sure what they expected. He'd long since concluded that woman were too complicated and it was simply less hassle to have a few fun dates and move on before things got too serious.

It wasn't like that with Kerry though. He didn't have to pretend with her. She'd known him since he was a boy for pities sake so what was the point in pretending he was someone he wasn't – she'd see through it in a heartbeat. She got him; she understood him; she didn't continually moan at him or try and change him; she loved him for who he was or at least he thought she did.

He thought fondly back to their teenage years when they would sit around and chat for hours; the two of them had a right old laugh and managed to put the world to rights - in their own heads at any rate. Was Kerry the real reason he could never settle with anyone else? Was she the reason things were never going to work out with Angela? Maybe his heart had belonged to Kerry all along since before he'd even kissed her, before he'd ever had the tremendous privilege of making love to her. Having her in his life again after all this time was the best thing that could have happened to him.

He knew now he'd never meet anyone that could compete with her. So why the hell hadn't he just told her? With hindsight he could see he'd been too busy telling himself to keep his distance, telling himself not to get too close, telling himself he was going to get hurt again, telling himself not to fall in love with her, that he hadn't even allowed himself to see that he was already in love with her. He always had been. He always would be. His heart had belonged to Kerry all along - he'd just been too damned foolish to admit it. And although the knowledge scared him half to death he could no longer deny how he really felt about her.

Why had it taken something like this to make him face up to his feelings? He should have told her on their weekend away how much he loved her. It was on the tip of his tongue so many times but at the last minute he'd always retreated back into his shell and left the words unsaid. He was ashamed of how he'd treated her, ashamed he'd turned and walked away from her even for a minute when he'd found out about the baby; he hoped and prayed she'd never find out what a coward he'd been. How could he have done that to the woman he loved more than anyone else in the world? How could he have believed that this situation was anything like what had happened with Angela? This was the love of his life; the mother of his child! For the first time that thought thrilled him instead of frightened him. She would be a great Mum he thought fondly. Anyone could see how good she was with kids. Laurie's children adored her. She had the patience of a saint, answering questions he would have long since lost patience with; taking the time to listen to them and getting to know them. He just wanted her to wake up so he could tell her how he felt about her. Please God let him have the chance to tell her. Please let her wake up and remember him; let her be alright.

Aidan must have dozed off but he awakened to the low, slow, moan of Kerry beginning to regain consciousness. She sounded like an animal in pain and it broke his heart that she was suffering so much. He wondered if he should call a doctor but before he got a chance to do anything her eyes fluttered open. He registered the confusion and then the fear on her face. Soothingly he tried to coach her away from the land of dreams and ease her re-entry into the land of the living.

'Hush now Kerry,' he whispered. 'You're ok. Don't try to move your head about. Don't strain yourself to see where you are. Close your eyes and relax and I'll explain everything to you.'

Kerry could hear Aidan's melodic tones as he soothed away her fears and eased her back to awareness. It was comforting having him here; holding her hand; whispering lovingly in her ear. Her head hurt like hell and the pounding in her skull was unrelenting but she tried to hold on to the gentle cadence of Aidan's voice and not allow herself to slip away again.

'You've had a bit of a bump to your head Kerry and you're in the hospital. You're going to be just fine but you'll need to take things easy for a day or two. Don't try and rush anything. It might take a little while for you to recover, and your speech might be a little confused at first but the doctors have said it's going to be just fine eventually; it's just important that you don't rush things and don't get stressed out. Can you squeeze my hand if you're hearing this?' Aidan whispered.

He felt her softly squeeze his hand and felt overjoyed that she could not only hear him but obviously understood what he was saying. 'Ok,' he continued 'that's the bad news out of the way. The good news is that I finally get a chance to tell you just how much I love you Kerry. I'm sorry I didn't tell you sooner. I think maybe it took you being ill to make me realise that I've always loved you. You are the most wonderful woman I've ever met; I love every part of you; I love your smile; I love your laugh; I love your beautiful mind and of course your gorgeous body; there's nothing you could do or say that will ever stop me loving you.'

Was she dreaming she wondered? She'd been dying to hear Aidan say those words for weeks but obviously it took her landing herself in hospital to bring him to his senses; but he didn't know, she thought desperately, he didn't know about the baby! He'd change his mind as soon as he realised she was pregnant. This was lousy timing she thought angrily, she was stuck here feeling like she'd just been hit by a bus unable to explain, unable to tell him that she hadn't planned it. He'd never understand, she thought miserably, as the tears leaked from her eyes and rolled slowly down her cheek.

'Now, now' said Aidan softly, 'these better be tears of joy because I don't want you getting upset' he soothed, gently wiping away her tears. Kerry opened her eyes, she needed to see him; she wanted to drink him in; she loved this man with her whole being and if he walked away from her because of the baby it would destroy her.

Aidan's eyes met hers. All she could see in his eyes was love; she knew then he meant what he said; he really did love her. They could have been so happy together she sobbed miserably. 'Kerry, Kerry, please don't cry' said Aidan gently, 'please don't cry, it's going to be alright I promise.' Aidan could see Kerry's face awash with tears her eyes full of fear and uncertainty. 'Is this about the baby?' he asked gently. He registered her shock. 'Kerry honey I know about the baby. They had to do some tests when you came into hospital and I found out you're pregnant. I'm delighted,' he said 'really, really pleased' he assured her. 'Of course our timing could have been a little better and I really would have preferred it if you hadn't knocked seven bells out of yourself because of it but its fine, more than fine actually,' he smiled.

Was she dreaming? Was this really happening? She couldn't believe it. She really thought he wouldn't want to know. Apart from the giant lump on her head, the neck brace, her inability to talk and ending up in ICU this was the best day of her life. She smiled at Aidan, her eyes alight with love as he gently dropped his head and kissed her softly on the lips.

Chapter 54

Cynthia was more than a little annoyed to learn that Brian had retained Kerry Ford as his solicitor whom by all accounts was one of the best divorce lawyers in the business. However she was confident that Arthur Allen would prove to be as ruthless and unrelenting a solicitor as she had been led to believe.

Certainly her first meeting with him had been very much to her satisfaction. He was just as scornful of the suggestion that Brian could hope to get a divorce on the grounds of adultery as she was herself. He had confirmed that if the only evidence of adultery was based solely on the fact that she had allowed an inebriated man to sleep off his drunkenness in her hotel room that the evidence was wholly inadequate. He had wasted no time in drafting a statement for Will Kerr to sign which he believed would be sufficient to dismiss any forthcoming petition for adultery. Cynthia was adamant that Will

Kerr's signature be obtained as soon as possible which was why she had insisted on personally tracking him down and ensuring he signed it there and then.

Cynthia felt that Will had been very ungracious indeed. He really should have been tremendously grateful to her for going to so much trouble but instead he was most disobliging. He had the gall to accuse her of ruining his marriage. It was a measure of how much she wanted his signature that she was able to restrain herself from telling him that she didn't give a damn about him, or his insignificant little wife and their inconsequential paltry marriage. How she had the wherewithal to stay calm and controlled after the weekend she'd just had she'd never know. She had to call upon all her reserves of charm to persuade him that they hadn't slept together and that he had simply misinterpreted her kindness in letting him crash out in her hotel room. Even then he had refused to do her 'any favours' as he termed it and it had taken all her powers of inducement to ensure she got what she wanted. If it hadn't been for the fact that she really needed his signature, there was no way she would have agreed to compromise.

Will's signature had barely dried on the statement before she had it back with Arthur Allen.

'Why Mrs Nixon you're extremely efficient,' complimented Arthur Allen standing to greet her for the second time that day. 'I really didn't expect you to have obtained Mr Kerr's signature so soon.'

'I am a woman of many talents Arthur as I'm sure you'll find out before long' she purred.

'Of that I have no doubt' smiled Mr Allen. 'Unfortunately, I have some bad news for you. I've just learned that Ms Ford has been involved in an accident and so it's unlikely that the actual divorce petition will issue until her return to work.'

'That's just not acceptable,' complained Cynthia. 'I thought I made it clear that I want this little misunderstanding dealt with as soon as possible' she protested.

'I understand Mrs Nixon, of course I do, and I will be writing to Ms Ford enclosing the statement and asking her to abort the case. However if she's absent from work, I'm afraid we are in limbo until your husband appoints an alternative solicitor or Ms Ford returns.' He explained calmly. 'Of course, on the plus side it does give us some time to evaluate the extent of your husband's financial assets and to confirm whether or not you are actually a Partner in your husband's business.

'I organised the Partnership Agreement myself Mr Allen. I wasn't actually in attendance when my husband attended to sign the paperwork but I have no reason to believe he didn't sign it.'

'Did he tell you that he had signed it Mrs Nixon?'

'You seem to forget Mr Allen that my husband is a moronic little man who would willingly sign his life away if the paperwork was organised and set in front of him.'

'Well if it turns out you are a Partner in the business Mrs Nixon then I can't see any reason for you not to retain your position as Practice Manager. However, if it transpires that you are an employee and not a Partner then your only hope of challenging your husband's decision is to threaten him with a case of constructive dismissal. Can you tell me again how he terminated your employment?'

'He said the Practice could no longer afford me and that the post was being made redundant.'

'I see' said Arthur Allen thoughtfully, 'You know Mrs Nixon it appears to me that his solicitor has coaxed him in exactly how to terminate your employment. He's been careful to bring the post to an end rather than to dismiss you for personal reasons.'

'Doesn't it amount to the same thing?' replied Cynthia angrily.

'Not at all' explained Arthur. 'It might seem that way because both scenarios mean an end to your employment but the law regards the two scenarios very differently. Your husband appears to be making a justifiable business case for a redundancy rather than waging a personal vendetta.'

'Of course it's a bloody personal vendetta!' Cynthia roared.

'All I'm saying' calmed Arthur, 'is that he has us on the back foot at the moment because he initiated this process. I would suggest we take this opportunity to gather as much information about your husband's assets as possible so that we know exactly where we stand if divorce proceedings do eventually issue. Information is power Mrs Nixon and I intend to gather as much information as I can. I don't like being caught unawares, so if there's anything else you think I should be aware of now is the time to say.'

For a moment Cynthia thought fleetingly of Jeff but as she was certain Brian was completely in the dark about him she didn't think it worthwhile even mentioning it.

'No' said Cynthia 'I can't think of anything. I've already told you what I know of our financial situation and so forth and of course I intend to stop him getting his divorce so I really don't think we need to consider the residency of the children. You seem to forget Mr Allen that I intend to stay married until it suits me to be otherwise.'

'Be that as it may Mrs Nixon but I intend to protect your best interests and therefore I won't leave any stone unturned.'

As Cynthia left the office of Allen and Boyce Solicitors she felt a headache coming on and as usual it was all Brian's fault. Thankfully Brian had been so fixated on proving her adultery with Will Kerr he was completely oblivious to the truth. She grudgingly admitted that she had been so engrossed by Jeff that she had momentarily taken her eye off the ball. She had completely missed the signs that Brian was planning this little coup. She wasn't about to make that mistake twice. She would have to ditch Jeff. It had been fun while it lasted but as far as she was concerned that little fling had ended the minute she received the letter from Brian's solicitor. Given the fact that Brian was already suspicious of her infidelity she couldn't afford to be caught out now.

She was still seething at the way Brian had spoken to her. How dare he, she thought venomously. He needed to be taught a lesson and she intended to see that that he was brought to heel. She would tear him to pieces one bite at a time until he was left with nothing; no children, no home, no wealth, no Practice. Divorce would be the least of his worries by the time she had finished with him. She didn't care what she had to do; she would destroy him.

Chapter 55

Kerry had finally been moved out of ICU and into a normal ward; she still felt as if she'd been hit by a giant double decker bus. Her head ached and she'd been poked and prodded, scanned and drugged more times than she cared to remember but her main concern was her inability to string a sentence together. She had the words perfectly formed in her head but so far her efforts to communicate them out loud had been a complete and utter failure.

Her neurologist was confident that her speech would return once the swelling on her brain had subsided but what if he was wrong? What if her speech never fully returned? She hadn't missed his comment that in most cases patients make a full recovery. That meant that some didn't. Maybe she would be one of the unlucky ones whose speech never fully returned. The more she thought about what that would mean for her career and her life the more fearful she became. The Occupational therapist had told her not to try so hard, that her best chance of regaining her speech was to allow her brain to relax and do its job. But it was impossible to relax knowing what was at stake.

And then there was Aidan. She was desperate to explain things to him, to let him know that she hadn't planned on getting pregnant, to find out how he really felt about it. Was he putting on a brave face for her because he felt sorry for her? Was he just waiting for her to recover before he went into meltdown? She couldn't believe he was being so reasonable, she had fully expected him to abandon her once he found out about the baby; maybe he was just waiting until she was well enough. The thought sent panic bells ringing in Kerry's head. She wanted to talk things through with him so badly that it was driving her to distraction not being able to explain how she was feeling; to let him know she hadn't meant for this to happen and, of course, to tell him how much she loved him.

The other thing she noticed was that her visitors felt compelled to talk endlessly rather than endure silence. She felt like a bloody therapist, except she was the one lying on the couch. Franco had gleefully shared the intricate details of his sex life with his Piloxing instructor and all Kerry could do was blush bright red and cast apologetic glances to the woman in the next bed. However, behind the bravado she could see just how devastated he still was that George had walked out on him. He was a man nursing a completely broken heart and Kerry was only just beginning to realise the extent of his pain.

She owed Franco so much.

If it hadn't been for him coming to her rescue on Friday night she realised now that she could have died. Imagine if he had tucked her up in bed with a hot water bottle like she wanted him to. She shuddered at the thought of what might have happened.

Franco was keen to reassure her that he was absolutely delighted about the baby and wanted her to know that 'if that Aidan buggered off' he'd be there for her. He told her he'd always wanted to be a dad and he'd be more than happy to help her raise the baby. She knew he meant it too. Other than Aidan she couldn't think of anyone she'd want more to be a dad to her baby. She really was spoilt having him as her friend. He would make a wonderful dad she thought sadly. It was just a shame he may never be given the opportunity.

Strangely the thought of not keeping the baby had never even occurred to her. She was already a little bit in love with him/her and even if Aidan walked out on her right this minute she knew she would never consider getting rid of their precious baby. Yes she'd been stunned to find out she was pregnant and in hindsight passing out and hitting her head a great wallop certainly hadn't been the best reaction to the news, but now she'd had a chance to take it in, she was thrilled there was a tiny baby growing inside her. She was going to be a Mum! She couldn't believe it. She never imagined that it would happen the way it had but did it really matter that she hadn't got things completely right? This baby would be loved and wanted and Kerry was delighted that she was getting the chance to experience motherhood first-hand. For years now she'd accepted that having a baby was something she'd probably never get to experience and it was only now that she was pregnant that she fully realised how much it meant to her.

Then there was Laurie. She was glad Laurie was so delighted that she was going to be an Auntie, she would have hated for her relationship with Aidan to come between her and her best friend. Laurie was convinced that Aidan and Kerry would live happily ever after and Kerry just prayed she was right.

Kerry was impressed that Laurie was coping so well without Will. She certainly seemed to be adjusting to his absence surprisingly well. In fact Kerry could see glimpses of the 'old' Laurie re-emerge. She knew Laurie would survive without Will in her life but she also knew that Laurie was still in love with him despite how much he had hurt her. When Laurie explained that she'd called with Brian Nixon on the way to the hospital and that he was now 'absolutely convinced' that Cynthia hadn't slept with

Will, Kerry felt sure that Laurie would run straight back to him and all would be forgiven. Laurie had surprised her though. She was determined to take her time and think things through. She admitted that while she couldn't have forgiven Will if he had slept with someone else that there were still issues she needed to deal with before she decided if she was going to take him back. She said she was determined to figure out what she wanted first and that if Will really wanted their marriage to work he was going to have to be prepared to make some lasting changes.

Kerry was dying to tell her she was doing the right thing and encourage her to take her time and put herself first for a change but the best she could do was scribble a 'you should talk to him' on the notebook Laurie had brought her. For all her bravado she knew that Laurie was dreading talking things through with Will. Laurie shook her head at Kerry's suggestion. 'That's the last thing I should do Kerry. You know what he's like. He's such a charmer, if I give in and talk to him he'll have me back in his arms and back in his bed before I even know what's hit me. I really need to be strong and the only way I can do that is sort out what I want first and make it clear I'm not budging. Otherwise I'll be back to square one and it'll all have been for nothing. He needs to appreciate me Kerry. He can't just go on thinking only of himself. It's time he put my needs first for a change.'

Kerry couldn't agree more.

By the time Laurie left Kerry was totally exhausted and was only too glad to finally get a chance to sleep. She had the loveliest dream. She dreamt that Aidan was dropping little feather-light kisses along her collar bone and then oh so gently he kissed her full on the mouth. So tenderly she felt like she was melting into him. He was whispering how much he loved her and finally she was able to tell him how much she loved him too. She didn't know how long she slept but when she awakened Aidan was there grinning from ear to ear.

'Hello gorgeous,' he said lovingly.

Kerry momentarily forgot she couldn't speak and attempted to ask him what he was looking so pleased about but once again only a babble of words emerged from her lips.

Seeing that she looked so dejected Aidan planted a kiss gently on her lips. 'Don't worry Kerry love, you're going to be fine Kerry. Do you know how I know?' He asked.

Kerry shook her head.

'You just told me you loved me', he said delightedly.

Kerry looked confused. She was pretty sure she hadn't been able to say anything of the sort.

'You were sleeping', said Aidan 'and I got distracted by the sight of your gorgeous mouth and couldn't resist kissing you and that's when you said clear as day 'I love you" he grinned.

Kerry remembered that part but she thought it was just a dream. Was he serious?

'Sweetheart don't you see what this means?' he grinned. 'You can talk. You're going to be alright. The Doctor was right, you just need to relax and the words will come. It was probably because you were half asleep that you stopped trying so hard and nature took over. Whatever the reason I've never been so glad to hear those three little words.'

'Of course, maybe it was just my great kissing skills' he grinned. 'Do you think I should maybe keep doing it, just to test the theory of course?' he joked.

Kerry smiled delightedly; thrilled that maybe her speech would come back after all.

As Aidan leaned over, gently covering her mouth with his, he kissed her so tenderly and so deeply Kerry felt certain he could conjure words from her lips. This time when Kerry felt light headed she knew it wasn't the bump to the head that was causing it.

Chapter 56

Laurie meant it when she told Kerry that she was determined not to slip seamlessly back into Will's world. She had already begun to make plans and was actually feeling more confident and positive about her future than she had in a very long time. Of course part of the reason she was feeling so upbeat was the fact that she now believed that Will hadn't slept with Cynthia Nixon. It was like a great weight had been lifted from her shoulders. The thought of Will having sex with anyone made her shudder but the fear that it had been her arch nemesis, Cynthia Nixon, had definitely made it worse. She only hoped that someday that woman would get what she deserved. How Brian Nixon had stayed married to her for so long she didn't know. She was delighted when he told her that he was finally seeking a divorce and then she immediately felt guilty wishing that on anyone, especially their two boys.

Time had given Laurie some perspective and she could now see that even though Will hadn't actually been unfaithful, it still didn't excuse his recent behaviour. She now realised that she wanted his respect just as much as his love. It was no wonder he had felt at liberty to treat her like his general dog's body and skivvy if she had inadvertently allowed herself to slip into that role. It was no surprise that Will had assumed he would automatically be allowed back into their home and back into her bed now that she knew he hadn't had an affair? Laurie had to admit that it gave her no small amount of satisfaction in telling him she hadn't made up her mind whether they still had a future together and showing him the door for the second time in as many months.

It was time Will realised things had changed, and more importantly that she had changed, which was why she had spent the past week diligently typing up her CV and applying for a few jobs based locally. She was delighted when one of them replied inviting her for interview. Out of the several jobs she had applied for this was the one she wanted most. The pay was good, it was close to home and the hours appeared to be fairly flexible. The problem was she hardly knew what being a 'Personal Assistant' entailed never mind convincing her would be employer that she could do it. However her determination to prove to Will that she was more than just a wife and mother gave her the boost she needed to invest in a new power suit and obligatory high heels and take herself off to the first job interview she'd had in years.

Conversely Will couldn't help feeling frustrated that Laurie was still refusing to talk things through. He knew if he could just get her to open up to him that they could sort things out. He had convinced himself that once Laurie knew he hadn't been unfaithful she would forgive him, but that hope had backfired spectacularly. If anything Laurie just seemed more determined than ever to prove that she could survive without him. He always assumed he was the strong one emotionally in their relationship but if that was the case why was he so bloody miserable? It was more a question of whether he could survive without Laurie than the other way around. The truth was the longer they were separated the more time Will had to reflect on what he had lost. Maybe his intentions to bring back the old Laurie had worked a little too well. He had forgotten just how fiercely determined the old Laurie could be. Once she had made up her mind about something there really was no stopping her. Had she made up her mind to move on without him? Did she really need him at all he wondered?

If Laurie was testing him she was beginning to test him beyond his limits. Some days he felt so angry he just wanted to march in and tell her that none of this was his fault and she'd just have to bloody well get over herself; then in his saner moments he'd realise that actually this was his fault. Alright, so he might not have slept with someone else but he had certainly been letting his marriage slide for some time; he hadn't been pulling his weight; he'd left Laurie to cope with the house and the kids while he'd quite happily walk out on the chaos and return a week later. Travelling on business was his get out of jail free card; he'd been able to justify his inability to help out around the house; he convinced himself that his role was to make enough money to provide for them all, but if he was being completely honest, he really didn't make much of an effort even when he was at home.

The truth was he hadn't wanted the hassle. Who the hell would want to spend hours cleaning the house, sorting out laundry, doing dishes, helping kids with homework, making meals, doing the shopping, changing nappies? When he was at home all he wanted to do was sit down and relax, maybe play with Shane on the X-Box or have a beer and watch a bit of telly. He certainly couldn't be bothered doing any of the hundreds of mundane jobs that Laurie nagged him to do.

The thing was though he was beginning to see that maybe that hadn't been fair to Laurie. In fact if he was being entirely honest he had known all along that he wasn't being fair to Laurie. The problem was that it had mattered more to him that he got to do what he wanted than it had to make sure his wife was ok. When he looked at things objectively he realised that he always put himself first because he was the most important person in his life; whereas Laurie always put herself last because she was the least important person in their family.

If only she would give him another chance he would prove to her that he really had changed. He would help out more, give her more time to herself, act more like a loving husband and father than the selfish prick that he had been. He realised that maybe he'd never get the chance to show Laurie how much better he could be and maybe she would never take him back, but he needed to know one way or the other. He couldn't go on living in a state of limbo staying in cheap hotels, visiting the kids only when Laurie left the house for the afternoon.

If their marriage was over he needed to set up a proper home; a place he could call his own and somewhere for the kids to come and stay with him. And yet the thought of moving on crippled him with pain. How could he ever move on without Laurie and the kids? He wasn't cut out to be a single parent. He wanted to be at home with his wife and their children. He wouldn't give up on that dream just yet. He had one more surprise for Laurie, it would be his last attempt to win her back. He just hoped it didn't backfire.

Chapter 57

Three weeks after the accident and Kerry was making good progress. Thankfully her speech had almost returned to normal but her Doctor was insisting that she didn't return to work for another few weeks. He was concerned that the stress of catching up with her case load and dealing with clients would undo a lot of the progress she had made over the past three weeks. The problem was that Kerry was finding it more stressful being at home twiddling her thumbs, knowing that her caseload was getting bigger by the day, than being at work sorting through it. As a compromise, her Doctor had agreed to allow her to work from home a few hours each day and Kerry was doing her best to take things easy.

She and Aidan had finally been able to have a long heart to heart a week after she got out of the hospital. He'd admitted that he did have a bit of a wobble when he found out she was pregnant but, in her book, it hardly seemed to matter now. He'd proven his love to her in a thousand different ways since she'd got home from the hospital. He was reluctant to leave her side, he was her daily companion and they had slipped into an easy routine. He had insisted that she wasn't left alone, especially at night, for the first fortnight. Maggie had been amazing, looking after Michael while Aidan played nursemaid. He'd brought her breakfast in bed every morning before popping back to check on Michael and then heading off to work. He'd call back with her at lunch time and if he wasn't able to be there he'd set up a rota of visitors to ensure that she wasn't left on her own for more than a few hours at a time.

They'd talked a lot about their future and she didn't know if she or Aidan was the more excited about having a baby together. Kerry was thrilled that Aidan seemed to want the baby as much as she did herself. Aidan was hoping for a little girl but really Kerry didn't care as long as it was healthy and well. They still hadn't fully worked out where they would live after the baby was born but as Aidan pointed out they had plenty of time to think about it and after the turbulent few weeks they'd just been through they were both determined to slow things down and simply enjoy being in love.

Kerry had never felt happier. She couldn't believe that she was finally with the man of her dreams and that she was going to have a beautiful baby. Right now, despite her head injury, Kerry knew that life couldn't be more perfect. They had decided not to tell Michael about the baby until she'd had her first scan in a fortnight's time. Kerry still had a lingering fear that all the tests and scans she'd been through had harmed the baby, and even though the Doctors had told her that the risks to the baby were minimal she knew she wouldn't rest content until she had her twelve week scan. She'd told herself that if the scan was fine then she'd stop worrying and she'd promised to Aidan she'd wait until after the scan before going back to work full time.

Chapter 58

Cynthia couldn't believe that Brian had moved out. While she couldn't physically stop him she was damned sure she could make life as difficult for him as possible. If he thought he could treat her like this and yet continue to see his children he was very much mistaken. She had already spoken to her solicitor instructing him to inform Brian that the children were extremely upset that their father had abandoned them and that they didn't want any contact with him. She had also made it clear that the children would continue to reside with her and that if he wanted to see them he would have to get a court order. If there was one thing guaranteed to have Brian come crawling home with his tail between his legs it was the knowledge that she wouldn't let him see the boys. Of course she had made sure that the boys knew their father had abandoned them. Naturally they were upset but she had made it clear that it wasn't her fault.

She explained that he was welcome to move back home anytime he wanted and if he didn't love them all enough to do that then he wasn't worth bothering about. If Brian thought he could get away with treating them like this he'd have to learn the hard way that Cynthia wasn't standing for it.

Finally after three and a half stressful weeks her solicitor had telephoned to advise her that he had heard back from Brian's solicitor. He had refused to speak about it over the telephone and insisted she make an appointment to see him.

'Mrs Nixon, how lovely to see you again.'

'Do you have some news?' asked Cynthia bluntly.

'Indeed I do,' said Arthur Allen 'and I'm afraid it's not good.'

'Not good?' asked Cynthia. 'You mean my moronic little husband is determined to press ahead with this?' she asked

'I'm afraid so Mrs Nixon. Ms Ford sent through the Petition for divorce today and your husband is indeed seeking a divorce on the grounds of adultery.'

'I don't believe this' said Cynthia scathingly. 'I thought you sent her the statement from Will Kerr denying adultery.'

'I did Mrs Nixon but I'm afraid that it's no use.'

'No use?' replied Cynthia indignantly. 'You've

changed your tune. You agreed with me that he would never get a divorce on the grounds of adultery based on such inconsequential evidence.'

'I did indeed Mrs Nixon but you see Mr Kerr is not listed as the co-respondent on the divorce petition.'

'What do you mean?' asked Cynthia puzzled.

'The name on the divorce petition is someone by the name of Jeff Orr.'

Cynthia's face paled and she was compelled to drop into the seat she had earlier refused to accept.

'But he has no proof,' said Cynthia shocked 'he can't have.'

'I take it you do know Mr Orr then?' said Arthur Allen.

'Yes' said Cynthia.

'How well do you know him Mrs Nixon?'

'I…umm, I would say he's just an acquaintance' mumbled Cynthia.

'So you're saying there is no truth in the allegation that you have been having an affair with Mr Orr?'

'Well,' said Cynthia regaining her composure. 'there's unlikely to be any solid evidence to that effect.'

'Ms Ford indicated that you might be of that opinion which is why she sent through some further evidence with the Petition.'

'What sort of evidence?' asked Cynthia warily.

'I don't know.' said Mr Allen 'I haven't had an opportunity to view it yet. I had my secretary contact you as soon as I received the Petition but I've been tied up at court all morning. Would you like me to view the content of the CD first Mrs Nixon?'

'No, no whatever it is,' said Cynthia 'I want to see it. Let me assure you Mr Allen its highly unlikely to be anything incriminating.'

As the content of the recording began to roll, Cynthia who was never lost for words, was momentarily stunned into silence. She felt her face flush as the images of her and Jeff flashed up on the screen. It was one thing indulging in a little fling but it was quite another watching yourself do it in the sober light of day. 'I think you can stop the tape now', she cried agitatedly as the images of her naked body flooded the screen.

As Mr Allen looked at the stilled image of his client astride the man on the recording he turned to her with a face like stone.

'Well Mrs Nixon it looks like your husband has incontrovertible evidence of your adultery after all. When you told me you were a woman of many talents

I didn't realise this was what you meant. You've lied to me Mrs Nixon and I don't appreciate being made to look like a fool.' He snapped angrily.

Cynthia was paralysed with shock. She continued looking at the image on screen, for the first time realising she was every bit the whore her mother was.

Jeff looked so young; fresh faced, muscly, lithe and lean. She looked ancient in comparison. Old enough to be his mother she realised; and there she was straddling him, degrading herself like a common tart, her face etched in fake ecstasy, every wrinkle clearly visible. She looked old, she looked like the forty three year old mother of two she really was.

When had that happened? She still felt like a twenty eight year old. Until today she had fooled herself into thinking she still looked like a twenty eight year old. But staring at that image in all its startling technicolour she saw herself for what she really was. A washed up old tart, whoring herself out for pleasure. She realised she was seeing herself for what she really was for the very first time and it had shocked her to her core.

The on screen images continued to play back on a loop in Cynthia's mind even though the tape had long since been paused. Her hands were trembling; she felt her stomach roll violently; she needed to get out of here; she couldn't bear to be reminded of what she had just witnessed; she needed to pretend this had never happened.

Had Brian viewed this tape she wondered shocked? Was this why he thought she was a vile, disgusting whore just like her mother? At this moment she felt every bit as dirty and revolting as he believed her to be.

She could never allow this video evidence to be shown in open court, it was the one thing that would utterly destroy her.

Perhaps you could never hope to escape your past; perhaps you could never really rewrite your future. She'd been fooling herself; creating a fantasy lifestyle, a happy ever after illusion that in reality could never conceal the dirty girl she had always been.

Mustering whatever dignity she had left, she dazedly prised herself from her seat.

'Tell my husband he can have his divorce' she intoned dully, 'as long as this recording never sees the light of day.' As she walked unsteadily from the office feeling every one of her forty three years her only thought was how quickly she could lose herself in a bottle of gin.

Chapter 59

How the hell did people ever manage to spring surprises Will wondered admiringly? He had been planning this surprise for Laurie for weeks now and he felt like a complete wreck. He had cajoled and bribed as many people as he dared to help him and he still wasn't sure he could pull it off.

Kerry had promised to have Laurie where she was meant to be at the correct time; Maggie had been working tirelessly to sort out the children and even his new boss Chris Canton had got firmly behind him once he realised what Will was planning.

Will was so stressed that he thought he might spontaneously combust at any moment, any one of a hundred things could go wrong and the possibility of him actually getting everything right was slim to none. His nerves were completely shot to pieces but at last the day had arrived, everything was organised to the best of Will's ability.

This was it, all or nothing. If Laurie still didn't want him back after today then he'd have to accept her decision and somehow find the strength to move on.

When Kerry had phoned Laurie earlier in the week to tell her she was treating her to lunch, Laurie had readily agreed. They'd decided to meet in Titanic Quarter at a lovely little restaurant Kerry had been to before.

'This place is gorgeous' said Laurie delightedly as she joined Kerry at their table.

'I know and just wait 'til you try the food,' said Kerry. 'I'm salivating at the very thought of it' she said delightedly.

'Well now, you are eating for two after all' grinned Laurie.

Kerry looked away. Was it just Laurie's imagination or was Kerry hiding something.

'Kerry is everything alright?' she asked fearfully. 'Have you had your twelve week scan yet?'

Kerry couldn't make eye contact. There was definitely something wrong.

'Yesterday' said Kerry at length.

'Well how was it?' asked Laurie cautiously.

'I was a complete wreck,' said Kerry 'and the more agitated I became the more Aidan pretended to be all cool, calm and collected which frustrated the hell out of me. But Laurie there's something you should know. The scan didn't go exactly as expected.'

'Shit I knew it' said Laurie. 'There's something wrong isn't there.'

'I......I...... promised Aidan I wouldn't say anything.' said Kerry. 'We haven't quite got our heads around it ourselves yet.'

'Come on Kerry, you've got to tell me now, if I know what's wrong I can help, if you don't tell me I'll just worry myself sick.'

'Listen Laurie I don't want you to worry, thankfully it's nothing we can't deal with. The scan was going really well and then the radiographer left the room saying she needed to get a Doctor and Aidan and I knew something wasn't right. When the doctor arrived back in Aidan kept asking him what was wrong. Oh Laurie, I was so frightened. All I could think of was that the drugs they gave me had damaged the baby and I kind of zoned out. I just couldn't bear to hear there was something wrong. I knew Aidan was talking to the doctor but I didn't know for sure it was something to be concerned about until Aidan passed out. I think it must have been him hitting the floor that brought me back to reality. I started crying and between Aidan lying spark out on the floor and me bawling my eyes out the poor nurse didn't know who to deal with first. It was a minute or two before I was coherent enough to realise what the doctor was telling me.'

'Oh Kerry please tell me it's nothing serious' demanded Laurie.

'Well maybe you can tell me if it's serious or not ?' replied Kerry solemnly.

'What do you mean?' asked Laurie puzzled. 'I wouldn't have a clue.'

'Yes, you would' said Kerry smiling. 'Its twins!'

'Oh Kerry, Kerry thank goodness. Bloody hell I thought there was something wrong. You nearly gave me a heart attack.'

'I'm sorry,' said Kerry smiling 'I didn't mean to worry you I didn't even want to tell you at all just yet.'

'I can't believe it.' said Laurie. 'I just can't believe it.'

'You can't believe it?' said Kerry 'try being me. First I find out I'm pregnant, pass out and end up in hospital and then we find out its twins and Aidan does the exact same thing' she laughed.

'Oh I'm so happy for you' said Laurie. 'Having twins is amazing! Mum always said twins ran in our family I guess this proves it.'

'I'd have been quite happy with one,' said Kerry.

'I'm not sure how we're ever going to cope with twins.'

'You'll be fine' said Laurie. 'We'll all lend a hand. Michael will be delighted.'

'I know,' said Kerry smiling. 'I think we're going to tell him at the weekend.'

'Who would ever have guessed that six months would make such a difference to our lives?' said Laurie at length. 'When you told me you liked Aidan I never would have dreamed you and he would make such a go of it. For a while there I thought Aidan would never allow himself to fall in love. I'm so happy for you both' she said tearfully squeezing Kerry's hand tightly. 'You make an amazing couple.'

'Believe me,' said Kerry earnestly 'I never dreamed I could be so happy either. I thought I'd end up a staunchly independent, lonely old woman, with no partner and no kids. Mind you it could so nearly never have happened. I keep thinking what if I'd hit my head an inch lower down she shuddered. There'd be no babies and no Kerry and Aidan. It could all have ended so differently. I can't tell you how grateful I am to be alive; to be able to talk normally again; to have the chance to love the people who really matter.'

Laurie sighed. 'I know what you mean she said thoughtfully. I guess it's not about how much money you have in the bank or how successful you are. At the end of the day it all boils down to the relationships you have with the people you love. I know I want a measure of success in my own life but nothing will ever bring me as much success or as much happiness as my children and the people I love.'

'Does that include Will?' asked Kerry carefully.

Laurie considered her reply for a long time. 'Will has been part of my life for so long' she said at last 'I can't imagine ever being with anyone else and I guess I think maybe it's time we had that heart to heart to see if we have a marriage worth saving.'

'For what it's worth' said Kerry 'I think you'd always regret it if you didn't try again. When you meet the right person Laurie its worth holding onto them even if it isn't always plain sailing. You and Will have always been good together, sometimes it's easy to lose sight of that when life gets in the way, but that doesn't mean it's not worth fighting for.'

'You know if you ever get tired of the legal work you could always take up counselling' said Laurie smiling. 'You're a great friend Kerry. Now let's get out of here and walk off that fantastic lunch.'

'I've never really been around the titanic quarter in Belfast before,' said Laurie as they strolled along the docks. 'They really have done a marvellous job selling this place to the tourists.'

'I know' said Kerry. 'It's still hard to believe that

half of Belfast used to work in these shipyards building some of the most famous ships in the world.'

'Oh look at that' said Laurie distractedly. 'I didn't realise they had opened up the port to cruise ships' she said delightedly.

'Yeah they've done that for a while now. Aren't they amazing' said Kerry looking in awe at the fabulous luxury liner in front of them. 'Shall I see if I can blag us a tour?' she asked Laurie mischievously.

'Ha' said Laurie throwing her head back laughing. 'Not even you could swing that one Kerry.'

'What are you trying to say Laurie? In all the time you've known me have I ever failed to blag us into a club, or a bar or free drinks, or hotel upgrades?'

'No, but this is entirely different' said Laurie. 'This is a cruise ship Kerry not some fishing boat. They're not just going to let you on for a nosey around.'

'Do you want to bet?' said Kerry eyes glistening mischievously.

'I wouldn't want to rob you of your money so easily' said Laurie grinning.

'Ok a tenner says I can get us on that thing for a quick tour.'

'You're on' said Laurie laughing 'but you'll never do it.'

'You wait here while I work my magic' said Kerry laughingly. 'I wouldn't want you to spoil our chances by your lack of faith.'

Laurie rolled her eyes as Kerry approached the porter and began chatting to him in earnest. There was no way Kerry was going to pull this one off thought Laurie amusedly as she watched her friend chat away nineteen to the dozen, hands gesticulating wildly while the poor man looked shell shocked. I bet it's not every day a civilian tries to persuade him to let them board the ship thought Laurie smiling.

Five minutes later Kerry was back looking very pleased with herself.

'We've got twenty minutes.' she said smugly.

'You're not serious' squealed Laurie. 'Is he actually going to let us on board?'

'Tut, tut Laurie I thought you knew better than to doubt my powers of persuasion and by the way you owe me a tenner.'

As they made their way up the gang plank Laurie was still in a state of shock that Kerry had pulled this one off. The cruise ship was amazing. They couldn't even begin to take in the extent of its luxury in twenty minutes but what they did see had them gasping in awe; luxurious ballrooms; a cinema; at least ten different restaurants; six swimming pools; a bowling alley; a casino and everything finished to a standard that screamed luxury and opulence.

'Wow this is amazing' said Laurie for the umpteenth time. 'Can you believe this?'

'I had no idea it would be so luxurious' said Kerry as they stood on the upper deck looking over the wharf below.

'I wish we didn't have to leave.' said Laurie longingly.

'Well since we only have five more minutes I'm going to make use of the ladies before we go' said Kerry promising she'd only be a minute.

Five minutes later and Laurie was beginning to worry that Kerry had got lost. She was just about to go in search of her when a familiar face appeared at her side.

'Will' stammered Laurie 'what are you doing here, what's going on? Where's Kerry?'

'This' said Will gesturing around him 'is your final surprise' he said smiling.

'Whhaaaaatttttt?' asked Laurie in astonishment. 'What do you mean? I still don't understand what's going on' she stammered.

'Ok Laurie so here's the thing' he said capturing both her flailing hands and pulling them tightly towards his chest.

Laurie could feel the warm heat of him and her

hands involuntarily itched to run over his taut chest, it was as if they wanted to fit back into the old well-worn routine. This man still made her heart beat faster she realised as he drew her in with his eyes. 'You're Mum and Kerry have been helping me plan this little surprise for weeks now he said earnestly. I'm taking you on a cruise' he said smiling.

'You're what?' shrieked Laurie. 'There's no way I'm going on a cruise Will. Firstly, we can't afford it, secondly I'm not abandoning my children and thirdly I'm starting my new job on Monday.'

'What? Wait! You've got a job.' Will asked disbelievingly.

'Yes Will I got a job. I am more than a wife and mother of our children you know. Didn't you think I was good enough?'

'Good enough?' said Will shocked. 'Laurie I think you're amazing! The most beautiful, intelligent, loving, sincere, hard working woman I have ever met. Any employer would be glad to have you working for them. I'm just surprised that's all. I hadn't realised you'd been looking for work. Congratulations' he enthused hugging her tightly. 'You never cease to amaze me Laurie' he said earnestly and Laurie could tell by the way his eyes lit up with pleasure that he really meant it.

'Where are you working?' he asked

'I'm Brian Nixon's new PA she said grinning. Three mornings a week. Apparently it's the role Cynthia had before he sacked her although she had the much more glamourous title of Practice Manager. Seemingly he had to alter the job description slightly to avoid Cynthia suing him for constructive dismissal.' she said gleefully.

'Wow look at you' said Will. 'You're glowing Laurie. You've no idea how much I wanted to see that sparkle back in your eye. I'd almost forgotten that amazing smile of yours, it warms my heart just to see you light up' he said holding her tenderly. 'I'm sorry Laurie, I'm really, really, sorry for how I've treated you. I guess I hadn't even realised I'd been taking you for granted until it was too late to put things right. I know you deserve someone who's far better than me but the thing is Laurie I love you; I love you so much that the thought of never being with you again makes me want to shrivel up and die; some days I miss you so much that I have to stop myself from begging you on bended knee to forgive me and give me another chance. I can't live without you Laurie, I don't even know who I am without you! You give me direction and hope and most of all you remind me that there's nowhere I'd rather be than with you and there is nothing else under the sun that will ever fill this massive hole I have in my heart....but you.'

'This,' he said gesturing with his hands 'is my

last hope, I was hoping I could persuade you to give me one more chance and I promise you, I PROMISE you Laurie I will never, ever mess you around or take you for granted ever again. So please, please say you'll come on this cruise with me, please give me a chance to beg your forgiveness over and over again because you see I want you back more than I want anything else in the world.'

'But Will' said Laurie desperately, 'even if I agreed to go with you, what about the children?' This was so typical of Will she thought angrily, as usual he was so focused on himself and what he wanted he had entirely forgotten to think about the children and who would look after them. Despite his words he hadn't really changed at all she thought angrily pulling away from him.

'Laurie wait. What's wrong?' he asked, dismayed that she was going to walk away from him even after he'd laid his heart his heart bare. 'Laurie the children are here. You don't need to worry about them.'

'What?' shrieked Laurie in astonishment. 'The children are here?' she asked.

'Yes' said Will 'they're happy as larry in the kids club and crèche.'

'I.......I........ I......don't understand this,' said Laurie faintly. 'I think maybe you better explain this to me. I can't take it in.'

'OK' said Will. 'Sorry. I didn't mean to upset you. It was meant to be a surprise. Ok let me go back to the beginning. Do you remember the night of the charity auction when you accidentally bid £10,500 for a luxury cruise?'

'I don't think I'll ever forget that night Will for more reasons than one' Laurie answered.

'Sorry' said Will 'but the point is - this is the luxury cruise.' He said carefully.

'But Will,' she cried 'we can't afford this! And anyway the cruise was just for two people not our whole family'.

'Hush, hush now Laurie' he said holding her close to him. 'Let me finish, I really can explain' he said simply.

When Laurie was calm again Will continued. 'I had a chat with Brian Nixon shortly after the auction. Brian was certain that his wife had set the whole thing up deliberately taking a bid that you had never actually placed. Brian was determined to pay for the cruise himself …. '

'No' interrupted Laurie. 'We are not taking that man's money; he's already done more than enough for us I am not having him pay for this.'

'Laurie please' said Will finally exasperated. 'Please let me finish.'

'Ok' she nodded.

'Well, as I was saying, Brian offered to pay for it himself. Obviously there was no way I could let him do that and I told him as much. He wasn't happy about it - said it was his wife's fault and that as she wouldn't pay for it he felt he should. In the end though he realised I wasn't budging and agreed to let it go. The only problem was I couldn't pay for it - well not unless I wanted to re-mortgage the house and I wasn't keen to do that. I stalled the charity's request for payment for as long as I could but eventually I ran out of time. Just when I had accepted the idea that I'd have to get a loan from the bank Brian came up with a solution.'

'Please tell me you didn't take a loan from him' Laurie wailed.

'No, no I didn't' appeased Will. 'You see, the day Brian called round looking for you we had a long chat. He told me that he'd started divorce proceedings against his wife on the basis of her adultery. Apparently Cynthia was fixated with the idea that Brian believed her to be having an affair with me. Brian knew that she wasn't, and unbeknown to Cynthia he had concrete proof that she was having an affair with some bloke called Jeff who's a fitness instructor at Cynthia's gym. Anyway, to cut a long story short, Brian was convinced that Cynthia would come to me looking for me to sign a statement confirming that I hadn't had an affair with her. He was right. A few days after later Cynthia found me and brandished a piece of paper under my nose demanding that I sign it. If I hadn't spoken to Brian beforehand I would have been quite happy to sign the damn thing confirming I had never had an affair with her but thanks to Brian I insisted that I wouldn't sign it unless……..'

'Unless she paid for the cruise' squealed Laurie delightedly.

'You got it' said Will grinning from ear to ear. 'As per Brian Nixon's instructions, I made her transfer the funds directly into my bank account, signed the statement which was totally worthless to her anyway and planned this as a surprise for you.'

'But what about the kids?' said Laurie, 'surely it must have cost a fortune to bring them along' she said doubtfully.

'Perks of the new job' said Will gleefully. 'You're not the only one with a new job. Meet the new sales director for Canton Medical Global.'

'You're working for Chris Canton?' Laurie asked incredulously.

'Yep' he said proudly 'and not only that but it means less travel so I can be at home more for you and the kids. I felt a bit guilty asking Chris for time off work to come on this when I'd only just started a new job with him but when he realised it was all as a result of that night at the auction he offered to pay for the kids to come with us rather than giving me my first ever bonus. I knew you'd be happier if the kids were here with us so I agreed.'

'You mean you planned all this by yourself as a surprise for me?' asked Laurie incredulously.

'Well I had a little help from your Mum, who's been working like a demon sorting out all the clothes you and the kids would need and of course I needed Kerry to get you here but other than that yes I did. I want this to work Laurie. I want us to be a family again. I don't want to lose you and I'll do anything it takes to prove that to you.'

'I want that too' said Laurie smiling. 'I love you Will Kerr, I've never stopped loving you.'

'You still love me?' asked Will incredulously. 'Even after all I've put you through?' he asked tearfully. 'I'm so sorry for being such a shitty husband Laurie. It wasn't until I lost you that I realised just how little I deserved you. I love you so much. I've missed you more than you'll ever know and I promise you if you give me one more chance I'll be the best husband I can possibly be. I want our marriage to work Laurie, not just for the sake of the kids but because I really, truly love you and I don't think I can survive without you. I think you're amazing' he said staring at her wonderingly. 'I'll never stop thinking you're amazing and I'll never stop loving or wanting you for as long as I live. Please forgive me?'

he begged.

'I think I forgave you a long time ago' she said pulling her husband close and holding him tight. 'I just needed a bit of extra time to find 'me' again' she said 'and I think I have. I feel more like how I used to be, more optimistic about us and our future, more certain that the choices we've made have been the right choices and even when we've got it wrong that we still have something that's special and unique and worth fighting for' she whispered.

'Does that mean I can kiss you now?' asked Will raising her face to meet his.

Laurie's face broke into a wide smile her eyes twinkling the way they had so often in Will's dreams, her mouth parted willingly to meet his and as he kissed her it felt like he was coming home, back to where he wanted to be and to the place he never wanted to leave. Only the noise of the cruiser leaving the port eventually drew them back to reality.

'I take it we're going on this cruise together after all' said Will as the cruise liner pushed away from the docks.

'I guess we are' said Laurie delightedly. 'You know this feels like the ultimate cliché' she said at length resting her back against Will's chest his arms folded tightly around her as they watched the port of Belfast fade into the distance.

'What?' asked Will 'they sailed off into the sunset?"

'I was thinking more along the lines of 'and they all lived happily ever after" she said joyfully turning to kiss him once more.

THE END

ABOUT THE AUTHOR

Jill Millar lives in the rolling countryside near Ireland's Causeway Coast with her husband Dave and their three kids. Jill left a career as a busy lawyer to focus on being a full-time mum and (un)domestic goddess in 2011.

Love, Lies and Laurie is her first novel which has been brewing for some time over good coffee and even better company.

Printed in Great Britain
by Amazon

44064445R00262